Tijuana Crossing

TIJUANA CROSSING

A NOVEL

B.H. LUFT

Talos Entertainment Ltd.
Toronto, Ontario, Canada

First edition (ebook) June 2019
ISBN 978-1-9991284-1-8 (paperback)
ISBN 978-1-9991284-0-1 (epub)

Cover and interior design by Marijke Friesen
Cover photos: Landscape: Laurens Hoddenbagh / Shutterstock.com;
Truck: Keith Bell / Shutterstock.com
E-book formatting/design by Stephanie Small
Edited by Chandra Wohleber
Proofread by Martin Llewellyn

Talos Entertainment Ltd.
105 Blantyre Ave., Toronto, Ontario M1N 2R6 Canada

Tijuana Crossing is entirely a work of fiction. Characters, some places, and all incidents are products of my imagination, and any references to historical events, real people, or real places are used fictitiously. Resemblance to actual events or persons, living or dead, is entirely coincidental with three exceptions: There was an extraordinary woman and some family members who ran an orphanage and whom I had interviewed on tape. The woman is known to the locals and most of the older racers simply as Momma Espinosa. I have based my orphanage and its owner and other orphanage characters very loosely on this amazing woman's fortitude and courage and I hope my imaginary version of her is seen as a loving homage to the work that she was doing. Also, the protagonist's timely and helpful hideout in La Paz was loosely based on a wonderful restaurant we discovered just off the main streets where a small film crew and I had a fantastic, completely unexpected meal and enjoyed ourselves well into the next day. The characters there are entirely fictional, though. I have only heard rumours and stories of Mike's Sky Ranch and am not even sure it really exists. On the other hand, I spent way too much time in Hussong's Cantina in Ensenada. *Tijuana Crossing* is very loosely based on my experiences filming the Baja 1000 off-road race, research, and my trips through the Baja peninsula during the late 1980s and early '90s.

I've tried to make the travel times and locations as authentic as possible and have taken a menagerie of the hundreds of wonderful characters I met over the years and painstakingly made them into very real, sometimes hateful or lovable, but hopefully believable human beings.

I have always loved Mexico and its people and cherish the times I have spent there in the past and will hopefully spend there in the future. My wish is that one day Mexico will come to realize its full potential, offering its citizens prosperity, hope, and the quality of life that all of its citizens deserve. It is a beautiful country.

Thank you so much for purchasing my book; I consider it an honour. I hope you enjoy reading it as much as I enjoyed creating it.

—B.H. Luft

In memory of my mother, Irene (Renee), and my grandmother Bella, simply known as Granny to the rest of the world. Who always loved and supported me unconditionally.

For my sons and daughters:
Lane, Dylan, Austin, and Genevieve.
I'm pretty sure you know how much I love you but I wanted to say it anyway.

Bonus pack: Kathryn and David.

And also for my stepfather, Doug McCorkindale.

All the racers and crew of the Baja off-road teams who spent many hours with me so I could understand their world a little better, and the hardworking and dedicated camera crews and all others I met over the years working in the Baja. You made my work and time there so much more enjoyable.

CHAPTER ONE

There comes an inescapable time in everyone's life when it is deemed appropriate by the karma police that they confront their past and their future simultaneously. Unfortunately for Cal Redman—a real menace to women, the bane of their existence, a goddamned thick-hipped, confident son of a bitch—this came at a time when he was already having trouble with his self-destructive present, which was about to become unfathomably worse.

All his could-have-beens were now never-will-bes. Unshaven late-afternoon brunches had replaced his early-morning jogs, and feeling sorry for himself was one of his favorite pastimes. If Cal's present life were a song, it would be in the country genre, probably a down-and-out oldie by Merle Haggard or the Louvin Brothers.

✳ ✳ ✳

This is it, definitely my last race as a crew chief, Cal thought as Bob (his only one true remaining friend) and he navigated their way out of their no-frills Spanish-style hotel. Step by crumbling step into the siesta-quiet, sun-drenched late afternoon of the not-so-sprawling metropolis of Ensenada: the start line for the twenty-fifth running of the infamous Baja 1000. The gentle whisper of a breeze combining traces of diesel, wood smoke, tequila and dog urine relentlessly swirled dirt through the heart of the low-rent shopping district, but still felt cool and welcoming on their faces as they moved forward. Another compliant step towards their favourite watering hole taken as effortlessly as they had taken one a hundred, maybe a thousand times before. (Who counted and who cared?) The two hopped off the final boot-worn, paint-peeling concrete step of the hotel's doorway like giddy hopscotching children and headed toward Hussong's, speculated to be the oldest still-thriving drinking hole in all of the Baja, possibly even in all of Mexico or North America, at one hundred and twenty-five years old. Hussong's was the birthplace of the margarita! If you valued your time there, you would not even think of arguing this point with the bartender. For Hussong's was still the best place in town to have a few of those overly salty, lemony refreshments and a lot of fun. Especially while the Baja 1000 was in town. When a place is that old, who can argue with its history anyway? And here it was once again, just a short, dusty limp away.

The limp: another small piece of the painful collection of collateral damage that seemed to be piling onto Cal's once barnyard-broad shoulders, that had started to weigh on him after the crash that had ended his finally starting-to-pay-off successful racing career only two years earlier. Bob, on the other hand, was actually happy not to be in the navigator's seat again and was enjoying the moment. They never talked about that stuff. Bob felt that to do so would somehow be letting Cal down. "Go all pusillanimous on him," as Cal would callously put it whenever Bob was feeling in a maudlin sort of way.

As the pair entered the exalted place of pilgrimage, shutting out the fading sun behind them, Bob, who had no idea his best friend would soon come to prominence (not in the Baja 1000 winners' circle but on Mexico's most-wanted list), was offering Cal his latest piece of advice.

"I know this is a touchy subject, little buddy, but you're now the crew chief, no longer the Lone Ranger out there driving with just you and me, and as such you should be leading by example. So tonight, take it easy on those margaritas, and the women, and let the older and wiser generations get a good night's sleep. We have a very early, long and exhausting day coming up tomorrow, not to mention the next forty-eight hours, so when I suggest it's time to skedaddle out of here you'll follow my lead, my attempt at showing maturity and wisdom, and exit with me, right?" Bob stared at Cal, hoping for an affirmative sign of acknowledgement. A simple nod of the head or tip of the hat would have sufficed. However, when Bob saw Cal's familiar devilish grin, he instinctively knew he would have some trouble getting Cal out of there early that night.

"That was not a rhetorical question." Bob sighed.

Cal adjusted his oversized mirrored aviation glasses that made him look like a fly; he had always thought they looked cool and had made them an entrenched part of his racing persona.

"It was a great day of tech inspection and pre-trial runs, I'm feeling lucky tonight. Carpe diem." With a wink, Cal was engulfed in the already noisy and smoke-filled establishment.

CHAPTER TWO

It seemed like ages ago that the crew had repaired the car and Turbo had come and gone, yet only thirty minutes had elapsed since his successful departure. Although problems of a mechanical nature could still happen to the Stallion, Turbo had made it past some of the most treacherous and barren landscape. As the drivers wound their way south to La Paz, there would be more towns and the distances between those inhabited areas would be shorter. It would normally be Cal and Bob's job to be at every stop. But Cal decided he would now tell Bob what he couldn't tell him the night before at Hussong's: that he had already told the Old Man this was going to be his last race, his last pit stop, and then he would turn the reins over to Bob.

"A quick beer before we head south?" asked Bob as he popped the tabs on two cans.

"Sure," said Cal, "but then I'm straight on my way to the finish line to watch the end of the race for a change and have nothing more to do with this race." Cal took the beverage from Bob and smacked the two cans together. He uttered the customary "cheers" and took an absolutely marvellous long, slow gulp.

"I needed one of these an hour ago." Cal grinned.

"Are you serious?" Bob asked.

"Bob, you can run the show on your own. You're the best mechanic on the circuit and there is not a crew chief out there that would not pay top dollar for you tomorrow. Don't think for a minute I don't know how many times over the years some other owner has made you an offer and how lucky I was that you stuck with me," Cal said.

"That kind of flattery would normally buy you an awful lot of beers, but you're serious, you're really walking?" Bob choked out.

"Why don't you join me when the race is over?" Cal suggested. "We're too old for this life. If we're going to do anything, let's start our own training school or something. That I could handle. I like the thought of coming home to the same place for dinner every night and hopefully with the same woman. I would even entertain the notion of having a kid or two, but I know that'll never happen as long as we keep trekking our asses around to the most barren and dusty places on earth."

"Home for dinner, eh? That's it? That's the extent of your ambition right now? And anyway, dinner with who?" Bob scoffed.

"That's exactly my point—look around. How are we ever going to meet anyone worth coming home to every night to have dinner with when we're spending half of our life on the road or in the middle of a godforsaken desert? I know it might just be this romantic notion I've conjured up in my head, but it just seems like something I'm yearning for again."

"Well," said Bob, "because the last one worked out so well. Listen, I'm no quitter. I promised the Old Man I would work the whole race so I am going to finish the goddamned race. Yeah, I know how tough it is. As well as he's done this year, he's still a bit short on sponsorship money and crew, but he's never let us down once, and I'm sure not going to let him down, especially right now.

And what about our dream, our own team? You giving up on that now too, is this what you're really saying?"

"Shit, I don't know anymore. Look around, man! Do you honestly think we would figure out how to raise the grubstake to pull all this together: two losers from Frisco who barely scraped through middle school? Neither one of us can balance a chequebook!" Cal finished with a drag of his cigarillo and started coughing and threw the thing away.

Both men laughed. Neither realized this would be their last laugh together before the real shit hit the fan.

Interrupting this monumental exchange of emotions between these two bullhorns, a pickup truck rolled in close to where Cal and Bob were standing and jolted to a cloudy, dusty stop. The driver hopped out and asked loudly, "Is Cal Redman around?"

"Over here," Cal replied. "What's up?"

"I've got a package for you," the driver said. "Or rather, something well packaged," he added as he walked over and handed Cal a note. "Here. From the Old Man."

Cal took the crumpled note and read it silently:

Hey there, Cal; hope all is running well. Since this was your last pit, as you had informed me, I didn't think you would mind running Laura down to La Paz. She is the widow of a good friend of mine (whom I know you know all too well) and has decided to do her first article as a writer on the Baja 1000. I'll let her fill you in on the rest. (I'm sure you'll find it interesting!) I wouldn't trust her with anyone else but you. I hope you don't mind this one last favour. See you at the finish and hopefully we'll be enjoying a victory cerveza together this year.

Thanks,
The Old Man

Cal looked up just in time to see a woman step out of the truck. The rest of the crew stopped doing whatever they were doing to look at her as well.

"Bob?" Laura screamed, looking excited.

"Holy shit. Hey gal, give us a hug."

"You know her?" Cal asked.

"Sure do and so do you. That's Marty's widow, Laura."

"That's Laura? Wow, let's hear it for Weight Watchers." Cal looked shocked.

"In the flesh," Bob replied to Cal as he stepped forward into Laura's open arms. "What a treat seeing you again," Bob said as they hugged warmly.

"I'd better get going," said the driver, watching the scene. "I've gotta get this tank of gas all the way down to mile 800 or Turbo will be looking for a ride to La Paz and I'll be looking for a new job."

"You'd better get your ass in gear. Turbo left here over half an hour ago," Cal told the driver, who was already scrambling back into his truck.

"Well then, it's a good thing he has to take the scenic route while I got nothing but a beautiful two-lane highway all the way now." The driver left in a cloud of dust, his wheels kicking up a few buckets of sand before they caught and he sped away, scattering the onlookers in every direction.

"God, what a wonderful surprise seeing you here," Laura said to Bob. Her eyes had the sparkle of someone who had just come across an oasis in the middle of a desert.

"God, what a wonderful surprise seeing you here," Cal mimicked. "I have to spend the next sixteen hours with that? What the hell is the Old Man thinking?" Cal said to himself, but just a little too loud.

"What are you complaining about? Now I wish I was going straight to La Paz with you," Bob said.

"So do I, but you still give a shit and I don't, remember?"

"Hi, I'm Laura, I've heard a lot about you. It's a pleasure to finally meet you." Laura extended her hand to Cal.

"The pleasure's all mine," Cal said sarcastically. "I guess I'm your new tour guide for the second half of the race." Then he turned and headed for his truck.

"What's with him?" Laura asked Bob as they walked over to the truck more slowly.

"He's got a boulder up his ass because he isn't racing anymore and your new boy is," Bob said.

"My boy?" Laura sounded surprised.

"Rumour was you and Turbo are a number now," Bob said with a wink. "Sorry to hear about Marty. He was a hell of a racer and a great guy, too," Bob added softly.

"Well, come along now, little missy, or we'll miss the big finale," Cal called from beside his truck, doing a very bad John Wayne imitation.

Laura gave Bob another giant hug. "See you at the bottom, and I assure you it's just a rumour, about Turbo. There isn't anything going on there," she said, and then she strode over to Cal's truck and hopped up into the massive six-wheeler, as if she had done it a thousand times before.

Bob put his arm around Cal and leaned in, and in a quiet, serious tone said, "You take good care of her now and we'll all have a drink tomorrow night by the ocean, under the palms in La Paz."

"Never mind tomorrow, Bob, live for today, tomorrow is overrated. A lot of people won't even get to see it." Cal answered sarcastically back.

"Now you're contradicting yourself. You just said you wanted someone to have dinner with every night. That is a complete philosophical about-face. Seriously, I'm getting a funny feeling about this one. Just had some big shivers up my spine, and whenever that occurs, shit happens, and you know I'm always right, so you be careful out there, good buddy."

"Not to worry, I'm just going to take my time—chill all the way down, and we'll see you in La Paz. And you best get your honourable ass over to the next pit." Cal grabbed Bob's hand and they bumped collarbones.

CHAPTER THREE

As Cal jumped in, Laura handed him a stack of papers and files that had piled up on the passenger seat. Cal shoved them under his seat, with some force as it was already crammed with other garbage.

"Excuse the chaos but this cab has been my ride, office, restaurant and bed for most of the past twenty-four hours."

"Judging by the smell it wouldn't take much to convince me of that," Laura said sarcastically, and then realized she probably shouldn't have said anything. But I'm sure it'll be nice once we clean it up a bit."

"Clean it up? Not until we hit La Paz, no time for that. She may be a bit untidy, but this is the best running truck you'll ever seat your ass in," Cal said rather matter-of-factly as he eased it into first gear.

Cal's brand-new Dodge Ram diesel sounded like an eighteen-wheeler as it rumbled from the now half-abandoned pit stop. Cal could almost justify the work and the upgrades he had done to it under the debatable tax category of "I needed the upgrades for work." Nevertheless, other than having it raised up for the extra ground clearance, which had come in handy from time to time, all the other bells and whistles, such as the chrome package, metallic paint, pipe, transmission and heavy-engine upgrades, had all really been done for show.

Laura and Cal rode in silence for the first twenty minutes or so, until they reached the paved highway, finally leaving the makeshift, bumpy dirt road that had led to the midway stop.

The tension was a little more uncomfortable for Laura than for Cal. Cal just went into his cave. Laura kept glancing over, wondering what to say, but ended up opting for the safer element of silence and looked out her side window or straight ahead.

When the Ram hit smooth (by Baja standards) pavement Laura reached into her bag and pulled out a small tape recorder, a pen and paper.

It was a luxurious ride of sorts. The soft glowing lights of the dashboard and plush leather seats the likes of which she had never had the luxury of settling into before felt pretty relaxing, she had to admit. She was trying to imagine what it was like to be Cal driving around in such a big rig all day long. She could tell he was quite proud and comfortable with the truck.

"Well, I guess this is as good a time as any. Shall we get started then?" Laura leaned in and turned the radio down a few notches, but she left it on enough that you could hear the static-riddled song just a bit in the background. She thought this would add a nice touch to the interview. Laura held the tape recorder close to her mouth.

"Captain's log—Star date—November, umm, twelfth I think, I've lost track, nineteen ninety-two."

"What's all this?" Cal asked with a big grin as he looked over at Laura.

"This is your time to shine; this is your fifteen minutes of fame. You're being interviewed for ORM." Laura smiled back.

"Wow, I'm going to finally be in *Off Road Magazine* after all these years. Is this the retired, rather-washed-up has-been portion of the article?" Cal was trying very hard not to succumb to Laura's warm smile. As pretty as she was, Laura had a way of putting just about everyone at ease as soon as she started talking to them.

"Hardly," she replied in her usual soft but confident voice. "I know we didn't talk much when you were racing against Marty."

"Yes, sorry to hear of his passing, hell of a racer," Cal jumped in.

"Thank you. But it's racer-world protocol for the wives not to get too friendly with the other drivers, or even the ladies for that matter. Just the way things unfold in this world." Laura looked down at her pad for no particular reason. Cal could tell she was holding back a tear, but chose not to say anything.

Clearing her throat, she finally looked up again.

"I miss him dearly, every day. It's funny how we don't ever think about a person that way when they are here. You just go about your busy lives, then one day they are suddenly taken from you and it's like wow, this giant void yet filled with pain. It gets lonelier and hurts more each day for a long time, and then one day—you don't realize it until later—but you actually got through a day without crying and maybe even laughed. Then slowly you move forward again." After clearing her throat she began again and clicked on the recorder.

"This is Laura Thompson and as stated earlier, this is November twelfth, nineteen ninety-two. We are just leaving the halfway point of the historic twenty-fifth running of the Baja 1000 and I am now riding down to the finish line in La Paz with a long-time veteran of the race Mr. Cal Redman."

Laura passed for a moment before starting the recorder again. She knew she had to choose her words, her questions very carefully. She had to tread carefully so as not to upset or offend her subject in any way.

"So, Mr. Redman," Laura started in.

"Call me Cal."

Laura hesitated for a second.

"Okay, Cal, I understand you got started in off-road as soon as you could drive. What got you interested in the sport?"

"Well, even before I could legally drive, I don't know what all your readers would be interested in, but I grew up in northern Alberta, Canada. My dad was a travelling salesman so he was away a lot. We had a huge open valley behind the house. Pops bought me a dirt bike when I was about twelve thinking it would keep me busy and out of trouble. I spent a lot a time on that thing just out back so I guess it worked."

There was a moment's silence; Laura had not expected Cal to stop talking so soon. She found there was a charming dichotomy in how he was somewhat awkward talking about himself but brash at the same time.

"How did you make the transition from backyard dirt biking to making a living at it?"

"Well, that took much longer than I expected but it all started that summer, when I got the bike. I was out riding one day, and I dropped the bike pretty hard. I was having trouble getting it going when this kid slightly older than me appears and asks if I need any help. That was the moment I met Bob and the day my life would head off on its trajectory to here. Bob was from San Diego and was visiting some relatives in the neighbourhood for a few weeks. He said he could hear the bike so he would walk over to a nearby maple and sit there and watch me ride. At thirteen he was already working on cars and bikes at his local garage, it's what he liked to do. Well, he not only got the bike going he came over to the house the next day and made some seemingly simple modifications that made the bike so much better to ride. I couldn't believe it."

"San Diego is a long way from northern Alberta. Have you been friends since then?"

"Pretty much. As it turned out, my dad took a management position with the company in San Francisco a year later, so Bob and I spent a lot of time driving up and down the coast until one day we were old enough to buy our first buggy and we started racing together in the summers. So we were mostly just on the road together during the race season. Man, that guy could fix anything, including a few of my broken hearts along the way."

Cal choked up a bit as he looked over at Laura and smiled.

"So fast-forward a few years, you and Bob are now crew chief and mechanic for Edwards Racing, your racing career cut short due to an accident, I heard?"

Cal looked sideways at Laura, no readable expression on his face. She wasn't sure if she had offended him with that question or if he just was caught off guard by it.

"Okay, that's fine for now." Laura broke the silence. "I'm much more tired than I thought. There will be lots of time for questions later," she continued as she shut off the recorder and folded up her notebook.

"It's okay, I'm sorry. Yeah, we are working for the Old Man now, as we like to call him on the team, and trying to keep cocky, upstart young racers like your Turbo in the race. Yes, sad but true, life does not always turn out the way you hoped. But we hope to have our own team one day, and maybe even race again?" Cal's answer had more than a tinge of bitterness to it even though Cal thought he had done his best to cover it up and Laura regretted having brought up the subject so early on in their time together.

"'My Turbo'? What the hell is with you and Bob? I spent an evening interviewing him over dinner and he took me out for a ride in the 'Stallion,' as he calls it, since you guys like to give everything a handle. It can't be just a 'race car.' And now everyone thinks we're an item. Really, this is like being back in high school." Laura leaned back in her seat with her arms folded around her body like metal strapping and stared out the window.

Luckily, Cal did not have one of his satirical responses at the ready and so they drove on in silence.

Laura was enjoying the quietness of the "red-eye flight." She knew she should be taking advantage of the situation, asking Cal tons more questions and making plenty of notes for her article, but she had not realized how tired she was until she got so comfortable, and now would be just as happy to curl up, go to sleep and wake up in La Paz. She could ask him plenty later on.

Cal, on the other hand, had been coddling a bottle of tequila since he put the truck in drive. After feeling the tires hit tar, he knew he could now make some real time and took an extra big gulp of the stuff he called the "Drink of Souls." For the first time since he'd cracked open the bottle, he gestured to Laura to partake in a swig, as if travelling with an old buddy. Not saying a word, Laura looked at Cal and shook her head with an emphatic no, not realizing she would have gained a few thousand brownie points with the cantankerous, aging fart by simply pretending to accept his offer and faking a swig. Cal, feeling Laura was just trying to be superior, took it as a personal rejection, not knowing her real reasons for turning it down. Not a lot of women Cal had been hanging around with lately turned down a swig of good quality Tequila. He took a long, slow, dejected draw off his half-finished cigarillo. "Do you know what I think is the secret as to why tequila is so powerful and mysterious?"

"It would be amazing if I did," Laura quipped back, sounding a little annoyed. She'd been thinking she was going to get off easy, put her head back, close her eyes and get some much-needed rest. "Considering that we've just met."

"They say that every time a Mexican dies"—Cal looked at Laura intently for a second, considering what he was about to say—"their soul becomes the seeds of a new cactus, and those souls get transferred into every bottle of tequila. That's why this stuff is so damned amazing."

"I'm speechless. I really have no idea how to respond to that."

"So the Old Man's note said this was your first article for the rag. Unfortunately, nobody ever reads those things. They just look at the ads, ogle the chicks and check out the standings. So you want to be a writer?" Cal said with a smile, knowing he had completely caught her off guard with his previous observation.

"I am a writer," Laura whispered back quietly as if she wasn't sure of her answer, her head still turned away, looking through the side window as she watched the statuesque giant cacti pass by, lit only by the chilling bluish soft glow of the full moon and the side of the headlights. "I just haven't been published yet."

"Is that your standard Wednesday-night writing-group mantra?" Cal jibed. "You sure you wouldn't like some? If you're going to be a serious writer, you must adopt your own brand of venom, your own trademark as it were." Once again, Cal passed Laura the bottle. Once again, she politely declined.

"I've drunk enough venom from every trademark on every bottle imaginable to write three novels. It's time I focused on the writing part," replied Laura, still looking out the side window, trying hard not to emit any emotion.

Cal held out the bottle a few seconds longer before his hand dropped to his side. He continued to stare at Laura, lit only by the full moon that was trying to press in through the heavily tinted windows and the very soft glow emanating from the dashboard. Cal usually had the dash lights setting on high because he envisioned it resembled the cockpit of a jumbo jet at night. But with Laura in the cab, he had it turned way down low. At that moment, he noticed for the first time how truly beautiful Laura's face was and, in particular, what a stunning profile she possessed. In this lighting, sitting cross–legged, her head tilted against the window, he would have pegged her age at twenty-something if he didn't know any better. Then his eyes drifted downward as he took in her whole body. Her long shiny chestnut-brown hair shimmered, heaving softly with every slow, gentle breath she took.

Laura, oblivious to Cal's stare, turned to look in his direction. Their eyes locked and, for an instant, they reached one of those understandings, neither one knowing what the other was thinking, an awkward yet pleasant moment. Laura grinned. Cal wasn't sure: Had he been busted or had he managed to look up at just the right time? Laura was thinking this ride was almost perfect, marred only by Cal's arrogant attitude and the crackling Mexican music on the radio.

"Do we have to listen to all this static? Surely, there must be a better station or do you have a cassette? If it wasn't for the music, this would actually be quite a pleasant ride."

"Cassette, I can do way better than that. This mother has a CD player in it. Speaking of static, I'm sorry I was a little ornery at the beginning of the trip there."

"Just a little, ya think?"

"You should get me on a bad day."

"I can hardly wait."

Noticing a little smile, a crack in the armour, Cal loosened up. "You caught me and Bob at a bad time as it was, and I was looking forward to booking off and riding down to La Paz alone and then you showed up, so really, just bad timing, I'm sorry. Some people think I'm a pretty nice guy sometimes."

"So does that mean you'll change the music, Mr. Nice Guy?"

"If you're in the right frame of mind, it isn't bad. The static starts to blend in with the music and adds to the character of the song, and it's a hell of a lot better than the static you were giving me about the static." Cal noticed he had prodded a smile out of her again.

"But hey, if you don't like it, no problemo." Cal leaned over to change the station. In the process, the cigarillo fell from his mouth and rolled under his seat.

"So what's your real story?" Laura asked.

"Real story?" Cal sounded surprised.

"Yeah, why are you so bitter? A walking exemplar of 'tragic loneliness,'" Laura said pointedly.

"You've known me what, precisely fifty-five minutes?" Cal said, looking at his watch. "And you have me already pegged as bitter and lonely. What makes you such an expert at personality diagnosis?"

"Well, I'm certainly no expert on personalities, but hey, do I know bitter," Laura said as she went back to gazing out her window. Cal continued to adjust the radio and simultaneously rummaged around for his cigarillo, periodically taking his hand from the radio to keep the truck on the road.

"Okay, off the record."

Cal gave up on looking for his cigarillo for a few seconds, and recited:

"How happy is he born and taught
That serveth not another's will;
Whose armour is his honest thought,
And simple truth his utmost skill!"

"That's very profound," Laura offered. "Did you pen it?" she asked, and turned to face Cal with a look of sincere interest.

"I wish I had." Cal grinned. "That, my dear, is Sir Henry Wotton, a superb bard to the likes of which I could only aspire. I do however possess a glove box full of crumpled-up sheets of pathetic diatribe, if you wish to give some of my stuff a read."

Cal realized he had just invited Laura to examine his life, as he resumed trying to find the missing cigarillo, which had now married up with a menagerie of garbage—fast-food wrappers laden in grease and receipts burning quietly but efficiently under his seat and filling the cab with smoke.

With neither one of them overly worried about the cigar or the smoke at this point, Laura opened the glove box and peered inside. "How lovely. A handgun snuggled in so cozily beside your poems. When you're not in the mood to wax poetic, you can just go out and shoot something; a true Renaissance man . . . Um, I don't wish to push the panic button just yet, but it's getting awfully smoky in here. Is everything okay over there?"

Coughing, Laura realized she had to lower her window to let some of the thickening smoke escape. She had just now realized that something other than the cigarillo was burning: a full-fledged fire was raging underneath Cal's seat.

"Very cynical, Mrs. Thompson, maybe there is a writer in you after all. And I think I have this under control, just need to lift the mat up." Cal lifted his head long enough to respond and to take a quick look at the road, then went back to searching for the smouldering culprit, but burned his hand this time and had to pull it away.

Laura was extremely nervous now; she could see the flames blistering under Cal's seat, the rubber floor mat had caught fire, and the smoke was turning a thick black. Laura could tell the situation was out of control. Cal was trying to keep his cool but could not see clearly enough to drive, he had to put his window down, and Laura got upset.

"Damn it, Cal! Just pull over so you can throw out the cigar, last night's dinner and the rest of the garbage that's burning under there and get back to driving!"

"I would, darlin', except I can't," Cal replied, annoyed.

"This is a forty-thousand-dollar four-wheel-drive truck. What the hell do you mean, you can't just pull over? Isn't this exactly what you bought it for so you could just pull over wherever the hell you felt like it?"

"We're in the middle of the Baja desert, with no soft shoulder to pull over onto. The grade is a foot straight down right here, and I'm hauling a five-hundred-gallon drum in the back full to the brim with high-octane fuel. If I pull over here, even if I'm lucky enough not to roll the truck, it'll sink into the sand quicker than the Buffalo Bills at Super Bowl time and we'll be stuck there until morning. I'm waiting for the next driveway, rancher's back road, intersection or just for the road to level out a bit. Hopefully sooner rather than later," Cal said, trying to get a little sympathy, but receiving only the sound of exasperation and a roll of Laura's eyes.

With her window down and her face tilted toward the breeze, Laura could smell the cacti. The cool, dry desert air whipped her hair around her face. She willed the sensation to calm her, but her frustration kept building. "I'm worried we're going to crash, you're all over the road from too much to drink and now we have a campfire burning in the truck, so if you can't pull over, then can you just stop and put the fire out!" Laura shouted at Cal.

"There are a couple of semis barrelling down the road behind us, so no, I can't just stop. I thought I was just going to be looking for a cigarillo, not putting out a toxic catastrophe."

Cal put his window down as he eased off the gas pedal a little. He reached under his seat and tried to pull the mat out, but he forgot that he had set the tequila bottle on the floor and he bumped it, knocking it over. Tequila flowed into the inferno. Within seconds, the flames were leaping up between Cal's legs and licking the sides of his seat.

"There are some work gloves right behind you on the bench

seat, can you put them on and pull this floor mat out?" Cal said, trying to sound calm.

Laura went to work as quickly as she could. Found the gloves, undid her seat belt and leaned over as far as she could, practically in Cal's face; she could smell the alcohol and tobacco on his breath.

"You smell like a cheap motel," Laura said with a tinge of disgust.

"Well, I must say, you smell pretty damn good for a gal who's been out in the Mexican desert all day."

Laura glared at him for a split second before she reached down to grab the inflamed mat. Ironically, there was a faint reflection from the flames growing below them reflecting in Laura's eyes, which made her look like a crazed she-woman about to bite his head off. The expression (yes, incorrectly quoted, but Cal preferred his own version) "Hell has no fury like a woman's scorn" jumped into Cal's head. With her head buried deep into the space next to Cal's right leg she held her breath and pulled as hard as she could to unclip the mat from the floor. Cal could barely see anything now, and the fire was starting to feel hot even through his boots.

Using both hands, Laura tried to lift the flaming mat up and throw it out the window but was struggling with the clips that held it to the floor. Finally she had to abort and bring her hands up. Even with the gloves on the heat was too much for her.

Both tractor trailers behind them were on their horns now, as Cal had slowed down considerably.

"What's their problem?" Laura asked huffily.

"They have nowhere to go, too many risers and bends right here, and of course they don't realize that we have a campfire going on in here. Hang on tight, little lady," Cal muttered in his bad John Wayne style again.

"What? What are you doing?" Laura asked as she moved back into her seat and did up her seat belt.

"Let's see what this baby is made of." And with that Cal turned the wheel sharply to the left so as not to impede the trucks behind him, and crossed over the highway and into the ambiguity of the desert terrain. Laura felt what seemed like a thousand grains of sand hitting her in the face and pushed on the window control as hard as she could, hoping to make it go faster but the sand kept on pummelling her hard in the face, a stinging, sharp pain.

Cal had the sand and the fact that as the windows went up he could not see as the smoke quickly filled the cab, but before Cal could bring the vehicle to a safe stop, it came to a somewhat more abrupt stop than he had anticipated. The new Dodge Ram was now firmly squished in between two giant cacti. Neither Cal nor Laura could get their door open, but Cal managed to get the flaming floor mat out through the sunroof, and with all the windows now open the cab quickly cleared of smoke. Cal and Laura sat and looked at each other, neither one saying a word as Laura stared in disbelief at the humongous cactus that was determinedly wedged up against her side window, another on Cal's side so that you could hardly see out the windows, let alone get the doors open. Several attempts to move the truck in either direction failed, the vehicle intractably fixed to the cacti, only sinking farther into the sand, wedging the truck and their hopes of getting out of there in a hurry in even deeper.

The driver of the second semi that had been following brought his truck to an abrupt stop but after sizing up the situation as stable, decided to call the local authorities and then hightail it out of there rather than waste time sticking around and having to help fill out a report. It was not long after that call that Cal and Laura were hauled into the local police station for the night, while the police had to cut and tow their truck out.

What neither of the pair realized, was that this was not the end of a little mishap on the road to La Paz, but the beginning of the worst nightmare of their lives.

CHAPTER FOUR

An irritating *hiss* had been emitting from the harsh, glaring industrial light just outside the jailhouse window, keeping Laura awake most of the night. Finally, as the sun crept above the horizon, there was a loud *click* and the light and hiss simultaneously ceased to exist. The whitewashed stucco wall at which she had been staring for the past hour now looked cheerful and bright as it caught the first offerings of the morning sun.

Startled by a crash down the hall, Laura came out of her semi-conscious state as she heard Cal's voice for the first time since they had been incarcerated.

Cal (one cell over) was finally awake, and was staring across the hall at the police captain. As he read the name on the brass plate that was loosely nailed to the door just below the dirty glass, Cal flung his tin drinking cup (which he then discovered also contained a two-inch cockroach) through the bars of his cell. The cockroach scuttled away when it hit the floor of the captain's office, knocking the cup out of its way.

"Hey, Captain, what's the score here? You can let us out now. I'm awake, we're good to go," Cal hollered across the hall.

"Redman, you get your ass off that bench and get us out of here!" Cal heard Laura shriek at him from her cell next to his. Then Cal heard another voice, with a Spanish accent this time, coming from the other end of the hall.

"What's going on down there, everything okay?" the unseen voice asked.

The captain came out from behind his desk, opened his door and walked over to Cal's cell. "It's okay, Anthony," the captain said in Spanish, looking down the hall in the direction of the voice. "I'll take care of it. Go back to your paperwork."

Cal found himself staring in amazement at Captain Ambrose Gonzalez. At first, Cal wanted to laugh. He had finally come face-to-face with a real-live film-noir Mexican police captain. Short, fat, balding, and with a need to stick his chest out to prove his manliness. He also fondled his pistol a lot (which made Cal very nervous) or periodically twirled his thin handlebar moustache. Cal decided it was best to keep his sarcasm to himself for once, as it might land him in a great deal more trouble than he was already in.

"Hey, *que pasa*? Why are we still in this place?" Cal asked as politely as he could.

"Yes, Señor Redman," the captain said, rubbing his chin with his left hand, resisting the temptation to twirl the moustache yet again.

"You and the lovely lady are free to go as soon as you pay us the two hundred American dollars that is the going rate for causing damage to one of our historic and rare giant cacti. Actually, in your case that will be four hundred, as it seems you caused considerable, maybe even irreparable damage to two of our most prized tourist attractions down here."

"That's fine," replied Cal, relieved. "I'm sure we can muster that up between us."

"That's good," mused the captain. "Because that is just the beginning. Then all we have to worry about is"—he flipped through his notepad—"drunk driving, which is a mere five hundred, in cash, of course, so we can avoid the time and embarrassment of court. Oh, yes! I almost forgot. There is also the issue of the gun in the glove box. As a veteran racer you should know this is very unacceptable in the Baja. This alone carries a minimum of two thousand US dollars or a short stay in one of our lovely federal prisons. That sentence is set at the discretion of the judge of the day." The captain inserted a dramatic pause for effect. "And the removal and the towing of your truck back to the station here. Sergeant, can you bring Mr. Redman's total bill, please?" After a moment of studying the handwritten sheet, the captain looked at Cal.

"Three thousand American dollars. Yes, we can just round this off to three thousand." The captain smiled slyly.

The captain and Cal stared at each other for a few seconds, and Cal realized he had to calm down and gain control of the situation.

"I gather you won't take Amex, Visa or MasterCard for this?" Cal asked with a grin. Then Cal noticed the bottle of tequila on the captain's cabinet. "Why don't we go into your office and discuss this like gentlemen?" suggested Cal. "I'll buy you a drink."

"Hey, what about me?" The two men heard Laura's concerned voice from next door.

"You don't drink."

"I'm happy to start again if it'll get us out of here."

"Hold your horses, little lady, let me deal with this. I'll have us out of here in no time."

"Right, just like you got us down to La Paz," Laura snapped at Cal, as she sat back on the wooden bench in exasperation.

"Don't try anything funny," Gonzalez said as he let Cal out of his cell and ushered him across the hall into his office.

Gonzalez took two dusty, sticky shot glasses out of his cabinet, gave them a light blow and wiped them with the rag that he'd just cleaned his gun with, and poured two generous shots. Both men swallowed the entire contents of their glass in one gulp.

Cal held out his glass. Gonzalez smiled, poured two more shots, sat back and put his feet on his desk.

"So, Mr. Redman, how are we going to remedy the severity of this expensive little misfortune?"

"You're not serious, are you? I don't carry that kind of cash on me," Cal retorted with a half smirk as he helped himself to another shot.

"Why would you think I am not serious, Mr. Redman?" the captain inquired. "Do I look like I'm joking?"

"Call me Cal."

"Okay, Cal," he drawled. "Why would I not be serious? Because you're a gringo or were once a famous racer, I should just let you go?"

"No! Because I don't have that kind of money on me and I've probably lost my job by now anyway."

"How much money *do* you have on you?"

Cal leaned forward and felt for his well-worn, weathered wallet. Of course it wasn't anywhere to be found.

The captain opened up his drawer and pulled out Cal's wallet.

"Okay, *you* tell *me* how much I have." Cal frowned.

The captain thumbed a small row of bills (although he already knew how much Cal had) and looked at Cal.

"You have two hundred and fifty American and another few thousand in pesos." The captain frowned. "That will barely cover the tow charge. You'll have to do much better if you want to get out of here anytime soon."

Cal sat quietly for some time, weighing the captain's question.

Finally, he said, "Let me check with accounting," and he stuck his head out the door.

"Oh Laura, darling, how much money do you have on you?"

There was a moment's silence. Then they heard an exasperated, "About five hundred in my bag."

"Actually, four hundred and eighty," said the captain. "Her bag is in our safe."

"Would you take that for now?" asked a hopeful Cal. "It's almost eight hundred American."

"No, not nearly enough," replied the captain. "It's an insult," he added, "especially after we may have saved your lives and your beautiful truck out there."

"If I can get to the next pit stop I could get another thousand US from a friend of mine."

It was the captain's turn to be silent. "That's the best you can do?"

"That's the best I can do today," Cal said.

"The girl stays here until you come back."

"That's fine," Cal said. "She's a royal pain in the ass anyway."

"My sergeant, Ramiros, will go with you."

"What for?" snapped Cal. "I'm leaving Pebbles behind as a security deposit. My ass wouldn't be worth two wooden nickels if I didn't come back and get her." There was a long silence between the two men, then a slow grin broke out on both their faces.

"I see," said Cal, understanding slowly dawning in his cranium. "You'd like some time alone with Pebbles, to get to know her better."

"If it's not too much trouble, since I am letting you off the hook for roughly two thousand dollars—a savings of over one thousand."

"Hey, no trouble at all." Cal grinned. "Just throw in the rest of that bottle and we'll be on our way. It'll be about three hours. I'll need something to drink."

"It's your liver," Captain Gonzalez admonished as he handed Cal the half-empty bottle of tequila. They stepped out into the hallway.

"Ramiros!" snapped the captain.

"Yes, sir!" replied the sergeant. He jumped out from behind his desk. Cal noticed the sergeant had strategically angled his desk to catch the maximum amount of light coming in through the single tiny barred window in the hallway. Cal also noticed a picture of a very beautiful Mexican woman beside a simple clay pot with a blossoming flower in it. He sized the sergeant up as a gentle, thoughtful person.

"You're to escort Mr. Redman here to wherever it is he has to go to get the money for his and the lady's release and bring him back—with the money, and preferably alive, understood?"

"Understood, Captain," the young sergeant respectfully replied.

"Here, take the new cruiser," said the captain as he flipped Ramiros the keys.

"Thanks, Captain!" Ramiros graced him with a wide smile.

The friendly tone of the male bonding going on in the hallway was abruptly interrupted by the stark, frightened voice of Laura who had caught smidgens of the conversation. "Cal Redman, there is no way in hell you're just leaving me here! Not in a million years!" Cal walked over to Laura's cell and stood in front of her.

"Listen up." Cal spoke in a low voice so as not to be overheard by the captain and his sergeant. "I don't have time to explain, but I want you to pretend to be really pissed off at me as I walk away."

"Pretend!" Laura raised her voice. "I don't have to pretend, I am pissed off at you!"

"Quiet down," Cal ordered. "I don't have any choice. You only have to stay a few hours." Cal turned and walked towards the two police officers.

"You better come back, Redman, or your ass won't be worth the shit that's in it!" Laura screamed as Ramiros and Cal left the building. Laura ran over to the window at the back of her cell, put both hands on the bars, went up on her tiptoes and watched Cal and Ramiros walk to the truck. Then Laura heard the *clang* of a key being inserted in the locked door behind her. She let go of the bars and turned to see the captain, who was also escorting a bottle of wine and two glasses. He entered her cell.

CHAPTER FIVE

Cal attempted to make conversation with the sergeant as they walked towards the truck. He asked Ramiros if he liked his job.

Ramiros replied by asking if Cal liked being "a washed-up racer arrested on several trumped-up charges in the middle of nowhere." That was the extent of their conversation until they reached the new police truck.

Cal waited for Ramiros to unlock the passenger door. As soon as he had, Cal slammed the half-empty bottle of tequila down hard on Ramiros's head. Ramiros dropped to the gravel driveway with a heavy *thud* so loud Cal thought the captain might hear it.

"It's a really nice wine, Santo Tomas Cabernet Sauvignon. Made here in the Baja, 1989. I've been saving it for just such an occasion," the captain said as he entered Laura's cell.

"I'm sure it's a lovely wine, but it's late November so I'd rather be drinking a light Beaujolais Nouveau poolside right about now, if you don't mind, and more to the point, I was trying to tell you,

you did not have to send Cal out for the money. I'm sure I could have covered whatever the bill was with my credit card or a Western Union transfer," Laura offered.

"An unregistered gun is an automatic two years minimum in Mexico. It's best these things are kept quiet and paid in cash or gratuities right here." Gonzalez leered as he poured the wine, his two gold tooth caps glistening in the tiny bit of sun that was slowly creeping into Laura's cell.

"Gratuities?" Laura said, truly grasping the severity of her situation.

"I was hoping you would understand." The captain demonstrated deep sighs. "Relax. You'll see I'm a very nice guy to spend some time with."

Laura cast a glance at the captain's wedding ring. "I'll be sure to let the missus know how lucky she is."

"Gonzalez. My name is Ambrose Gonzalez."

"Well, Ambrose, I'll be sure to let Mrs. Gonzalez know what a gentleman you've been," Laura said crisply. She was hoping he would catch her meaning and go away. She realized, though, that this might not have been the first time the captain had been in this situation and that he did not care what idle threats of infidelity she presented him with.

The captain and Laura heard the engine roar as Cal and Ramiros drove the truck away from the jailhouse.

"Here, enjoy your wine," Gonzalez said sternly as he handed Laura a glass. "It seems we'll have most of the day to ourselves."

Laura lifted the glass towards the captain and then brought it to her mouth.

"Cheers," she said with a nervous smile as she took her first tiny sip, trying not to let too much wine in and all the while trying to think of a way to avoid a physical confrontation with the captain. She was in good shape but knew she would be no match for the captain if he forced himself on her. She hoped she could keep him interested in light talk and drinking until she could concoct a plan. She figured friendly and polite would buy her time.

✳ ✳ ✳

Outside, Cal had backed the truck down the jailhouse parking lot revving the engine as loud as he could to make sure the captain heard the truck leaving, giving the false assurance that he and Ramiros were on their way to obtaining the required cash to spring him and Laura free.

Pulling the truck over at the end of the driveway, Cal found Ramiros's handcuffs and put them on the sergeant for good measure. Then Cal found a tire iron in the back of the pickup, grabbed it and walked quietly back to the jailhouse. He found the window of Laura's cell. He could see and hear Laura and the captain as he knelt near the far side of the window, well out of sight. He could hear Laura trying desperately but politely to change the course of what was on Gonzalez's mind.

Luckily for Cal and Laura this was a very old, small jailhouse, usually reserved for one-night stays by the local drunks or criminals awaiting transfer to a larger facility. The jail itself was a very simple adobe structure, built in 1947 in the traditional Mexican style. The holding cells, of which there were only three, were below ground level to help keep them cool and only metal bars were used in the windows—no glass—to allow for ample airflow. There would normally be a few more officers milling around but they had all been dispatched to various locations throughout the Baja because of the race. The place was unusually quiet, partly because it was set back off the main highway about five hundred feet, then hidden down in a small gully, surrounded by a gravel parking lot and nothing but cacti and scrub for miles. Very isolated and very difficult for anyone to make a swift getaway by foot.

Cal waited for the captain to take a drink of his wine, then tossed in a small pebble that hit Laura. She turned quickly to see Cal, who gave her a brief wave and then leaned out of sight again. Laura, completely relieved, let out a big sigh and moved closer to the window.

She took a gulp of her wine and held out her glass to the captain. "Would you mind filling it up again?" she asked. "I'm thirstier than I thought."

The captain grinned from ear to ear like the Cheshire cat. "*Sí,* now that's more like it," he said heartily as he leaned over to pick up the bottle. Laura took the opportunity to look at Cal. He was spinning his finger around in circles, mouthing the words, "Turn him around! Turn him around!"

"What's so interesting out the window?" Laura heard the captain ask as she looked back at him quickly.

"Nothing, it's just such a beautiful day. I thought we could go outside for a while. It's a little dank and musty in here. I would feel much better if I could take off some of these clothes I've been in all night and lie in the sun. It's not like I'm going to try and run away. From what I recall, we're in the middle of nowhere."

The captain went motionless for a moment as he contemplated the image of Laura barely clothed, covered in suntan lotion, lying on one of the chaise longues on the patio out back of the jailhouse.

Gonzalez laughed. "That is a lovely thought," he said, and moved in closer as he refilled Laura's glass. Laura responded by also moving in closer. Playfully she tipped her glass to his before taking a small sip.

"I suspect the men will be at least several hours before returning, so why don't we enjoy that time instead of being cooped up in here?

Laura put her glass down, placed her hands on the captain's shoulders and backed him up to the wall under the window.

"There, now you stay there. Close your eyes. I'll slip into something a little more appropriate for an afternoon on a patio, and then we'll go outside and enjoy our wine."

Laura went over to her bag, which was sitting beside the bed, and started to rustle through it, hoping that how she had placed the captain was what Cal wanted and that he would do whatever it was he was going to do soon.

She pulled a top out of her bag and held it up to look at it.

"I think this will do."

She lifted her T-shirt over her head, exposing her impressive formations, barely covered by a lace bra.

"Close your eyes," Laura instructed.

Gonzalez, in a complete state of disbelief at his reversal of fortune, closed his eyes but stumbled forward. To get him back into position under the window, Laura leaned forward and put her arms around him. Gonzalez, slightly shorter than her, buried his head in Laura's bosom. She slowly backed the two of them up so that Gonzalez was against the wall under the open window again.

When Laura looked up, she saw Cal doing everything he could to hold back his laughter.

"Now?" she mouthed quietly but forcefully. Cal cupped his hand to his ear, pretending not to have heard her.

"Now?" she said a little louder. The captain began to move his head around in her cleavage and his hands started to become active up and down her back, which made her shiver with repulsion.

"Now?" asked Gonzalez, surprised, without looking up. "I thought you wanted to go out to the patio."

"Yes, now!" yelled Laura as she looked up at Cal who had had enough fun and was ready with the tire iron. Quietly manoeuvring it through the bars, Cal struck a hard blow to Gonzalez's head.

CHAPTER SIX

As Cal and Laura ran out to Cal's truck, Laura noticed Ramiros slumped over, handcuffed to the steering wheel of the police cruiser.

"You didn't have to go to all this trouble. I could have gotten the money to cover the fines," Laura said, huffing as she hopped in.

"Well, I don't know how much experience you have in these situations, darling, but I've been in a few over the years. In case you didn't notice, it wasn't just about the money, honey, it was also about you." Cal started the truck and hit the highway as fast as he could.

"What do you mean, it was about me?"

"It's not that the captain didn't want the money, but he wanted to have time alone with you as well. Have you checked your bags and your wallet? They know exactly how much money and anything else of value you had on you." Cal concentrated on steering the truck straight ahead as fast as he could. "If it wasn't for you, the captain would have taken my few hundred bucks, put it in his pocket and kicked me out of there at the first sign of sunrise without so much as a coffee."

"Slow down, we're going to end up in the ditch again," Laura said as she looked about for her purse. "My purse. They've got my little handbag. We have to go back!"

"Not on your life. I figure we have a few hours to get our asses as far south as we possibly can before someone figures out something is wrong there. I pray they'll just let this thing blow over, but somehow I doubt it. I'm sure they'll at least come looking for us until dark or another emergency occurs."

"Stop this damn truck now!" Laura insisted as she pushed her left foot down hard on the brake pedal.

Cal fought the truck hard so as not to lose it again and brought it to a screeching halt. Cal glared at Laura, eyes blazing. She had gone too far in hammering on the brakes, endangering their lives. Laura's eyes blazed back at Cal just as fiercely, neither flinching.

"Everything I own is in that bag and I'm not about to leave it in some godforsaken Mexican hellhole in the middle of nowhere. So either we go back and get it or we sit here and wait for them to find us." Laura pulled the keys from the ignition before Cal realized what she was up to.

"Are you nuts? Do you know what they'll do to you if they catch us now?" Cal asked. "I imagine there will be cops all over this place very soon when they realize the phone isn't being answered and nothing's getting done."

"If I was that captain I would be more afraid of what I will do to him if we meet again. But whatever they do to me it won't be nearly as painful as what they'll do to you," Laura responded in kind.

"Exactly my point, so I'll make you an offer. Forget your bag and I will buy you whatever it is you think you need when we hit La Paz. There are some nice stores there."

"It's not about the clothes. I brought that bag from the cell. But everything important to me in this lifetime is in my handbag and I'm not about to leave it behind."

"It means that much to you?" Cal asked with genuine concern.

"It means everything," Laura pleaded.

Cal held his hand out, expecting Laura to drop the keys in it, but all he received was silence and a stare that cut like daggers. "I'll need the keys if we're going to drive back, or were you planning on walking?" he asked.

"You're not as tough as you want people to think you are," Laura said quietly as she plopped the keys back into Cal's hands, showing a small victory grin.

CHAPTER SEVEN

Cal and Laura made quick work of transferring an unconscious Ramiros from the police cruiser to Laura's old cell, where Captain Gonzalez was lying, way too still, on the cot. Cal checked his pulse to make sure he was alive. The unconscious officers looked like discarded mannequins from a uniform store, and they'd be none too happy when they eventually woke up.

Cal found Laura in the captain's office, rummaging around in his drawers. "I can't find my purse anywhere." Laura grimaced.

"Hey, you got your suitcase, fifty percent isn't bad," Cal said hopefully, trying to get Laura to cheer up, to look on the bright side so they could just *get the hell out of there.*

"Funny, but this isn't a percentage thing. I'm not leaving without that bag," Laura said, distracted. She noticed a small metal safe in the corner. "I wonder if it's in there," she said.

Cal looked over at the safe. "Did you have anything of value in your purse that would make them want to lock it up?"

"To me, yes; to them, not really—a few hundred dollars."

"Well, if it's in there, we'll have to wait for them to wake up and then we'll have to bargain with them for the combination, but I'm not particularly keen on that scenario."

"Is there any chance we could break it open?" Laura asked. "It's not that big."

"From what I understand, when it comes to safes, size really doesn't matter, unless you happen to be toting some dynamite?"

Laura laughed a little for the first time since being brought to the jailhouse. Suddenly she was aware that something had just been transmitted between them. Was it pheromones? She wasn't quite sure which scientific phenomenon it was she had experienced.

Cal pulled a large Swiss Army knife from the pouch on his hip.

"That's overly zealous, don't you think?" Laura asked, half-laughing, getting back to her normal self, much to her own amazement considering the circumstances they found themselves in.

Cal ignored her as he flipped open the largest blade and moved swiftly through the aging adobe building, cutting all the phone lines. Laura followed.

"Ooh, I feel like I'm in a spy movie," Laura said as they approached the safe, back in the office.

"I don't know about being in a spy movie, but I do know we're in a hell of a lot of trouble now, so the more time we can buy ourselves, the better chance we have of getting to someplace safe. We'd better figure out what to do pretty damn quick."

"I'll check all the drawers and cabinets to see if they have the combination written down anywhere," Laura suggested. "Who knows, right?"

"Well, I sure hope whatever's in your purse is worth risking a few years in a Mexican jail for!" Cal said as he headed off down the hall. "I'm just going on a little expedition to see if I can find a good-size hammer or nuclear warhead. I'll call a friend of mine in

North Korea and see if he can get his hands on something really powerful for us."

Cal returned a short time later with a crowbar and a small hammer. "Any luck?" he asked as he entered the office.

"Nah. How about you? Anything resembling a nuclear warhead?"

"All I could come up with was this old hammer and a crowbar," Cal said with disappointment. He sat down in the captain's chair looking disgruntled.

"Well, let's see. We have a hammer and a crowbar—"

"And Grand Marnier," Laura injected quickly.

"What?" Cal asked.

"Grand Marnier," Laura repeated as she reached into the cabinet behind Cal and pulled out a full bottle of the liqueur.

"And what exactly are we supposed to do with that?" Cal asked as he swivelled around in the chair.

"Umm, we could set the safe's doorknob on fire to weaken it, knock it off with the hammer, then stick the crowbar in the gap and pry open the safe," Laura said with confidence. "It doesn't look that strong."

"Lady, either you've been watching too many really bad made-for-TV movies or the accident did more damage than first we thought."

"I'm fine and unless you come up with a better idea I'd like to at least try it." Laura pranced over to the safe, quite proud of herself. "Do I have to grovel, or are you going to help me?"

Cal pushed himself out of the captain's chair, strode over to where Laura was standing and grabbed the Grand Marnier. After he guzzled down a few gulps, he doused the knob with it, made sure he got some inside the handle as well, took out his lighter and lit the whole thing on fire. They watched it burn for a few moments. When the fire went out, Cal suggested they repeat and then try knocking the handle off. Laura liked that Cal was willing to try, but even she could now see that this might be a silly idea.

Cal handed the hammer to Laura.

"Swing away until your arms fall off, it isn't going to do any good."

"Oh, and I was just thinking you liked this idea."

They'd only used half the bottle so far, so Cal took another swig.

Laura took her first hard swing with the hammer, then another. On her third swing, Laura used so much force the hammer flew from her hand and landed between the wall and the safe.

Hot sparks flew off the flaming doorknob, hitting Cal in the forehead and sending him back on his haunches. He manoeuvred so magnificently he didn't spill a drop of the Grand Marnier. "God, I can't believe this!" Laura exclaimed.

"Why not? I told you it wouldn't work, but if you like we'll light it again and I'll take a few swings."

"That may not be necessary. Come look!"

Cal quickly evaluated the excitement level in her voice and hurried over to the safe. Seeing nothing, he looked up at Laura. "What's so wonderful?"

"I think this is the combination," Laura said as she pointed to a small silver sticker on the back of the safe. "It says, 'Remove this sticker and keep in a safe place.'" Then it gives these numbers: 21 right, 33 left, 43 right."

"Let's give it a try. Stranger things have happened." Cal tested the knob for heat. It was barely warm, so he leaned towards the dial and began to turn it. "What was the last number again?"

"Forty-three right." No sooner had Laura said it than Cal was pulling the heavy metal door open. They both stared in amazement as they looked inside and saw not only Laura's handbag, which she grabbed right away, but also an excessive amount of American money in stacks; too large a number of neat bundles of cash for such a tiny Mexican jail in the middle of nowhere in the Baja.

Laura quickly inventoried her purse and was relieved when she realized everything was intact. She then looked at Cal suspiciously, watching him finger the stacks of bills. "What are you doing?"

"I'm counting the money," Cal replied. "What does it look like I'm doing?"

"I can see what you're doing, the question was more rhetorical. What I want to know is why."

"I was just a little curious as to how much was in each of these bundles," Cal said as he finished counting. "Ten thousand each, and there are ten bundles so that makes—"

"One hundred thousand, Einstein," Laura finished for him.

"I know that's a hundred K." Cal snorted as he snatched Laura's purse from her hand and started to stuff the money inside.

"What! Are you nuts? Breaking out of here is one thing. I was even going to leave them all the cash I had on me and suggest you do the same in hopes they'd just forget the whole thing, but stealing their money is a whole other stinking kettle of fish."

"First off, what the hell is a stinking kettle of fish, and secondly, honey bunch, I can guarantee you this is not their money! If we relieve them of some of their guilt, they will be more apt to leave us alone in hopes that we won't tell anyone from whence it came," Cal said as he kept on stretching into the safe and shovelling the money into Laura 's purse.

"I may have done a lot of dumb things in my life and made a lot of mistakes but I am not a thief. So regardless of whose money it is, one thing for sure is that it's not ours and it sure as hell isn't going to be yours."

"Was everything in your purse?" Cal asked.

"Yes, everything," said Laura.

Cal sat back on his ass, looking very dejected. "Okay. Jiminy Cricket, you're right. Somewhere in the deepest, darkest recesses of my prefrontal cortex something is agreeing with what you're saying, so I guess it makes sense." Cal slowly began to place the stacks of his *early retirement* back in the safe with a forlorn frown on his face.

"God, you look like a little baby about to cry." Laura giggled.

"Hey, I'm putting it back, aren't I? Quit teasing me before I change my mind."

"Trust me on this one, Mr. Redman. I may have just saved your life," Laura said gravely.

"Well, at least prolonged it." Cal managed a small joke, but could tell that Laura felt a real concern for his safety this time and that it was not just another slight against his degenerate personality.

The drawn-out silence between Cal and Laura meant they were both deeply contemplating the harsh reality of their situation. All joking aside, they knew that they had limited time to come up with some distance and a plan. In addition, if the two officers were not already awake they soon would be, and they'd be as mad as pissed-off hornets.

CHAPTER EIGHT

Cal's once shiny new truck looked like it had been in the Baja 1000 and lost badly. Covered in dust and newly acquired dints and scratches from hitting the cactus and rolling over, it looked like a grizzled veteran, but even so it cruised effortlessly towards La Paz and that was all either of them cared about at that point.

It was still only mid-afternoon and Cal did not like being on the open road in broad daylight. He knew at some point other officers would be reporting to the station and would discover Ramiros and Gonzalez. He had no idea how much leeway they had, but it would definitely be more if no one knew which way they were heading.

"I have half a mind to turn us around and try and get over the border by morning. We won't stop until we hit the first Starbucks. My treat," Cal said, breaking the silence that had enshrouded them since leaving the jailhouse.

"I wouldn't worry about them," Laura said dreamily as she lifted her head from where she'd been resting it on the window frame and looked at Cal.

"I've heard they kill gringos down here for less than what we just did," Cal said as he eyed the bottle of Grand Marnier he had taken along with them, now nestled between the seats.

Laura saw where Cal's eyes were focused and grabbed the bottle before Cal could even think about it. "We're lucky to be out of there and I'm in no hurry whatsoever to go back so don't even think about taking a drink," Laura said as she stuffed the bottle in her bag. "And as for going back north, I think we're okay, for now anyway. They obviously have broader financial issues to deal with. I find it hard to believe they would even worry about the obviously petty amount of money they were trying to squeeze out of us. I think we've seen the last of those two, and I think they'll be happy to have seen the last of us as well. I know they'll be really pissed at us, but other than those few bruises on their heads, we didn't really hurt them. Their egos will be hurt more than anything. We left all that money, and I am sure they do not want to draw any attention to that issue." Laura finished her monologue, content with her conclusions, and rested her head gently back against the window. She closed her eyes.

Cal looked over only to find her fast asleep. He considered slipping the bottle out of Laura's bag but thought better of it. Instead, he lit himself a cigar, slipped in a Los Lobos CD and decided it would be best if he could find a place to hide the truck from view and take a little nap himself until the sun went down.

Aside from needing the rest and figuring it would be better if they drove at night, he did not want to be alone in his head right now anyway. He instinctively knew this was not a good time to be inside himself. This usually led him down a darker path he always regretted taking later. He wondered where that other path was. The path with colourful flowers tossed about gently in the sunny afternoon breeze. Grassy shores along a slow-moving river. Why could he never find that path? He knew that with Laura sleeping he would just start to brood—from why he had never won "the big one," to why he and his brother did not get along. From why he still missed his father so much to his divorce and what he was going to do with his life. Not to mention the question of why he was starting to enjoy having this nagging Sleeping Beauty beside him.

Cal spotted an overgrown farmers' lane that looked like it had not been used much of late. He pulled in and found exactly what he was hoping for. He pulled the truck over behind a pair of high rolling hills and the sanctuary of some heavy brush. Confident he had found a secure hiding place, he shut off the engine. He leaned over and as gently as he could, trying not to wake her, he tilted Laura's seat back so that she rested more comfortably. Adjusting his own seat, he settled in for what he hoped would be a few hours' rest, before a long drive through the relative safety of a Baja night.

✴ ✴ ✴

It was about 7:30 a.m. before Cal, worn ragged from driving all night, found a restaurant that looked hygienic enough to eat in. He pulled the truck around back just in case the police were out looking for him, but he was really hoping that Gonzalez had been as happy to see him and Laura gone, as they themselves were to be gone. In addition, he hoped the two officers would be so busy with the Baja 1000 festivities that they would not have the time or resources to pursue them. Cal gave Laura a shake and suggested that if she wanted to freshen up he would order for them. As they stepped inside the creaking wood-and-stucco structure, with its dust-coated windows and unattended dying plants, Cal quickly sized the place up and realized this might not have been the perfect place for a safely digestible breakfast. The server came right over with coffee and menus. Cal was starving and would have loved to chow down on some bacon and eggs but having been ill a few times from eating them in places such as this he felt it best to stick with pancakes. After ordering, he spotted the morning paper at an empty table nearby and began giving it a read. It seemed like quite a while before Laura sat down. The food had already arrived.

"It's nice of you to finally join me. I must have forgotten to mention that this isn't a formal brunch." Cal shovelled another forkful of pancakes and syrup into his mouth.

"You were married for how long? You can't have forgotten already that any woman worth her weight in lipstick wouldn't be caught dead this time of day with last night's makeup on," Laura replied.

Looking at her plate, Laura studied what she assumed had been, at one point in their short history, steamy, hot and fluffy pancakes. Even Laura did not realize how long she had been gone.

"I know they are not what you ordered but I went with my gut feeling here. No pun intended! I'll certainly sleep a lot better on the next leg of the trip knowing that you're behind the wheel with fresh makeup on and a somewhat safe and nutritious breakfast in you."

Laura ignored Cal's sarcasm and got excited about his last comment. "You want me to drive?" Laura asked just before she mmmmm'ed through her first bite. "It actually tastes better than it looks."

"Yeah, you can drive, can't you? Just until we can find another suitable place to hide out for the day. I'm exhausted."

"Yes, I can drive. Nevertheless, that was Marty's biggest fear so he never let me drive anywhere. He was so worried that he would die in a car accident with someone else at the wheel. He hated being a passenger. I'd never really quite understood how he could feel that way, until spending time with you driving."

Laura gave a saccharine smile, and then squeezed in another delicious bite. "Wow, these are either some of the best pancakes I've ever tasted or I'm just plain starving."

"My God, sarcasm and wit this early in the morning!" Cal took another sip of coffee, grimaced, shoved his chair back, stood up and walked towards the flimsy screen door. "I'm going to go out to the truck and see if I can get anyone on the radio. Although I'm not so sure it's a good idea, I'm going to listen for a bit. We were too far away earlier this morning but we might be close enough here."

"Do you think we'll make La Paz sometime today? I'm sure the magazine is wondering why I haven't checked in for two days."

Cal looked at his watch and brought his foot back in through the door. "I wouldn't worry just yet, there may not even be a winner at this point, but unless somebody has removed two hundred or so miles of the worst hairpin curves and mountain roads you've ever been on, don't hold your breath. We'll be lucky to get there by three or four this afternoon and I am still not sure it is safe to drive during the day, but so far, we seem to be okay. Maybe we'll get lucky and this will just blow over. Though you spending a half hour dressing up for this place did not help. Eat up."

"Grouch," Laura snarled as she picked up Cal's newspaper and went back to enjoying her breakfast, hoping to make this break last as long as she could.

Cal came back a few minutes later carrying the bottle of Grand Marnier. He poured a long shot into his coffee.

"That's disgusting, I thought you were going out to check the radio," Laura said, taking the short-lived smile off her face.

"I did, and we're still too far out, and the coffee is disgusting. This makes it drinkable," Cal retorted. "Besides, you're driving."

Laura sized up the situation as pragmatically as she could and realized Cal was probably right, no harm would be done and she for sure was not about to give an inch on his everything-had-to-be-just-perfect theory.

"You're right—enjoy yourself," she said with a big smile.

Cal could not believe how agreeable she was being, but was not about to change his good fortune by saying anything.

"By the way," Laura continued, while Cal showed an uh-oh-here-it-comes look on his face, "while you were out supposedly getting us back in touch with current affairs, I noticed an interview with one of the police officers from the station on TV." Laura grimaced. Just then, a young lad dropped off a bundle of newspapers by the door, and Laura ran over and grabbed one. "I can't read Spanish but I can spell my own name and they mention you two or three times. Does this mean anything?" Laura handed Cal the paper, open to the first page where their names appeared. She waited a few seconds as Cal read in silence.

"Well, what does it say?"

"Hold your horses, I can read Spanish but not that fast. But I can tell you it isn't good."

"What do you mean it isn't good?" Laura asked, concerned.

"I mean, we-may-as-well-be-on-Mexico's-most-wanted-list not good. We, my darling, have been charged with the theft of one hundred thousand dollars and a few other incidentals like concealed weapons, breaking out of jail and, let us not forget, assaulting two police officers."

"I thought you put the money back."

"I did. You saw me put it back. Now let's get the hell out of here. I can read the rest of the article when we're not sitting still," Cal said angrily.

"You don't have to get so snippy. I was just making sure."

CHAPTER NINE

After a few minutes of silence, Laura, with her eyes steady on the road, making sure Cal was happy with her driving, could not contain herself any longer. "Well, what does it say?"

"'The armed robbery was reported late last night by the captain of the Baja North Federal Patrol,'" Cal read out loud. "The captain says he is lucky to be alive. 'We were brutally attacked, knocked unconscious. They seemed like such a nice American couple. We were just trying to help them, make them feel comfortable after their accident and then found ourselves tied up like Christmas pigs and left to die. If Sergeant Ramiros's wife, Alessandra, had not come by with his dinner when she did, we would both be dead!'"

"Dead! Give me a break."

"'I noticed the money missing shortly after I returned to the jailhouse from the hospital,' the captain is quoted as saying. When the sergeant was asked why such a large amount of money was in the safe at the jail he said that only the captain could answer that question. He said that he was not aware that such a large amount was being kept in the safe. 'Right now, our concern is to catch the two Americans who did this.'" Cal finished reading and looked over at Laura.

"But we left all the money, didn't we?" Laura snuck a look over at Cal, who remained silent. "Cal, didn't we?"

There was no response from Cal. He took a sip of his coffee and continued to read the paper as if he hadn't heard her.

"Cal, answer me."

"Maybe one bundle of hundreds got stuck in your purse although I *thought* I took them all out," Cal said sheepishly.

Laura lifted up her purse and looked inside. She could barely see the half bundle of bills tucked way down at the bottom of her purse. She exploded. "I could kill you! What the hell were you thinking?"

"It was like half a bundle, out of a hundred. They owe us at least that, for what they put us through. Besides, they're saying over a hundred thousand has gone missing but only ten fell into your bag," Cal said, trying to downplay the fact that he knew he should not have taken any of the money.

"Ten, as in ten dollars fell into my bag?!"

"Possibly ten grand, we were in hurry, I'm not quite sure," Cal replied purposely not looking at her.

"What are you going to do now?" Laura asked.

"What, like I have a plan or something? I found out the same time you did. Remember? Coffee, pancakes then the newspaper from hell," Cal said defensively, finally looking up at Laura.

"I think we should go to the police," Laura suggested firmly.

"The police," Cal repeated in disbelief.

"Yeah, we'll go to the police in La Paz or a city like Tijuana and turn ourselves in. Tell them you were going to take the money but changed your mind, and thought you had put it all back. They'll believe us," Laura said, not quite convinced herself.

"Remember those other nice police? They are the reason we are on the run right now. *Oh, hi, officers, excuse me but my name is*

Laura. I'm the nice girl you guys are looking for, from that news-paper article." Cal mocked Laura's voice. "*Let me tell you that firstly, the captain wasn't very nice. He was going to rape me and we didn't take that money after we knocked the two of them out,*" Cal continued.

"Okay, okay, knock it off," Laura said in a nervous voice.

"Look," Cal said softly, "this is serious shit we're in. We are now just two innocent gringos who have been set up very conveniently like two lambs being offered up to the slaughter."

Cal went on. "Those two cops know we didn't take that money—well, not all of it anyway. I'm sure they're the ones that are up to something, and I'm sure they'll stop at nothing to keep us quiet. This is not about a measly ten thousand or us busting loose."

"I feel like we're in a Quentin Tarantino film or something." Laura fought back the swelling tears. "This is for real, isn't it?"

"Let's see. Gun, missing money, two Feds who have been bopped on the head, tied up and totally embarrassed and are likely under a lot pressure from whoever owns that money to get it back, and are now VERY pissed off. Hell, they don't even care about the fines anymore. My guess is this is for real. Someone has set us up and we are in some deep shit here."

Laura started to weep in earnest, making it hard for her to drive.

"Do you have any magic in that purse of yours?" Cal asked softly, hoping to stop Laura's sobs.

"Sorry, no magic," Laura said, tears streaming down her cheeks. "You have no idea how this could affect the rest of my life," she wailed.

"I swear I will not let anything happen to you. I will find a way to at least exonerate you." Laura could hear the sincerity in Cal's voice. "I promise," Cal finished, and he touched her hand. He reached into the glove box for a tissue and wiped Laura's eyes dry as she tried to keep the truck steady.

Laura sniffled and smiled half-heartedly through her weeping. "I want to believe you," she whimpered. As Cal gave her eyes another dab, she fought back more tears and shifted her focus to the long road that lay ahead.

"Okay, we'll find a way to at least get this money back to them without giving away our location. We'll enclose a very sincere handwritten note, explaining that this is all we took, sorry, discovered had fallen in your bag, and we didn't even mean to take it, and apologies for the knocks to the head. I am not sure how we will accomplish this though. I need some time to think about it. Therefore, you focus on driving and I will put my tired pea brain to work on an apology letter and how to get it into the right hands, whoever that might be." Cal glanced over at Laura as he finished spelling out his plan A and he could tell she may not have even heard a word he had said, she was so focused on driving.

CHAPTER TEN

Sitting at Captain Gonzalez's desk at the jailhouse was Jorge Molina, a high-ranking colonel with the Baja police force. The room held several other officers, including Gonzalez and Ramiros.

"This certainly embarrasses us all," barked Molina, extremely angry with the two officers. "Everyone is asking what that kind of money was doing in such a small jailhouse to begin with. I do not care how you find those two, just find them! Now, Captain, you and I have some explaining of our own to do. Carlos wants to see us both right away." Gonzalez fidgeted, looking very nervous.

"Don't worry, Colonel, just reassure Governor Vita they'll be caught soon. Nobody hits me on the head like that and gets away with it," Ramiros injected.

"Well, good luck, Sergeant," Molina said, looking Ramiros dead in the eyes as he stood to leave.

"Luck, Colonel, is for fools and matadors, not police officers."

With a broad smile, the colonel patted Ramiros on the back to show his appreciation for Ramiros's bravado. Molina was still smiling as he and the captain left the jailhouse for their appointment with the governor.

✳ ✳ ✳

After a few hours' drive, the captain and Colonel Molina approached the governor's house. They drove past the two guards with machine guns. "Relax, Captain," Molina assured Gonzalez. "Carlos is a fair man. He'll be fine once we catch those two thieves. We have nothing to worry about."

Carlos Vita was a well-educated, sophisticated and experienced politician and businessman. At fifty-two years of age, he had accomplished more than even he had expected. He had a reputation for being a hard-working politician and a hard-nosed executive. *Most* of that business was legitimate, but *fair* was not an adjective that people who knew him well would have used to describe him.

The governor's country home was a massive architectural beauty done in traditional Spanish-colonial style. It was perched on top of the only hill for miles, which afforded the governor beautiful vistas of well-kept gardens and meandering, well-groomed, shaded paths. There was only one road in or out of the compound, and it was about a quarter of a mile long, lined with beautiful cacti and perfectly manicured lush and fragrant rose bushes. It was also heavily guarded all the way from the guardhouse right up to the mansion's doors.

As the car approached the main entrance to the house, they could see Carlos through the magnificent French doors to his study. He was seated behind his large Mexican mahogany desk, which was strategically situated near the doors to allow him the pleasure of surveying his kingdom whenever he looked up from his work. He liked that he could see who was coming long before they could see him.

✳ ✳ ✳

"You may leave us," Carlos said with a wave of his hand, dismissing the two bodyguards who had escorted the captain and the colonel into his sanctum. Turning to his guests, he offered them a drink and moved over to the bar.

"No, thank you," said the colonel.

"Tequila, *por favor*," said the captain, perhaps too eagerly.

The colonel shot him a dirty look to let him know that he was somewhat displeased with the captain's decision to accept the offer. He had hoped that, for once, the captain would hold his drinking in check and stay sober for just one important meeting.

"So it seems we have a little problem, gentlemen," Carlos said softly, but with an edge. He poured the captain his drink, and poured himself a refreshing glass of ice water.

"Here you go, Captain, 4 Copas. Some of the finest tequila Mexico has to offer. It takes almost ten years to make one bottle," Carlos enlightened the two men.

"It's a temporary setback, no big thing," said the colonel quickly.

"Excellent," said Carlos as he clinked glasses with the captain. "So I will have my money on time, per our agreement? This little 'setback,' as you call it, will have no effect on my investment?"

Carlos had always prided himself on his keen sense of character and his shrewd ability to read other people's minds, which was why he was so suspicious when "a temporary setback, no big thing" rolled off the colonel's lips.

After a sip of his drink, the captain tried to reassure Carlos that he had made the right decision when he chose the officers of Baja North Federal Patrol for his new business venture. "Just as we agreed, Governor," the captain forced out.

Carlos walked out from behind his desk, gesturing expansively. "Look around, gentlemen. Do you see a lot of people here?"

The colonel and the captain looked but said nothing.

"No, you don't, and the reason you don't is I allow very few people to work here, and the ones I do, I would trust with my life. I trust no one, especially two lowlifes like you. How do I know you did not concoct this story of a washed-up racer and his little whore? How do I know you are not trying to keep the money? Didn't you sell the whole shipment?" asked Carlos.

"Yes, everything has been sold now, over three million American dollars' worth. The money is in a safe place in Tijuana," replied the colonel.

"So what's the problem?" Carlos was beginning to lose his temper. "Let these Americans keep the spare change for now, and you go get the millions—which is what I'm really concerned about—from Tijuana."

The colonel cleared his throat and prepared to tell the rest of the story. "They not only took the one hundred thousand in fundraising money, they also took the key to the safety deposit box at the bank."

"Box! What box?" demanded a very frustrated governor.

"There's a safety deposit box in Tijuana. It contains a sheet of paper that has the secret account numbers into which the buyers deposited their money. For security reasons, we never met them. It also has a list of names detailing the profit disbursements." The colonel looked sheepish. His skin had paled considerably since his arrival, as if someone was slowly sucking out his blood.

"*List?* There is a list of names? So the whole world can read who gets a share of the money? This list—am I on this list?" The governor was not pleased and displayed this by smashing his glass against the wall behind him. As long as he had known him, the colonel had never seen Carlos lose his temper. "You two should be sentenced to a slow, painful execution on some old medieval device that has been around for a thousand years. And I happen to be the proud owner of just such a device, prepare to become quite intimate with it if you do not make this problem go away as quickly as possible.

"Please, Governor. I have a wife and two children."

"Don't grovel," the colonel said to the captain.

The colonel finally spoke up, trying to defuse the situation. "We didn't anticipate anyone would steal the key. We put our distribution list in the box with the account numbers because we thought it would be a safe place to keep it. We did not want to carry it on us so we left all monies in their various accounts at the bank, and put the account numbers and the list with the names on it in a safety deposit box. The key to that box was in our safe. We were waiting for the balance of the final payments, and then we would go pick up the money from the bank and distribute it. The buyers knew whom they were buying from so there was no trouble. After they picked up the first half of the drugs, they deposited the money over a few days into a bank in Tijuana. We thought we had planned this out very well. No one would be able to trace any of us to the account. When we checked the safe after Mr. Redman and his woman friend escaped, we saw they had taken the hundred thousand and the packet containing the key to the safety deposit box. In addition, the box not only contains the codes to get the rest of the money out of the bank, but also a copy of the list of who gets how much. We really thought the list would be safe at our place. It happened just the way I've explained it, I swear."

"So this safe place, the 'bank in Tijuana' as you call it really isn't that safe anymore. How did you come to have such a large amount of money in your safe at the station?" The governor turned his attention to this little detail.

"It takes a lot of floating untraceable cash changing hands on the spot to make these big deals happen, Governor. It started out as much more. That's just what was left," Gonzales answered, finally speaking again without sounding sheepish.

"I see: a tidy untraceable little bonus for you two I suppose it would have been!" the governor added, looking distraught and angry as he distilled all this new information concerning this particular problem into his ever-growing portfolio of nuisance issues he would have to deal with. "I was hoping this would have resolved itself by now, but I can see I am going to have to take a personal interest in this. That will be all," he said.

At a wave of the governor's hand, a security guard entered the room to escort the captain and the colonel out.

CHAPTER ELEVEN

As Cal and Laura motored down the relatively desolate Baja 101, Cal's brain was fluttering as fast as a hummingbird's heart. He was trying to think what they could do to get out of this mess.

"There's a gas station up ahead," Laura observed.

"We don't need any gas. In case you haven't noticed you're riding in a gas truck carrying five hundred gallons of fuel in the rear tanks."

"Precisely," said Laura with a smile. "What is it that you can't get for hundred-mile stretches during the race around here?"

"A decent coffee?" Cal asked.

"True," said Laura with a grin. "But I'm talking about Texas crude: gasoline."

"Why would we want to sell the gas?" asked Cal.

"It's not that we want to sell the gas, particularly," Laura replied. "But the Feds will be looking for us in this truck. We need to find a new mode of transportation, a different ride, and I have an idea."

"And this brilliant idea is what?" Cal asked.

"Trade this truck with all the gas that's in the back tank so they can sell it. In exchange, we get the loan of someone's car for a few days. They'll bank more tax-free George Washingtons than they'll see in a year of working."

"And what of my dream truck?"

"Well, if you don't get your precious truck back, when you get home you can claim it was stolen. You have insurance, don't you?"

As they neared the station, they counted about thirty cars and trucks sitting two abreast in line waiting for gas. A handwritten sign propped up by a garbage can in front of the station read, *Sorry, no gas until 2 p.m.*, but the 2 had been scratched out and replaced with a 4. Laura pulled the truck up alongside the gas station office and eased it into park.

Cal put his hand on the door and was about to step out.

"Where are you going?" asked Laura as she reached for her door handle.

"I know the plan now and I speak better Spanish than you," Cal said snobbishly.

"Yeah, but I have these," Laura replied, putting one hand under each breast and lifting them up. "And if anything, they'll think they got a better deal because this is a garage and I'm a woman."

Cal took his hand off the door and leaned back in his seat, contemplating Laura's statement. "They certainly are very nice looking and it now appears they will be well worth every penny you spent on them," Cal said sarcastically. For one fleeting moment, Cal was ashamed of being a man and especially of himself for falling into the macho stereotype so easily.

"This set is as genuine as they come, Cal, honey, and you're just jealous because you know you'll never be personally introduced." Laura laughed as she slid out the door.

Cal admitted to himself that he was a bit curious to see if Laura could pull this off. Laura got down from the truck and, as if she was on a modelling catwalk, strutted through the front door of the office while Cal tilted his seat back and watched her go to work.

✳ ✳ ✳

Laura positioned herself so she looked her best as she approached the attendants. *"Hay alguien que hable ingles?"* she asked politely with a big smile.

"I can speak a little bit," replied one of the young lads in his best broken English.

"How would you like to help me and my friend out while we help you out?"

"How?" the young man replied.

"We will trade you the truck out there with all the gas in the back tank in exchange for the use of whatever it is you're driving. Moreover, the clincher is, you're free to sell the gas. Someone will bring back your ride in a few days and pick up the truck." Laura spoke slowly, politely and with a big smile.

"I lend you my car for a few days, for the use of the truck and the gas in the storage tank, which I can sell. That sounds okay, but how do I know you'll bring my car back?" The kid was trying to sound smart or at least concerned.

"I don't mean to be presumptuous but I'd wager a guess that even without the gas, and as banged up as it looks, that truck is worth a lot more than whatever it is you're driving. Am I right?" Another huge smile spread across Laura 's face.

"You have a good point, señorita," he said with a somewhat embarrassed smile, realizing he had missed the obvious. "How much gas is in the tanks?"

"I'm not sure, but pretty close to full. You can go have a look if you like."

"It's okay. I would like to drive the truck anyway."

"Then we have a deal?"

"A deal," the young man agreed, and shook Laura 's hand.

As Cal witnessed the closing of *the big deal* from the confines of his truck, he marvelled at how Laura seemed to be helping by taking control of the situation and not crumbling under the pressure. He had never met a woman quite like her before and found himself fascinated by the duality of her persona.

On the one hand, she was this beautiful, sensuous, sometimes flirtatious woman and on the other hand, she could be a very astute, cool-headed confident person who seemed to possess the smarts to accomplish anything she might wish to tackle in life. Cal had heard of this type of woman before but had never really taken the time or the opportunity to get to know one. Most of the women he met or gravitated towards were one-dimensional except in matters of their figure. Except his ex-wife who had given up on him after several years of marriage. When he looked at Laura now he thought of her as someone different, someone he would actually like to know on another level. He was starting to enjoy her company. He had not felt this way in many years.

CHAPTER TWELVE

Sergeant Ramiros—Anthony, Antonio, or Tony depending on who was addressing him, was very fit and stood six feet tall. He was also very handsome by anyone's definition so he stood out in most situations and his muscular build and chiselled good looks were a definite asset to helping him get on in life. In addition, he was an intelligent, thoughtful person and a pillar of moral strength; he often fought hard for those he believed to be good, but who maybe had been led astray or had made a bad decision or two. He was always kind to the young kids, who he thought were "just being teenagers," and tried to give them a break and talk to them before coming down hard on them. His approach differed somewhat from the shoot-first, ask-later gun-happy environment that prevailed around the quarters.

The captain relied heavily on the sergeant to keep everything running smoothly at the jailhouse but also tended to keep him in the dark about many of the side business deals that cropped up from time to time around the jail. He was painfully aware of Ramiro's superior intellect and of his position on life's moral high road. This frightened the captain on many levels but mainly on the one that Ramiros could not be bought, and eventually might threaten the captain's position within the force. The captain was secure for now; he knew he was invaluable to the smooth running of the colonel's special supplementary projects.

This often bothered Ramiros, who was vaguely aware of the less-than-legitimate goings on around him, but was also smart enough to know he had to keep quiet about certain things lest he lose his job, or squash his chances of advancement. Ramiros had come to accept that this was simply the way of his world.

He picked his righteous battles very carefully and decided that he could turn a blind eye to a few of the captain's misdemeanours in exchange for a little job security for him so he could take care of his wife and, one day, their family. His dream was to make captain and run the jailhouse the way he would like to see it run, but for now, he knew he had to pay his dues. Work hard and keep his mouth shut.

Happily married to the prize of Ensenada, Anthony thought his life was good. He would work as a sergeant at the jailhouse until the captain retired, which he figured would happen sooner rather than later, because of all the extra money the captain seemed to be making, and then he would become captain.

What Anthony did not bargain on and—what he was about to learn the hard way—was that evil people were capable of doing good things, which is what often makes them so hard to recognize, and good people were capable of doing evil things, which makes it hard to assume anyone is completely innocent, or free to cast the first stone.

✳ ✳ ✳

In his entire short-lived career as a police officer, Anthony had never been on the receiving end of a hostile venting from a superior before; his work record was exemplary. As Anthony listened to the colonel on the other end of the phone his palms were sweaty and his voice shook. He suddenly felt as if his very job and his comfortable, secure, future life were all at stake here.

"I understand, Colonel," Anthony said as calmly as he could but noticeably shaken by the chain of events. "I thought that maybe you would have given me more men. The race is still on and almost all the officers are down in La Paz. Only having six men to try and find these two is a joke."

There was a long pause.

"No, Colonel, I did not mean the whole thing is a joke. I said six men to cover all the Baja is a joke. They could have gone north, south. They could be in the desert or hiding along the coast." Anthony took a breath. "*Si*, Colonel, after the parties are over. *Si*, I understand." Anthony was feeling the pressure, and wanted to calm the colonel down. "*Si*, thank you, and don't you worry, I will find them if it's the last thing I do, Colonel. You have my word on it." The colonel was getting louder on the other end and so Anthony pulled the phone a little ways away from his ear, and all the men in the room could hear him.

"Well, I have all the confidence in the world you will find these two, and when you do find them I will make sure they regret having taken the money, even before the police deal with them. I will make sure whoever took this money and treated our police so badly pays dearly. I want to see them first," the colonel finished, sounding almost exhausted.

Anthony understood the silence on the other end as a goodbye and he hung up the phone.

Anthony stood in silence for a few seconds as he looked around the room, studying the faces of the six officers who had been assigned to him. The nervous cluster included his best friend since grade school, Ramon.

"What are you all looking at?" he finally said. "I've got six men to cover the whole of the Baja."

"I've notified the border patrol along the US border and the airport authorities in Tijuana and Mexicana," said an older officer.

"That's good," said Ramiros, "but if I were those two, I would probably try to buy my way onto a small private plane that could take off freely from anywhere and land in Texas or any open field in America. I think you should call all the smaller airports right away and fax them the photos."

The timid officer nodded his head in agreement and headed straight off to carry out his new orders.

"May I speak freely, sir?" Ramon asked.

"When haven't you?"

"Sir," Ramon addressed him, again to let Anthony know that he was in control. "I think, for what it's worth, that they might in all likelihood try to make it to La Paz where they could get lost in the festivities and hope that this thing would just blow over, or where, with the help of some of their friends, they might easily buy a ride or a plane ticket out of Mexico."

"Not a bad thought," replied Ramiros. "However, I do not want to put all my men in one basket. I think we still have to wait and see if publishing their photos and the news articles turn up any leads. But just in case, Martin," Ramiros said, looking at one of the other obliging officers, "call the authorities in La Paz and tell them who we're looking for. The rest of you, think of anyone else you can call. Find out who their friends were in the race, did any family come down with them, call all the hotels and motels, B&Bs—there are not that many along the 101. They have to eat and gas up and stay somewhere. As for me, I have to go home now. My head is killing me and Alessandra insists I go straight to bed and get some sleep tonight. She is getting very worried about my head."

"Right, I couldn't agree with you more, Sergeant," joked Ramon. "If I had a wife like Alessandra I'd want to go home to bed too!" Ramon gave Tony an all-for-fun nudge. The other officers laughed as they left the room and set about their individual assigned duties in what was quickly building up to being one of the largest manhunts the Baja had ever seen.

"If we catch these two, I'll be promoted to captain way ahead of my time and that will be good for both of us," Tony said to Ramon as they headed for the police truck.

"*When* we catch them, Tony, not if—*when*," Ramon said with confidence as they hopped inside the beat-up, dusty-to-the-core, poor-excuse-for-a-police-cruiser of a truck. Ramiros was glad of one thing: that Ramon was driving so he could close his eyes and shut his brain off. Ramon and Ramiros had stayed friends through high school and joined the police academy at the same time. Ramon had been posted to a nearby town; but regardless the two had remained best friends and frequently got together. Ramon was the first officer that Ramiros had asked for when putting this team together and he had been happy to hear he was available. Likewise, Ramon was very happy at the prospect of being able to work so closely with his best friend again.

Tony leaned back in the passenger seat and was more than happy to let Ramon drive so he could rest his pounding head. The minute he closed his eyes he shut out the outside world and all he could think about was getting home to Alessandra and a good night's sleep.

CHAPTER THIRTEEN

Carlos Vita knew that he would have far worse problems than dealing with his new-found business partners and the bungling Feds if he could not retrieve the money and the list. He was hoping he would have some answers before he had to explain to his partners on this deal what was going on with it. "Yes, what is it?" Carlos said gruffly as he picked up his phone, resenting his secretary's intrusion.

"It's that Verner guy from US Border Patrol again. He insists on talking to you this time. He is asking to speak to you right away. He says it is important. I should put him through, yes?"

"Okay," Carlos said, a little less gruffly this time, feeling bad he was letting his temper get the better of him.

"Carlos—how is my friend?" The brash American voice boomed loudly on the other end of the phone with a very unfriendly intonation.

Verner Russell was an old-school Texan, recently put in charge of US customs at the Tijuana border crossing. But at age forty-nine he had finally come to the realization that if he wanted a comfortable retirement he would have to become a much more creative businessman, do more than just invest in and manage the small port-folio he'd acquired after working for what seemed like a pittance of a salary for twenty-five years. Being army-trained and all-American, it took him a while to come around to "creative business opportunities." It was not long after attending a VIP weekend-long party at Carlos's ocean-side-villa retreat, that Verner had learned of the power of his newfound friend and all that he could garner from that friendship.

The extra cash was the main incentive, and it was more than he had ever dreamed of stashing away for retirement, but Carlos's ever-changing, never-ending stable of very friendly and sexy Mexican women (who Verner heard from friends were the prettiest in all of Mexico) was a definite bonus. Verner quickly became one of Carlos's best contacts but still he was first a Texan, and then an American, and the wrong man to piss off. Verner had little to no sense of humour. It had even been rumoured around the crossing that there existed a secret pool of money, contributed to over the years from bets: if you could get the son of a bitch to laugh there was enough cash you could not even spend it living in the lap of luxury for a week in Los Cabos. His wife, Alice, was once over-heard somewhat jokingly telling a friend at a party that she was more afraid of not having his dinner ready on time than of having their house broken into.

Verner Russell kept his body in Special Forces form and stood ramrod-straight as he looked out from his cheaply decorated office. Two fingers of his left hand spread apart the blinds so he could overlook his chaotic kingdom of metal and rubber, the thick black smoke of diesel fuel spewing out of the hundreds of vehicles waiting to get in and out of Mexico while hundreds more people crossed on motorcycles, bicycles and foot all day long. This was Verner's world. Trying to separate the desperate liars and hope-fuls with false ID trying to escape to the American dream illegally from those who possessed legitimate visas and work permits. And Americans trying to get into Mexico to sell truckloads of illegal goods or escape the law or an ex-wife, or just to start a new life.

Verner's view was quite a contrast to the lush, glistening, poolside serenity he could picture Carlos surveying. Verner imagined Carlos leaning back, relaxing in his tufted-leather chair, appreciating everything that he himself could only dream of owning one day—at least before he had been introduced to Carlos.

"I'm well, Verner. How are you?" Verner could tell straightaway that Carlos's voice was not as confident as usual over the phone. It did not have that tone of the high-ranking government official in control of everything. Verner was already feeling that this conversation was not going to go well.

"Me? I am busy as usual. In fact, I have what seems to be one of your trucks here right now, only the driver says he's got no money for me," Verner said, as he glanced down, smiling, at his newly purchased snakeskin boots. He leaned over to give one of them a bit of a polish with the cuff of his shirt.

"We had a little glitch," Carlos admitted nervously.

"A little glitch? Well, what if we had a little glitch on this end and this truck happened to get searched right now?" Verner said harshly.

"Let's not be hasty. A lot of money will be coming your way shortly, but stopping and searching that truck won't help," Carlos said, trying to sound relaxed. Carlos outlined the story to Verner, downplaying the seriousness of the mishap and emphasizing how skilled and determined the Mexican police were.

"Any idea when?"

"You've always been paid in the past. This time will be no different."

"It had better be soon, Governor, and now with a little interest added, or there won't be any more trucks getting through for a while," Verner said sternly.

"As soon as we catch those two, you'll have your money," Carlos said.

"If you need my help, let me know. As in, why don't we just go blow open the goddamn box?" Verner asked with a smarmy air of cockiness.

"Well, we know which bank the boxes are in, but this is why the boxes are kept secret. The key to the main box is in the pouch, which has all the codes to the accounts. The captain at the station had not copied down any of the information. He just put the packet in the safe, he probably could not even remember which bank the safety deposit box was in if you asked him, let alone the number. He was waiting for the call that the rest of the money had been transferred. He was going to go get it then. In addition, even when they do find out which bank the money is in, they cannot access it without the other key or the box number. Not even in Mexico." Carlos was still feeling the squeeze.

"Bad timing on the little glitch, I guess is all then. You'll keep me informed, won't you?" Verner sounded a little less stern but the threatening tone was still in his voice. "I understand there's a lot more at stake here than just the money. I don't think I'd have to tell you the implications of that list falling into the wrong hands."

"You'll hear from me as soon as we get a break," Carlos assured him, and making that his closing, he quickly hung up.

Carlos waited by the phone for a second but when no callback came, he felt relieved and poured himself a large shot of tequila.

After listening to the *click* in his ear, Verner put his own receiver down. With a smug look on his face and the bearing of a man in control, Verner waved to the guards outside to let the truck in question pass without inspection; no sense in cutting off his nose to spite his face. He would just cut off Carlos, and probably a few other limbs too, if things did not turn for the better soon. Verner had only a few more years to sock away his "bonus money" as he called it. Nothing was going to come between him and his comfortable retirement, not after all these years, and not after all the bull and the ass-kissing he had had to put up with along the way. Verner had convinced himself: a handful of years of letting a few truckloads of narcotics through was not such a big deal. This was not going to make a significant difference to the war on drugs or homeland security. Verner's slight intervention was not going to change anything in America. However, it would have a huge impact on his retirement plans.

CHAPTER FOURTEEN

The amethyst-purple, seven-year-old two-door Nissan hummed down the highway, sounding like a giant whoopee cushion because of the brand-new Noisy Boy exhaust system he had just so proudly had installed. The tinted windows were rolled halfway down to let in as much wind as possible and the boom box speakers sitting in the back window thumped out some local band's CD that the kid had been playing. Laura and Cal were beginning to like the music and were bopping their tired heads and trying to sing along to the music. They were feeling a tiny bit relaxed for the first time in two days, knowing they had at least put off what might be the inevitable, that they had just bought themselves a few more hours of obscurity and hopefully enough time to come up with some kind of a plan.

"This was the best you could do for my truck and all that gas?" Cal asked, shouting over the sound of air whistling through the car.

"It's only for a day or two max! It's been redone in a custom shop here. It's got real Corinthian leather he told me," Laura yelled, patting the seats with a smile. "And the stereo is a hell of a lot better than the crackly piece of crap that was in your truck."

Cal noticed the traffic was slowing down and bunching up. They were getting close to La Paz. The police had set up a road-block and were checking all the cars going in and out of town. This was standard procedure during the race anyway, but Cal was sure they would also be specifically on the lookout for the two of them. Either way Cal did not want to take any chances, so he quickly pulled off the main highway and drove a few miles down a dusty dirt road until he spotted a partly demolished wooden shack just off to one side on a little rise. The shack hid the car well and they could see the checkpoint clearly about two miles down the high-way. They knew they were close but Cal liked the hideout and felt safe there, they were well hidden from view, but could see anything coming. Cal leaned over and shut the music off. "We'll stop here until it gets a little darker," Cal said.

"What difference will that make?" Laura asked.

"It'll be dark, for starters," Cal said patiently. Laura kept look-ing at Cal quizzically.

"It means they will have to use flashlights to look inside the cars. Moreover, it will be even busier than it is now, with more people coming in to party, so they will be under a lot of pressure to push the cars through quicker. Next to Christmas or Easter, this is probably the single largest event down here," Cal said, look-ing pleased with himself for giving such a detailed and practical answer. "I think it will work better for us all around. We can get some much-needed rest now and we can figure out how to get the money back to the captain without giving ourselves up."

Cal dug around in the gym bag that doubled as his suitcase and pulled out a sweater and a bottle of tequila. Looking rather trium-phant, he stepped out of the car, hoping that Laura would join him while he had a drink. Laura pulled her suitcase out of the trunk and placed it in the backseat.

"I'll take the top bunk," she said to Cal, throwing an old blanket she'd found on the backseat at him.

"You're all heart," Cal said, reaching for the flying object. Then he realized he might lose the tequila if he grabbed the blanket so he watched it drift aimlessly to the ground as it opened and the soft breeze caught it.

Laura, looking around nervously, took off her blouse and slipped on a sweatshirt. It was still a bit warm out but she had spent enough time in the desert to know it would get much colder as the sun went down.

Cal fluffed up his scruffy gym bag as best he could and placed it on his blanket-bed against the rear tire. He laid his stiff, weary body down and even though his duffle bag would have felt like a lumpy sack of potatoes to most people, to Cal it felt like a pillow in a five-star hotel, which he had had the pleasure of experiencing once. Putting on his special desert jacket, Cal felt comfortable for the first time in twenty-four hours and took no time at all settling in.

Laura poked her head out the window above Cal.

"And don't be getting drunk," she said, looking down at Cal. But to her surprise, the bottle rested at Cal's side unopened. His eyes were already closed tight and it appeared that Cal had drifted off to la-la land immediately. Laura laid her head down, feeling a little guilty about taking the backseat, but pleased about Cal going straight to sleep without taking a single drink. As Laura settled in, hoping to drift off to sleep as easily as Cal had, she unexpectedly found herself wondering what Cal dreamed about. Laura began to giggle at some of the silly images she was conjuring up in her head, having no idea what was making her think this way. Then she realized she had better stop whatever it was she was doing and get some sleep. "What does it matter what Cal dreams anyway," she told herself before a few more awkward images and a couple more chuckles helped to push her over the line into a deep slumber.

✷ ✷ ✷

A half day's drive away, Sergeant Anthony Cardenas Ramiros was also having the sleep of his life. He had not slept since he had woken up from the blow to the head that he had received from Cal. Anthony was still in a near-comatose state when Alessandra came quietly into the room, carrying a warm bowl of homemade soup.

"Anthony, honey, wake up. I made you some soup." Alessandra liked to use his full name. She tolerated it when friends like Ramon called him Tony but she did not think it did justice to his chiselled good looks and the presence with which he carried himself. How handsome he always looked in his uniform, she thought.

Alessandra sat herself down lightly on the bed and placed the soup on the side table. She stared lovingly at Anthony for a moment or two before she gave the seemingly lifeless lump a couple of gentle pushes to wake him.

"I made you some soup," Alessandra repeated, adjusting his pillows and propping him up. "Are you feeling any better?"

Tony's head was pounding but he did not want to tell Alessandra.

"I'm not going to feel better until I catch those two," Tony responded in a groggy drawl. "Has Ramon called yet?"

"No one has called. They know not to call, to leave you alone," Alessandra said, feeding Tony a spoonful of soup.

"How long have I been sleeping? I should be getting back soon or Ramon will be falling asleep in the chair," Tony replied, while Alessandra gently mopped away the soup that was spilling out the sides of his mouth onto his chin.

"Not so soon. Ramon wasn't whacked over the head with a bottle and he doesn't have a wife to go home to," Alessandra responded, wiping more soup away from Tony's chin.

As the nourishment started to take effect, Tony sat up straighter. As he did, the bedcovers slid from his shoulders, bunching up around his waist, exposing the full, solid form of his muscular physique. Alessandra's eyes followed the flow of the sheets that slid down his body, and then shifted to the thin line of hair that led to the rim of his underwear. As she looked back up, she caught Tony smiling at her.

Tony took the spoon from Alessandra and began to feed himself. Alessandra, still holding the bowl with her right hand, leaned in to Tony and as she gave him a slow gentle kiss she slid her left hand down under the tight-fitting elastic band of the black boxers. As Anthony grew large in her hand, she could see his chest muscles tighten and his soft, perfectly formed nipples, becoming more erect.

Alessandra loved it when they just lay together in bed and talked about their future. She and Anthony had met in high school and been in love ever since. They had never wavered in their commitment or attachment to each other and had managed to build a simple but happy life together in the tough economic climate of the Baja. They had managed to stay true to their dreams when many of their friends and family opted for less-than-legal ways of earning an income or had left for larger cities or found work in the hospitality industry down in Los Cabos. They were considered an ideal couple, the envy of their friends, with their own home, Anthony with a good job, many friends and family in their lives.

Alessandra's biggest wish now was to start a family of their own, just as the two of them had always discussed.

* * *

After they made love, Alessandra lay her head down gently on the moguls that formed the outline of Antony's firm stomach. With the slow pounding rhythm of Anthony's heart, she quickly joined him in a deep, motionless sleep.

CHAPTER FIFTEEN

Just before he awoke from one of the best sleeps of his life, Cal was lost in a dream. The type of dream that starts out happy; the sort you wish you would never wake up from, vivid and steeped in reality, rich with that wonderful texture of subconscious surrealism. Borderline out-of-body experience. Unfortunately, like most of the dreams he had been having of late, it ended as his worst nightmare: the reason why he was living the way he was.

From inside the cockpit of the off-road machine, the heads of the driver and passenger are flopping around vigorously as they approach the small Mexican town.

Bob's voice echoes deep inside Cal's head. "Slowwww doww-wwwn, Cal, slowwww dowwwwwn." Cal hears his name several times as the shaking of the truck becomes more severe.

When Cal woke up, he was lying on the ground; he was not in the middle of a race; he was not even in a car. He was also looking at Laura's concerned face rather than Bob's jovial mug.

"Cal, Cal! You're having a nightmare, wake up," Laura said, forcefully shaking him. Cal sat up. He could feel his cold sweat.

Laura had a bottle of water for him, and he gratefully took a few long, hard, audible gulps. "Are you all right?" She looked concerned.

"Yeah, I'm fine," Cal answered, sitting up even straighter. "Thanks for the water."

"You're welcome," Laura said, coming to the realization that those were probably the most polite words they had exchanged since they had met.

"What were you dreaming about that was so frightening?" Laura asked with genuine concern.

"I dreamt I was married again," Cal said with a grin, trying to lighten the atmosphere and avoid answering the question. After they'd looked into each other's eyes for a moment, Laura stood up, again noticing that the bottle of tequila still had not been opened. Cal caught Laura glancing at the bottle but decided not to over-react this time and instead just appreciate where her concern was coming from. Cal decided to break the awkwardness of the moment: "It's dark enough now; we should get going."

Cal pawed through his gym bag and pulled out a bright red baseball cap with *Skull Tobacco* embossed on the front and a well-worn blue jean jacket. He handed both items to Laura.

"What are these for?" she asked hesitantly.

"They're looking for a man and a woman in a pickup truck. We are going to be two men in a Nissan. It will be dark and they'll be in a hurry. Tuck your hair up in the cap and lie back. We'll put the tequila bottle on your lap and you'll look like you're passed out from drinking too much already."

"Red," Laura complained. "I hate red ball caps. Do you not have another colour? Red makes my skin look pale." Cal gave her the same look of frustration he had been giving her since they met. Without a word, Cal poured out half the bottle of tequila and then splashed some all over Laura, as she stood silent in amazement.

"It has to look like you drank it. But I know what you're thinking, *what a waste*." Cal liked that Laura laughed at his joke.

As the bright purple Nissan hummed its way to the checkpoint, Cal took a few long swigs so that his breath would smell as if they had been drinking all night long as well, and placed the bottle of tequila back on Laura's lap. She rolled her seat back, pulled the cap of bitter resignation from the fashion world down over her eyes, tucked her hair underneath it and put on her Academy Award–winning performance of a sleeping drunk, complete with a bit of snoring, sporadic snorting with the odd little snuffle thrown in for effect. It was all Cal could do to keep from laughing and getting them busted.

"We're looking for a black Dodge pickup up truck with a large industrial container on the back, carrying gas. Did you happen to see such a truck?" the police officer recited as he shone the flashlight in the car. "Doesn't look like he would have seen much," offered the officer after seeing Laura passed out with the bottle on her. "Start the party a little early, did you?"

Cal replied in his best Spanish. "It's a long ride from Mexicali and we've been following the race for two days already."

An impatient driver behind them honked his horn. The officer looked up and reacquainted himself with the long line of cars. "I hope he has enough left in him to enjoy the weekend festivities," the officer said with a smile, waving the flashlight in a sweeping motion to let Cal know it was okay to move on.

✵ ✵ ✵

Ramon had swung by and picked up Tony, and they were speeding their way down to La Paz, the police now aware about the truck swap at the gas station. But it was too late to have them picked up at the spot check going into La Paz, at least they knew the fugitives were more than likely headed that way, and would try to get lost in the crowds. Sergeant Ramiros also knew they would have to stay somewhere and would likely join up with a crew member from the racing team as all the hotels had been booked for weeks.

"I'll bet next year's uniform that's where they're headed," Ramon said. "With the number of vehicles that will be heading north from there on Monday they could easily hitch a ride out or arrange for a private plane by then."

"We'd better find them before Monday or we won't need next year's uniform," Ramiros answered gravely.

The Grand La Paz, a five-star hotel, was where Cal and Bob loved to stay during the weekend parties. Built along the ocean strip, it had a swim-up bar and hot tubs, and the manager had an innate ability to hire the best-trained and best-looking staff available. A day or two at the Grand always felt good, and regardless of the outcome of the race the Grand was a great healer of racers' bruised dreams and soiled relationships. Cal had booked there several months ago to make sure he would get his favourite room. But he was smart enough to know he couldn't go anywhere near it now; he could kiss that deposit goodbye.

Tonight, the crew, including Bob, had walked together to the poolside bar where they would start the night. As usual, after a few starters, they would end up at some loud and packed disco on the main strip.

Hiding in a bush near the bar as the crew came in, Cal heard his name come up more than once within the span of a few seconds. Bob, in the full throes of inflicting on the guys some long-winded joke he had likely told a hundred times before, was oblivious to the hissing and other secretive noises Cal was throwing in his direction from the shelter of the fully blossomed hibiscus shrub.

Cal had to pelt him twice with some little stones before Bob shut up and turned to see where those annoying little things were coming from. Cal stuck his head out from the bushes. It was a good thing no one had been listening to Bob's story because it meant nobody noticed he had suddenly stopped talking and dropped away from the group.

"Hey, I forgot my wallet in my room, guys. I'll meet y'all at the table in a few minutes," Bob muttered to their backs as he shrugged in disbelief that no one had been listening to his joke. Then he turned around and headed towards the hotel. Once the rest of the crew was out of view, he ran over to the bush and scrunched in as far as he could.

"What the hell happened, Cal? Everyone is worried sick about you two. I leave you alone down here for a minute and you become Baja's most wanted!" Then the amused look on his face changed to one of near panic. "Where's Laura?"

"She went to Turbo's room. She was supposed to meet him down here and get the story on him. Apparently, they're friends," Cal said, a little miffed.

"Turbo was really pissed when the Feds questioned him and he found out what Laura was up to," Bob warned.

"So Turbo's pissed. Big deal."

"Am I detecting peripheral jealousy here?" Bob asked teasingly.

"I have to admit she's been good company," Cal said reluctantly.

"How good?" demanded Bob.

"Good company, and that's all," Cal insisted. "We're going to meet in Turbo's room to figure out what to do from here. I'd sure appreciate your help on this one if you'd like to come to the brainstorming session," Cal suggested tentatively, remembering that he and Bob had not exactly parted ways the best of friends. He was hoping for a kindly response but was preparing for the worst.

"Oh sure, a few days ago I'm on my own, but now that you're a fugitive we're best buds again," Bob said with a grin. He wrapped Cal in a bear hug. Cal, not being the mushy type, cringed and pulled back a step.

"We'd better get up there before Turbo talks her into turning herself in or something stupid like that," Cal said with a shake of his head and a manly pat on the back for Bob. "That was one of her suggestions earlier on, and now that I'm not around she might just start thinking that way again," Cal added.

✳ ✳ ✳

Up in the fifth-floor room, Laura had scrubbed off two days' worth of grime and was starting to relax and feel like a woman again when Turbo's voice came rolling through the door, disturbing her much-needed peace.

"I can't believe you spent twenty-four hours with this guy, mostly in small, confined spaces and he didn't try anything! He has quite a reputation, you know."

Laura flung open the door and Turbo almost fell in, pressed up against it as tightly as he was. "Firstly, we were in separate cells and secondly, why would that be any concern of yours anyway?" Laura said firmly, standing there with nothing on but her underwear and a knee-length, Turbo-autographed Baja 1000 T-shirt.

"I was just making sure he didn't try anything, 'cause if he did—"

Laura cut him off in mid-sentence as she strode over to the counter and poured herself a sparkling water. "That's sweet, Gordon, but I can take care of myself. Anyway, he's just a sheep in wolf's clothing. He is truly a gentleman and he'll be coming here as soon as he hooks us up with Bob."

"Here?" Turbo shrieked. "Why the hell would he be coming here? You'd think he'd be trying to get his ass out of this god-forsaken place and just leave you alone after all the trouble he's gotten you in." No sooner had Turbo finished uttering these words than there was a knock on the door.

"That must be them," Laura said with a tinge of excitement in her voice. "So to answer your question, he hasn't left because they're looking for the two of us, not just Cal. If they found me," Laura continued, moving to the door, "with or without Cal, I would be spending at least the next two years of my life trying to escape from my worst nightmare."

"Don't open it," Turbo whispered fiercely as Laura reached for the handle.

"Let's make sure it's them. Who is it?" Turbo asked, nonchalantly.

"Bob," a voice bellowed through the door.

"Is Cal with you?" Turbo asked.

"Shush," came back at Turbo. "Just let us in," Bob whispered. Laura galloped over to the door and let them in.

"What the hell are you doing, asshole, trying to get us caught?" Cal was seething.

"*Us* caught?" Turbo argued back. "You mean, you! I, for one, think Laura should turn herself in. And if you were any kind of man, you'd go to the police and fess up—"

"Feds," interrupted Cal.

"Explain that Laura is innocent," continued Turbo, ignoring Cal. "Work this thing out yourself. Laura should be focusing on her article and on getting her son back. She didn't need this to happen."

"I didn't need this shit either and just remember, Gord-o, I could have left her there in that cell and been back in San Diego long before anyone even knew I was gone," Cal said. "And when several of the local Feds finished having their own brand of fun with her, they may have let her go or just decided to shoot her to keep her quiet or simply put her to work in the sex trade for a while.

"She wouldn't have been there in the first place if you weren't such a drunken loser!" Turbo shouted.

"Loser! Who the hell are you calling a loser? You've yet to finish the Big One in two attempts," Cal retorted viciously. "You were favoured to place in the top five this time, you have everything going for you, and you can't even finish."

"We blew a gasket just ten miles from the last pit stop. I was stranded for hours. Maybe if the Old Man had hired the right mechanics we would have had a chance," Turbo said with a smug expression. Cal leaned in to give Turbo a taste of his knuckles but Bob stopped him, stepping between the two angry men.

"Slow down, man. Like it or not, he's one of us and you guys are going to have to find a way to get along—for now, anyway," Bob said. He forced Cal to take a step back.

"He'll never be one of us," Cal said grimly, walking away from Turbo, towards Laura. "He's as useless as a lame duck."

"That's it! I'm leaving! If you think I'm going to help out, put my ass on the line for this jerk, you're nuts," Turbo said over his shoulder to Laura as he headed towards the door. "I told Laura she should go straight to the Feds and get as far away from you as possible. Hopefully she'll come to her senses and go with me to the police station when I get back," Turbo said sincerely, looking at Laura as he left.

Only seconds passed before the door opened and Turbo stuck his head back in the room. "And you'd better be long gone by the time I get back," he said pointedly, looking at Cal, "or I'll bring the Feds back myself."

"For God's sake, Gordon, if you're going to act like a little baby and not help us, then just leave," Laura said, stepping between Cal and Gordon, crowding Bob who was also still between them. She could see the two men edging towards each other again.

"Promise me you won't do anything stupid while I'm away?" Turbo asked Laura, staring at her like a puppy dog. "I'll leave you guys alone to plan your Great Escape but I think you are all making a big mistake."

"I promise not to do anything stupid, and I pray you won't either. Now, get," Laura said.

"Cal's right though, Gordy. They'd throw Laura in jail and just leave her there for a year before her trial even comes up," Bob said. "Did I ever tell you the story of my mother? I was fifteen the first time my mom brought me to watch the Baja 1000. The Feds pulled her over, supposedly for speeding."

"There's not enough time for one of your stories right now, big guy, but I'm sure Laura would love to hear that one someday," Cal said.

"They both should, it might help them to see why—"

"I'm out of here," Turbo said, cutting Bob off. "I'll see you when I get back," he said to Laura, closing the door again. Bob looked at Laura as soon as the door clicked shut.

"They held us for two or three days in the worst conditions I've ever been in. They would drag my mom away, down the hall to a private room and keep her there for hours. I can only guess what happened to her there. She was so traumatized she never would tell me."

Laura's eyes watered as Bob finished. "Okay, you've made your point," she conceded.

Cal handed Bob an envelope containing the $10k US he had "inadvertently" taken from the police station.

"Without going into too much detail right now, we would need at least a few beers for me to fill you in on everything. I need you or someone we can really trust to return this to the captain at the station where we spent the night—or better, the sergeant there, Ramiros I think his name was, something about him that I liked. I would trust him. I have enclosed all the info with the money.

"Ten fucking grand." Bob gulped. "That is a hell of a lot of money to be carrying around in an envelope."

"Not as much as it could have been. I'll explain it all later, but we're completely innocent of everything they are accusing us of."

"Well, almost everything," Laura interjected.

"Right, but when they get this money back, other than some trumped-up charges that I doubt they'd want to pursue, I think we'll be off the hook."

"If we can hide out until someone takes this money back or gets it to Sergeant Ramiros, I think we'll be okay, once he reads the note inside and realizes what's happened." Cal looked at Bob, who was still standing and staring, his mouth gaping in disbelief.

"What are you folks going to do in the meantime? Do you have any money?"

"I have a bit," Laura said. "Enough to help get us back to the US if we can clear this thing up soon."

Bob folded the envelope and put it in his back pocket.

"Well, aside from getting this to the sergeant we'd better get working on a plan for you two. I'm sure there are police buzzing all over here looking for you guys."

✷ ✷ ✷

Gordon saw two Feds at the front desk as he stepped from the elevator into the hotel lobby. Anthony and Ramon were showing their badges to the desk clerk along with pictures of Laura and Cal when Turbo approached them.

"Laura is innocent but Cal is guilty as hell," Gordon said, grabbing the officers' full attention.

CHAPTER SIXTEEN

"I think this meeting calls for a few cold ones," Bob suggested. "So I'm going to scoot on up to my room and get us a couple." Bob could see by the look on Laura's face he should maybe not have been so graphic with the story about his mom. He could tell that Laura was very worried.

Therapy didn't have to come by appointment only, Bob thought, so he leaned in and gave Laura a good old bear-sized Canadian hug. When Bob felt he had sufficiently helped to hold back the tears he could see welling up in Laura's eyes, they both let go with a big sigh. The two smiled at each other as Bob left the room. They had shared something precious that moment, something that restores faith in the value of simple human connection.

"What was that all about?" Cal asked Laura as the closing of the door instantly restructured the atmosphere in the hotel room.

"Something I hope you get to experience before it's too late," Laura said. She looked at Cal's bewildered face and wondered how anyone could have survived this long in life without having expressed any such emotion. Walking slowly over to the fridge, Laura was suspicious that Cal was staring at her. She quickly glimpsed down to make sure her nipples were not acting like beacons for souls lost at sea.

"What's that supposed to mean?" Cal was defensive, feeling a little misunderstood. He realized that he was making Laura uncomfortable, and shifted his eyes away.

"I don't know," Laura said, making an honest attempt to keep the irritation from her voice. "I just say things sometimes. I don't even know where they come from. I am way beyond frustrated right now. I cannot even explain it. My body feels like shutting down. I'm shaking. I just want to go lie down and get up later to find this has all gone away." She poured another glass of water and wondered if she would ever find a man who possessed Cal's good looks, confidence and sexiness, combined with Bob's sense of humour and emotional, caring side. "I guess that was a bit harsh, sorry. I'm going to finish getting dressed. Would you like some water while you wait for Bob to get back with a real drink? I'll just be a few minutes."

"Sure."

Laura handed Cal a bottle of water with a hesitant smile. "I guess you've certainly earned a beer," Laura said. "I almost feel like one myself." She leaned over and gave Cal a friendly hug and a peck on the cheek.

"Why don't you have a beer with us when Bob gets back?"

"It's a very long and private story, but one day, when we get out of Mexico, I'll fill you in on my colourful recent past," Laura said, disappearing back into the bedroom.

Cal was just about to settle on the couch when they heard the key in the door and Bob came bursting in, putting the double lock and the deadbolt on behind him.

"You guys have to get out of here, *now*!"

"What's up?" Cal turned and saw the scared look on Bob's face, an expression he'd rarely seen.

"Turbo is marching down the hall with two Mexican Feds. They were just stepping off the elevator and I heard their voices before I turned the corner. They'll be here any second! Get your asses out of here NOW!"

Cal put the water down and turned to go to Laura's bedroom but she had heard the whole conversation and was already there right behind him.

"How the hell are we going to get out of here?" Laura asked. She jumped as the doorknob rattled. "There's only one door!"

"I guess we'll choose door number two," Cal said, opening the balcony door and looking at the pool two stories below. "And you'd better not miss. Let's go!" Cal shouted, striding out onto the balcony.

"I can't go like this," protested Laura, drawing attention to the long T-shirt she was wearing—with not much else.

They could hear Turbo's key in the door as Laura was speaking.

"I don't think you have time to change, little darling," Bob said, leaning against the door, hoping to buy the fugitives some time.

Laura ran for the balcony. Just as she reached Cal, who was already poised to jump, crouching balanced on the railing, she glanced back at her bag on the coffee table.

"Forget it," Cal ordered, reading her mind, almost falling over as he tried to grab her arm. "That bag has already caused us enough problems." But it was too late. Laura had snatched the bag and was running back to Cal.

"Meet me at the truck on Monday morning," Bob said in a loud whisper to Cal, just as the force of the three men in the hall finally overcame the chintzy locks. They had managed to budge Bob but he quickly put both hands back on the door and with all his might and girth he got it shut again.

Laura reached for Cal's hand; he pulled her up on the railing and without even stopping to coordinate a plan or let Laura catch her breath he pulled her forward as they leapt from the balcony in one continuous motion.

✳ ✳ ✳

Seconds later, Turbo, Ramon and Ramiros burst into the room. The two Feds reached the balcony just in time to see Laura and Cal lift themselves, dripping, from the pool. Ramon pulled out his gun but Ramiros placed his hand gently on Ramon's hand and lowered his arm. The pool was full of guests. There was nothing for the Feds to do but jump or run down after them. They chose the latter.

As the officers turned to run out the busted door, Bob stood in their way.

"I suggest you move away quickly before you find yourself in more trouble then you are already in, my friend," Ramon suggested in a less than friendly manner.

"I have something to give you. You need to take a moment to read this," Bob said, pulling out the envelope containing the money.

"If that is money and you are offering us a bribe to let them go, we are federal officers and that would be a federal offence, which I'm sure would get you a lot of free time for thinking over the next few years," Ramon answered.

"Do you know a Sergeant Ramiros?" Bob was reading from the note inside the envelope.

Both officers stopped dead in their tracks a few feet from Bob.

"I'm Ramiros. Why?"

"You're Sergeant Ramiros?" Bob asked quizzically.

"Yes." Ramiros pulled out his badge and showed it to Bob.

"I'm supposed to turn this over to you. It's ten thousand dollars. Taken by mistake. My friends did not even know they had it until this morning. I am not sure of all the details but there is a note inside for you, they asked me to make sure you got this. I can only say that Cal said he trusted you." Bob handed Ramiros the envelope and stepped aside. Bob was trying not to show his relief at having at least bought the pair some time. He opened one of the beers and took a long slow drink as Ramiros read the letter.

The officers were agitated and perplexed at the interruption, they were worried Cal and Laura were getting too big a lead. However, they knew they had to investigate this development.

"I don't have time to read this now but I can tell you that there was more than ten thousand dollars taken. I wasn't even aware of what was in the safe, and if this is nothing more than a bribe, then your friends will find themselves locked up for an even longer time. Now please step aside," Ramiros said as he stuffed the envelope in his breast pocket. "My first objective is to catch those two. Whatever is in this letter we will deal with later."

"Look," said Bob, moving even farther away from the door to show that he was not going to stand in their path. "I don't know what went on that night but I do know those two people and if they tell me they played no part in the disappearance of some funds from your office and even that this money ended up in their possession by mistake, I would believe them."

"Maybe so," Ramon said, "but right now our job is to catch them, or alternatively, if they won't co-operate, our instructions, which in this case have come from much higher up than usual, are to kill them, which makes this a very unusual case, and so I guarantee you we will do one or the other. I doubt this letter contains any information that would distract us from our orders. Nevertheless, we will make sure it is read. Later," Ramon said as the two officers left—running down the hall to the stairway.

Bob slowly shifted his gaze and his thoughts to Turbo, who had been standing in the kitchenette area, quiet, in shock at what had just transpired.

"I surmise you will enjoy being suffocated to death by your own smelly underwear," Bob said, looking at Turbo with a sadistic grin.

✹ ✹ ✹

Down at street level a sopping-wet, bare-footed Laura was trying her best to keep up with Cal, who kept looking back to make sure she had not fallen too far behind. Cal hoped the market area would still be open and busy. He figured they had a good chance of disappearing into the crowd, they might even have enough time to buy some things for Laura to change into. She was attracting an awful lot of stares. It was a beautiful warm Baja night, cooled only slightly by the breeze off the ocean, with Full Moon Inc. supplying the lighting. Luckily, because of the race and the postcard weather conditions, the market was still full, with more bargain hunters than Cal had hoped for, which made him optimistic of a surreptitious escape, but before he entered the market area, Cal glanced over his shoulder again and noticed Laura slowing down, lagging way behind. He doubled back, put one arm around her waist and pulled her in the direction of one of the hundred makeshift stalls.

Laura, exhausted, dropped down on a wobbly wooden stool and strained to catch her breath. Cal spied some sandals hanging from the inside roof of the booth; he reached up and unhooked one of the more stylish pairs. "Here! Try these on," he ordered, handing the sandals to her. She took them and, huffing and puffing, held one up against her foot but then decided to examine the cheap footwear more closely.

"I can't wear these." Laura pouted, handing the sandals back to Cal. "They'll fall apart in minutes."

"Those are very nice, perfect for you," the old woman said from behind the counter in her monotonous, rehearsed phrasing, eyes drooping. Her nimble, wrinkled hands were stretching towards Cal, hoping to feel the hard, stamped surface of coins but instead they felt the smooth, clean texture of leather when Laura placed the shoes in her hands.

The old woman was reaching sadly to put them back on the hook when Cal noticed the market was filling up with police.

"How much? We'll take them," Cal said gently, ripping the sandals from the shopkeeper's hands and slapping them down on Laura's lap. To Laura he hissed, "This is not the time to be shopping for a fashion statement. Put these on and let's get the hell out of here!" Cal reached into his wallet and pulled out a handful of pesos, twice as many as the shoddy footwear was worth.

"I wouldn't be found dead in these under any other circumstances."

"You just might be if we don't get the hell out of here," Cal said, taking Laura's head in his hands and turning it so she could see the police thronging the market area. "This is no time to go shopping."

"Can I at least get a poncho?" Laura asked, pointing out to Cal that her soaked white T-shirt was sticking to her like clear packing tape. She had nothing on underneath except her underwear. "Why, I think you look amazing," Call said with a boyish grin as he grabbed a poncho from a nearby hook and tossed a few more pesos at the now very happy saleswoman. He threw the large garment over Laura's head and she strapped the sandals to her feet quickly.

"I know a place where we can hide out for a while," Cal said as Laura stood up, looking like a tourist.

"Would you like a sombrero to go with that?"

"Do ya think?" Laura asked, striking a pose.

Cal rolled his eyes. "This way," he said, and grabbed Laura's hand. They dashed to the east side of the market, which opened into the real downtown area with a long boulevard that ran beside the ocean's shoreline. Moving slowly now, and trying to look like they were regular old tourists shopping, they had almost manoeuvred their way safely through the market when Cal spotted two Feds coming towards them. At first, they tried not to overreact, not a hundred percent positive they had been spotted. They kept meandering with the crowd, but then one of the officers noticed Cal looking straight at him and the officers began to chase the two. Cal pulled the unsuspecting Laura hard to the left, jolting her off her feet. He almost yanked her arm almost out of its socket as they quickly veered into a nearby bar. Situated in the middle of the trendy market area, the bar was packed. As it was also awards night for the race, it was extra lively. Everyone was dancing and having a great time. Cal was hoping they could disappear in the crowd and find a rear exit. He spotted some people he knew and he and Laura joined them on the dance floor, using the dancers' bodies to shield himself and Laura from the Feds.

It was an extremely large bar with two levels packed to the rafters with partiers. The music was thumping loud and the lights were dim. Cal was hoping these conditions would buy them enough time to escape.

The two officers split up, darting through the bar. Cal and Laura hunched down and, looking a lot like two chickens out for a stroll around the coop, they made their way to the ladies' washroom, locking the door behind them.

"Now what?" Laura asked.

"Out that window," Cal replied, noticing a small opening halfway up the far wall.

"I'll never get through that," Laura complained. But at that moment, she and Cal could hear one of the officers outside the door asking if anyone was in the washroom and knocking repeatedly.

"Answer him," Cal prodded.

"What should I say?" Laura whispered as the officer knocked and again asked if there were any women inside.

"Tell him to wait a minute," Cal whispered.

"Hold your goddamn horses. I'll just be a minute!" Laura screamed out, startling even Cal.

"Let's go," Cal said, shoving Laura towards the window. Cal knelt down and Laura climbed up on his shoulder. He stood up and hoisted her towards the open window. Laura grabbed the ledge, pulled herself the rest of the way up and stuck her head through the opening. Looking down, she realized it was a six-foot drop to the ground.

"How do I get down?" she asked Cal, just as he grabbed her feet and pushed her hard through the opening.

"Fall lightly and roll," grunted Cal. He heard the *thud* of Laura's body and a big moan over the music and sound of the officer trying to break through the door.

Cal noticed a mop and pail in the corner. He turned the pail upside down and stepped up on it just as the officer came bursting through the door. Yelling, *"Detentes,"* the officer pulled out his revolver. "Please stop, señor."

Cal heard the *click* of a gun and froze in his tracks.

"Ponga sus manos para arriba y permanezca donde usted esta." The officer motioned for Cal to put up his hands. He approached Cal slowly and clicked on his walkie-talkie.

"Get your ass out here, Cal Redman!" Laura's voice come screeching through the open window sounding like a cat in heat on a hot summer night. "I can't wait to see you fall! That hurt like hell!"

The officer holding Cal at gunpoint was just about to ask his partner for backup when he was levelled to the ground from behind. Cal turned to see Bob lying on the officer, acting like he was drunk. "Sorry, mister," Bob said, laying all of his 260 pounds flat on the back of the dazed and confused cop. Seizing the opportunity, Cal sprinted out the bathroom door, bounced off some confused cooks and sous chefs and scrambled out the back door. He scurried around to where he hoped Laura was still waiting and found her, elated and surprised to see him come out that way. Cal kept running and suggested Laura do the same as he huffed and puffed, gasping for air on his way by.

Inside the ladies' room, Bob was rolling over the officer, almost getting up and then crashing down on him again, each time rendering the poor officer more helpless than the last and making it impossible for him to manipulate his pistol or his walkie-talkie.

With each "fall," Bob would apologize to the stunned officer more profusely, stereotyping the common drunk and slurring his words. "Exclude me, off-afather," he mumbled, holding back his laughter, playing the part of the town drunk as best he could, trying to buy the fugitives as much time as possible for the second time that day, and hoping he himself would not get locked up in the hoosegow in the process.

CHAPTER SEVENTEEN

Cautiously, Cal led Laura down an alleyway lit only by the single bulb hanging over the back door of the Restaurant Frattoria. A pair of cats scattered out of their way as Cal and Laura slunk along the wall to the half-open door.

Most of the overpriced canteens were situated along the beach strip. Frattoria was just off the beaten path, a few blocks from the ocean. It was worth the trek up a short rise for those seeking a beautifully decorated trattoria-style atmosphere: exquisitely prepared food, with light jazz or classical guitar filling the room quietly in the background. Pastel stucco with rough murals highlighted its textured exterior and the interior had been painted by local artists. A quiet, softly lit, stylish haven welcomed those who preferred a more refined night out than what was offered by the loud disco fare prevalent on the strip. Discerning patrons entered through its large wooden double doors.

✶ ✶ ✶

Tonight, Cal would not be entering through those large wooden double doors even though he had made a reservation. Crouched down low, pretty much on their knees now and peering into the busy kitchen the two fugitives could see the smoke, smell the victuals and hear the dinner preparations. Cal stuck his head in a little farther and spotted Mattie, one of the two flamboyant owners. Mattie was overdressed as usual, in pastels mostly protected by his starched pristine-white-with grey-checked-cuffs cooking jacket. Mattie was the one who did most of the cooking. He was very focused on flipping some exotic fish in a large smoking copper pan. Mattie was sipping a refreshing drink from his always-at-the-ready wine glass, admiring his own gastronomic genius, when he thought he heard his name being called from the vicinity of the back door.

"Psst! Mattie!" Cal said again, softly but hopefully loud enough to be heard this time.

"I know you missed your reservation but you don't have to come in through the back door," Mattie said with a wide grin. He was always happy to see Cal, regardless of the circumstances.

"I need a place to hang quietly for a while. Are any of your rooms available?" Cal asked, creeping farther into the kitchen.

"What is it this time? Loan sharks or just running from another girl?" Mattie asked jokingly. "I know—it's a husband!" At that comment, Laura shot Cal a look of either concern or interest; he was not sure which and was not about to inquire.

"Mattie! Where are my starters?" Randy's voice boomed from just outside the kitchen, at the entrance to the dining area. Randy was Mattie's front man on the tables and his life partner. They were both extremely handsome and had been together for so long they could finish each other's sentences. They were as comfortable as a set of old cottage sweaters. Randy never let an opportunity go by at a dinner party or any gathering of friends to point out what a fabulous cook Mattie was. Mattie proclaimed the virtues of Randy's ability to keep the restaurant hopping, and would also expostulate on how Randy could sculpt the atmosphere in an almost empty dining room on a Tuesday night so customers would feel as if they had been somewhere special.

"Hold on to your damn shorts, Randall! We have guests back here," was Mattie's response. "Today is your lucky day!" Mattie said, turning back to Cal and noticing Laura for the first time. "We were expecting my parents for the weekend, but my dad decided at the last minute he wasn't crazy about coming down for the festivities this year so they're not coming for a few weeks. The guest room is all yours, Callywag."

"Callywag. I like that. It suits you," Laura said light-heartedly, feeling better about their situation now that it seemed they had a safe place to stay for the night.

Mattie walked over to Randy with a starter plate of shrimp. "Guess who's here for dinner?" Mattie asked coyly.

Mattie and Randy lived above the Frattoria. You could hear the distant gentle rumble of the waves through their bedroom window; the sound lulled them to sleep at night or "helps us keep the rhythm" as Randy liked to say, "if we're feeling frisky."

They had one splendidly decorated guest room that faced the alley and had lovely dark mahogany French doors that opened on to a colourful garden balcony. Mattie liked to have the garden on the back balcony because the sun was softer there. The room was so beautiful guests often told the two men to send pictures of it to *House and Garden* magazine. They also had two large full bathrooms. They could afford this use of space as they did all their cooking and eating downstairs. The couple only had a very small kitchenette upstairs. The master bedroom was large and overly decorated in an eclectic blend of traditional Mexican plus whatever they felt like. Laura spent more time looking around the room and asking questions than she did focusing on getting some decent clothes to wear, which was supposed to have been the task at hand; Randy was making a serious attempt at helping her.

"Let's see if we can get you out of that . . . thing and into something a little less revealing?" Randy hinted, rummaging through his drawers.

"This wasn't exactly the outfit I had in mind for tonight, but we had to leave the hotel in somewhat of a hurry," Laura said warmly, knowing already that they would be friends.

"Now, don't take it personally. I think the wild look suits you," Randy said, laughing, as he held up a beautiful soft sweater against her. "But I think this will look much less risqué. So . . . what kind of trouble has he gotten himself into this time? I take it not the usual run-of-the-mill pissed-off husband?"

"This isn't the first time he's had to hide out here?" Laura looked shocked.

"Good heavens, no! He's like one of those feisty, wiggly salmon. Risking their lives, year after year, swimming up waterfalls, dodging bears and fishermen and maiming themselves on sharp rocks just to do a little spawning," Randy said. Changing to a near whisper, he added, "Trouble was, some of them were married." Then, back at his normal pitch, "But Cal's been less than particular since his accident and divorce. Try that drawer to the left," he directed Laura.

"Speaking of the accident, what happened? He won't talk much about it," Laura probed as she discovered that the drawer on the left contained women's undergarments.

After a dramatic pause Randy replied, "A year ago, he and Bob were in the thick of it, leading the race, coming into the town of La Rosa, the only town the racers have to go through the middle of because it's situated high on a cliff and there's nowhere else to go."

"You're sure Mattie won't mind if I borrow some of these?" Laura interrupted.

"Are you kidding? Any excuse to go shopping in Mexico City or San Diego! Take anything you need."

"Some of these might work," Laura said, holding up a matching bra and panties from Victoria's Secret. She had not been expecting to find anything like them in a man's dresser.

"We keep some of the things left behind by our guests. You know, for Halloween and such! They are all thoroughly cleaned."

Laura gave Randy a crooked smile but made no comment.

"Bob was screaming at Cal to slow down," Randy continued, "which is the norm coming into La Rosa, even though the streets are blocked off and everyone is usually watching the race. It's a huge event down here, the whole town loves it! The racers tend to slow down on the main street for safety and to let the spectators have a good look at the vehicles. They used to stop and sign autographs. Some would even have a beer and tacos at Momma Espinata's in the old days. Now everyone takes this race far too seriously.

"Cal could smell the victory this time and there was no way he was going to give up even a few seconds. Then out of nowhere, three kids darted out, trying to cross the road. The last one was kicking a soccer ball."

"Wow! These are great!" Laura said as she admired the undergarments now sitting comfortably on her frame. But the expression on her face changed from happy to concerned when she realized where the story was going.

"It was either hit the kid head-on or swerve onto this path that led down an embankment. Without any hesitation, Cal made the swerve but he still clipped the poor kid," Randy said with a big sigh.

"Oh my god," said Laura, bringing her hands to her mouth.

"Cal flipped his truck but he and Bob managed to crawl out. Momma Espinata was right there with her pickup truck. She often acted as the ambulance since the town didn't have an official one. She laid the boy down in the back on a bed she had made up, and she and Cal drove straight to the hospital in Ensenada. That saved the boy's life. But then Cal, aside from realizing he had not won the race, discovered he was in a lot of pain. It was not until the boy's condition had stabilized that Cal mentioned his leg and how much pain he was in to the doctors. The doctors examined him and discovered a fracture up near his hip. They had to operate on Cal right away. He might have been all right, but because he had waited so long to mention it, and in the meantime had moved around on it, he had made it even worse, and they had to remove a small piece of the hip.

"That's why he has a slight limp."

"But it seems like he can drive okay," Laura said, checking herself out in the mirror again, feeling better knowing that the little boy had lived.

"It's not his leg that keeps him from racing. He could have returned the next year. It's his edge. He lost it. That race was the closest they had come in fifteen years and he knew he could never just go full out again, and when you know that, you know you will not win. If you know, you don't have the will to win at any cost, then why race at all. He could not do it. But you, you could win a lot in that outfit," Randy said. "Perfect for a hot Mexican night."

"All dressed up and nowhere to go, and no one to go with."

Randy ignored Laura's negative response and held up the dirty, damp T-shirt she had arrived in. "Mattie will wash this," he said, moving towards the door.

"I'm sorry. I shouldn't have said that. I take it you and Cal are good friends?" Laura asked.

"We're more than just friends, honey," Randy said with a wink.

Laura gave Randy a quizzical look but did not know what to say.

"He's certainly not the same Cal he was a few years ago. He's a much darker and more bitter Cal, and he's been making more enemies than friends lately. He used to be the one who would always prop up everyone else. By the way, I just made up that line about the married women. It's a thing Cal and I do, getting each other into hot water."

"Don't give it a second thought," Laura said as they left the room. "It's not like we're together or anything, and besides, I know it's probably true anyway," Laura said softly as the two new friends headed downstairs.

CHAPTER EIGHTEEN

Cal and Laura sat alone in the now-deserted softly lit dining area of the restaurant, with its curtains drawn tight and the remnants of a fine meal still on their table. Cal had his feet up and his back against the mural-painted wall. Laura leaned back with her arms crossed, so relaxed she'd almost forgotten about the predicament they were in ... She could hear Randy and Mattie rustling around in the kitchen.

"I am so happy down here." Cal broke the silence. "I love the smell of this place. The combination of the sun, sea air, spicy foods grilling everywhere, and diesel from the cars, trucks and buses is unmistakably Mexico."

"Speaking of Mexico, these are not exactly the kind of friends I expected you to have," Laura said.

"And what's that supposed to mean?" Cal said.

"You know, they don't really fit in with the rest of your racing buds," Laura said, trying to be vague.

Mattie and Randy came out of the kitchen, laughing, carrying a bottle of twenty-year-old brandy and dessert.

"So, Unc, have you heard from your brother lately?" Randy asked, putting everything down on the table. "I don't exactly get a lot of fan mail from home these days. Uncle Cal here is pretty much my yearly update," Randy said, looking at Laura.

"Oh, *that's* what you meant by 'more than just friends,'" Laura said, laughing.

Cal looked bewildered as he turned to Randy. Randy simply shrugged.

"Wish I had some news, but I haven't really seen much of him this year," Cal explained, noticing the big smile on Laura's face. "What! Randy's my nephew, my brother Billy's kid. The two of them are less than close. Billy's a bit of a redneck."

"Oh, and what are you, slightly rouge?" Laura said sarcastically.

Randy and Mattie burst out laughing.

"What's so funny?" Laura asked.

"Actually, Cal is considered the sensitive twig on our macho family tree. He was considered 'the wuss' at family functions until it was very evident that I was taking over that handle. If it were not for Uncle Cal and Aunt Sandra, I would not have much of a connection to my family at all. Aunt Sandra and I are still close. We write a lot. I miss her but since they split up she doesn't come down anymore," Randy said, looking at Cal with a grimace.

"Well, I don't miss her," Cal said defensively.

"That's because you're still angry with her."

"She gave up too easily. I am not the one that left. Hell yeah, I'm pissed at her."

"Would anyone like more coffee with their brandy, or dessert?" Mattie interjected to try to change the tone of the conversation.

"You became impossible to live with. She wanted a different lifestyle and you were inflexible."

"She knew what she was getting into when she married me. I

did not become impossible to live with. She stopped believing in me and gave up too early," Cal insisted.

"Believing in you and being a realist about what to do with the rest of your life are two separate issues. You had a little trouble addressing her concerns," Randy said, more forcefully. Neither Cal nor Mattie had ever heard him comment on Cal's breakup with such attitude.

"I know! Why don't we retire to the balcony?" Mattie suggested, making sure things did not escalate. "That'll take the edge off."

Laura poured herself another coffee and wriggled in her seat to make herself more comfortable. "This is just starting to get interesting."

"Don't you have an article to write?" Cal said pointedly to Laura. "And when did you become a psych major?" He gave her a long hard look before shifting his steely gaze back to Randy.

"Well, Unc, it's pretty obvious that the long-term effect of the crash is having an impact on your frontal lobe. You're having a hard time separating reality from fiction."

"Wow, and you call this a normal lifestyle? Two gay bohemians running a restaurant in a tiny Mexican village at the end of the planet. I mean, really. No offence, Mattie, but I'm just making a point."

"Just read Professor Yorgy Simeroff's 1992 book *Trauma and the Uncertain Brain*. You're a classic case."

Cal jumped up from his chair, deadly serious and looking like he was going to pick a fight with Randy. "Classic case? I'll show you a classic case, Professor Randall!"

Cal put Randy in a headlock and started rubbing his head as if he was playing with a little kid. Then he forced Randy to his knees and began to tickle him. Randy was laughing and gasping for air, begging Cal to stop. Mattie and Laura breathed a little easier now and enjoyed the show of affection. Laura was surprised to see a side of Cal she would never have envisioned twenty-four hours earlier and took a nice relaxing sip of her cappuccino. Just then there began a tapping noise on the big front mahogany doors. It got louder. Luckily Randall had remembered to lock the doors after the last of the evening's customers had left. The knob started rattling, someone was really trying to get in. Mattie jumped up and rushed to the door and everyone else went silent. Cal and Laura skulked behind one of the large wooden dividers in the dining area accentuated with an expansive leafy balm plant hoping this would shield them from view. Mattie waited a moment longer before revealing the two Mexican police officers, who stared at him intently for the first few moments. Mattie recognized one of the officers as someone who had been to the restaurant, and offered up a "Buenas Noches, sorry we are closed." The officers responded in kind. "Unfortunately, we are here on official business this time," the older one added.

Cal, Laura and Randy could hear them chatting in Spanish, Randy decided it would be good if he went to the door as well. The second officer was much younger than the one who had eaten there, and informed Mattie that they had been instructed to look around.

"Case the joint" were his actual words. He introduced himself as Damon. "I learned that saying from watching American detective shows. I love it when I get a chance to say it for real."

Damon reminded the other officer that their instructions were to check all the rooms and buildings.

As Mattie and Randy tried to assure them that no one else was there, Damon gently pushed his way through and started to walk around. Randy offered the older officer a coffee and seated him at a table near the door, and then ran and poured him a coffee and one for himself to make the officer feel more at ease. Mattie followed Damon around like a puppy as he "cased the joint."

"Can you turn the lights up?" Damon asked Mattie.

"Really?" Mattie sighed. "It's so late, we were just going to bed," Mattie replied in a friendly voice.

"Please," said Damon in an equally friendly voice. "It looks like you were having a dinner party here."

As the lights came up (Mattie was careful not to turn them *all* the way up), Damon walked over to the table and looked at the settings.

"We often eat late after we close," Mattie said as he rejoined Damon, looking over his shoulder, wondering where Cal and Laura had gone. They were no longer crouched behind the divider.

"We had some friends over for dinner tonight. It's the only time we get to entertain, after the restaurant closes," Randy injected, raising his voice a little to be heard while he remained seated with the older officer by the front door. Mattie was busy still looking around for any sign of the two fugitives; then made a little gasp, barely audible, but Damon heard him and looked around at him.

Mattie could see Laura's toes sticking out from under one of the sets of floor-to-ceiling curtains on either side of the large windows.

"I just noticed we forgot to close the curtains, we always do before bed," Mattie said as he pulled the curtains in together (being careful not to expose Cal or Laura; in fact he was creating more camouflage for the pair). He gently tapped Laura's feet with his. Laura got the message and backed up as far as the wall would allow. Then Mattie moved around and did the same with the other two sets of large curtains to make it look routine.

Randy, who had been sitting awkwardly and quietly with the older officer, finally spoke.

"I have seen you and your wife—I presume—in here before," Randy said with a wry smile. Taking a chance and being a bit playful with the officer.

"*Si*, just my wife." The officer smiled back. "My wife loves this place; it's her favourite place to dine out."

"Well, then you shall be our special guests one night," Randy said, pulling his card out and offering it to the officer. "Tell . . ." Randy paused.

"Lucinda, her name is Lucinda," the officer said with a gigantic smile.

"Tell Lucinda to call me; we'll set a date, with some of your friends as well, of course." Randy tried to get the baited hook in farther. "We will reserve the big table by the window there for you and your friends; you will be our special guests." Randy could tell he had hit the right button.

"Words cannot express what this will mean to my wife, she'll hardly believe it when I tell her."

Mattie and Damon were now in the kitchen.

"Would you like to see the upstairs?" Mattie offered, hoping he would say no. Mattie worried there would be some tell-tale signs of the pair having been there. But he wanted to get Damon away from the windows.

"Damon!" the other officer shouted before Damon answered Mattie. "I can appreciate you wishing to do a thorough job, but honestly, it's almost midnight, and these two clearly have had a long day running this great restaurant. I have eaten here many times with my wife. I'm sure they would tell us if they had seen the fugitives?"

"Yes, of course we would," Randy blurted out. "If we see any-one suspicious we will call your offices right away."

"Damon, time to vamoose, I wish to be home in bed with my wife. Our shift is over," the older officer said as he stood up, look-ing at his watch and tucking Randy's card into his breast pocket.

Damon took a long look around and Mattie tried to position himself between Damon and the curtain without being suspicious. Damon did not say anything; he just walked around the rest of the big room very slowly, tapping his billy club gently against his hand.

"Okay, sorry to have troubled you," Damon finally said as he picked up his pace and headed over to the front door.

"If you see anyone suspicious at all, anyone who might be our couple, please call, we would be very grateful." He handed Mattie his card.

"Have a good night, I will be back again soon with my wife," the older officer said as the pair left the restaurant.

Mattie quickly turned the dimmers down on the lights and told Cal and Laura to slowly move back to behind the room divider. The officers could be watching from outside for a while.

Mattie and Randy started to clean up.

"What did he mean by 'I will be back again soon with my wife'?" Mattie asked suspiciously.

"Let's just say we have made a small investment in saving Uncle Cal and Laura's lives." Randy took a load of dishes into the kitchen smiling. He was more than pleased with his own ingenuity.

"I'm not sure I like the sounds of this, as if harbouring two fugitives was not enough!"

"We may have also purchased a lifetime of police protection as a bonus," Randy added with a smile at Mattie as he continued to clean up. "You'll see, it'll be well worth it; I'll explain later."

After a few minutes of very nervous waiting, Cal and Laura carefully slid out from behind the divider.

"That was close," Cal said after a moment of everyone just staring at one another.

"How did you get them to leave so quickly" Laura asked, looking quizzically at Marty and Randy.

"I just turned on the ol' Randall charm—and offered up a free meal." Mattie shot Randy a look of bewilderment.

"That's it?" asked Cal.

"Well, a free meal for the older officer . . . and his wife . . . and just a few of their friends."

Cal laughed aloud and Mattie stared even harder at Randy.

"Thank you so much," Laura said, giving each of them a big hug. "We owe you our lives."

✳ ✳ ✳

With the recent scare and sudden jolt back to reality it was obvious to all it was time to retire for the evening. Mattie and Randy said their good nights. Cal and Laura climbed the stairs to the guest room.

After changing into the way-oversized pyjamas she'd been loaned, Laura found herself staring uneasily at what seemed like an unusually small queen-size bed. Laura quickly surmised that it only looked that way because of the multitude of pillows that smothered it: that and the prospect of having to share it with Cal. As much as she was starting to appreciate him for who he was, as opposed to what she thought he represented and getting a peek of him through that thin veneer, she was still mad as hell at him and the idea of sleeping in the same bed was pushing the boundaries of her comfort zone.

"You looked great this evening," Cal, said hoping to warm the chill he could feel settling over the room.

"Thank you. Not bad, I guess, for throwing on someone else's clothes in a hurry," Laura said.

"I meant earlier, when you got out of the pool," Cal said with his wide boyish grin.

"Ha! I should have known," Laura said. Frustrated, she walked towards the bed.

"I was kidding, you looked beautiful tonight," Cal said quickly, trying to redeem himself. "Especially in that getup."

"Forget it. Too late. That brand of glue might stick to other women but it won't hold a toothpick to me. I am on to you. But if you promise to behave yourself I'll let you sleep on the bed just to show you what a nice person I am, in spite of my reservations," Laura said as she took all the pillows from the top of the bed and lined them up, down the middle of the bed.

"That's too bad," Cal said sadly, looking disappointedly at what Laura was constructing. "This bed reminds me of riding in a '67 Caddy with its old spring shocks and a heavy-duty suspension. It's got a good feel to it."

"Well, tonight it's going to remind you of the Great Wall of China." Finishing her task and rubbing her hands together, she was pleased at how much she had frustrated Cal. "There! That should provide a strong enough current to stop you from wriggling upstream."

"What the hell are you talking about?" Cal asked quite sincerely, a puzzled look on his face.

"The next time I get romantically involved with a guy, I'd like someone who keeps his hair neat and who isn't always wearing some worn-out baseball cap that his grandpappy gave him, or that has the name of his favourite beer or a chewing-tobacco logo on it. I'd like a man who won't make me feel like a four-cylinder engine short on oil every time we make love. He'll be sensitive, the strong, silent type."

"You should take the other side," Cal said to Laura when she had finished her long-winded monologue and was crawling into bed. "That side has a little dip in it down near where your hip is."

"Oh!" Laura said as she hopped out of bed and switched sides. "Thanks, I guess."

"What?" Cal asked, now smiling at Laura's frustration. "I'm just trying to show you what a sensitive guy I am. I'll work on the hair thing later," he added, taking his hat off and running his free hand through his hair.

✳ ✳ ✳

Morning came without incident and it was relatively quiet, all
things considered. It may have been Baja week, but most of the
transient population connected to the race and those locals that
found themselves caught up in the festivities were now nursing
well-cured hangovers or such. At the restaurant, there was an
atmosphere of solitude and contentment, of letting the present
eclipse the absurdity of the past few days. It was especially good
for Laura, who enjoyed the therapeutic benefits of helping out in
the kitchen.

The boys were busy; the place always did a brisk business every
Saturday night and this one was no exception. Like most of the
good restaurants in town, and even the not so good, they were
full to capacity all night. Laura remained busy working behind
the scene in the kitchen the whole evening until closing time. This
proved a wonderful distraction from their current situation and
time stood still for a brief moment, free of concern or worry about
what the future might hold. She kept herself so busy she had little
time to think of anything else. She felt guilty that she had momentarily forgot about her son, M. J., but quickly assuaged those concerns,
assuring herself there would be ample opportunity for her to deal
with that problem later. Cal stayed well hidden, as someone in
the crowd surely would have recognized him in a cursory glance
through the open kitchen window, or on a trip to the restroom. It
would be best if Cal remained obscured from view, they all agreed;
he could work on their escape plan and help with the cleanup after.
And so another nervous night came and went without incident.
There was an additional late-night meal for just the four of them,
more introspective conversations and drinks while the big hand
moved slowly down the right-hand side of the clock face that no
one seemed to be paying any attention to. The fugitives and their

accomplices were caught up in the spontaneity and carefree simplicity of the moment. Where did I go wrong? Why is my life not always like this? thought Cal.

The boys had briefly considered not opening for the usual Sunday-morning brunch but Restaurant Frattoria's brunch, considered the best in La Paz, was eagerly looked forward to by the after-church crowd and not to be missed. Sunday dinner would be a set menu, early and simple with a jazz duo on guitar and piano playing quietly in the corner. An abrupt closing on the final day of the Baja would arouse some suspicion. It was decided best to stick to the routine and drag their asses out of bed and get on with the show.

Monday was their day of rest. Frattoria closed. There was the shopping and various other duties but Monday was for rest, swimming and sailing if the gods were working in their favour.

Laura particularly enjoyed the continuous banter of the waiter and the chef, despite the pressure of the hot, hungry crowds waiting for food and the stress of always being at the ready in case the Feds showed up. Surprisingly, not once did police officers or armed guards come through the doors, although seen passing by on the street throughout the day just on their regular duties. The fugitives were ready to hide in a special cubbyhole in the back of the master bedroom's closet if necessary. It was a space the size of a small two-piece bathroom, which had made no design sense to the boys when they bought the place so they had just built a giant pine armoire around it and used the back part for storage. In case of emergency, as they now realized, it could also hide two or three people quite nicely.

✳ ✳ ✳

Again, Cal kept to himself most of the day, up on the patio, trying to stay out of sight and keep an eye on the alleyway for any surprise visits while keeping busy constructing a game plan for their escape from La Paz. Cal welcomed these days of serenity knowing that come Tuesday morning he and Laura would attempt to implement the plan he had been working on. This new master plan meant trying to stealthily connect with Bob at the truck to head north, and once again their lives would seem like a living nightmare. One from which either could not wait to awake from.

Laura, feeling right at home now in the kitchen, thought that maybe she could do this back home if they ever get out of here alive. She could open a place of her own; her son could join her when he was older, they could enrol in cooking classes, why not? But thinking of that made her think of her reason for being here in the first place.

"Do you have a word processor?" Laura asked after things quieted down in the kitchen. "I'd like to start work on my story today, not just keep making notes."

"Sorry, we're not that advanced here yet, but I do have an old typewriter you can use," replied Mattie.

CHAPTER NINETEEN

Monday morning brought a bustle of activity to all the hotel parking lots. It was one thing for the crew and trucks to be arriving at
different times when the race was on, but something else altogether
for sixty or so eighteen-wheelers plus a plethora of other race vehicles
and cars to be packing up and heading north, caravan-style.

The commotion of all the equipment being loaded onto the
eighteen-wheelers and then moving out at the same time was nearly
as exciting as the start of the race. Racers signing final autographs,
fans and tourists alike taking pictures, temporary lovers tenderly
kissing goodbye, exchanging numbers along with addresses and
empty promises to stay in touch.

✳ ✳ ✳

After hugs and kisses goodbye and promises to keep in touch with
the others more often, Cal and Laura made their way covertly over
to where they could see the team truck. It was that magical time
of morning when it's still dark but the sun is rising, the birds are
singing, and there's that strong scent from the dew on the plants

as you start to feel the welcoming force of the sun. It was also usually very quiet there at that time, with a few joggers, or employees coming to work, and even today there were remnant partiers still lingering in the hotel parking lots. Luckily, the fugitives found a comfortable, secluded spot among the crowds, in an old, disused laundry building where they huddled together to keep each other warm and grab another hour of sleep before Cal awoke, pleasantly surprised, spooning against Laura's warm body. Cal could not or would not allow himself to go back to sleep. He loved this feeling, the trust and the closeness. He had not felt this way in a long time. This was usually the time of day when he was leaving someone but now he wished Laura would not wake up! Cal wanted this moment to last forever. With his arms tight around Laura and his nose buried deep between her shoulder blades and her long soft hair just tickling the end of his nose, Cal watched the sun come up and was aware of his own heartbeat for the first time in a long time.

Bob showed up at the truck with the first crack of light, which was always his way. No matter how much partying he had done the night before, Bob was usually the first crewmember on-site. Cal could see him from a tiny window, as he and Laura stepped out from the security of the laundry building. Bob saw them coming and quickly opened the side door to the massive trailer for them. Cal grabbed Bob's fresh, hot coffee on his way into the darkness of the trailer that seemed to eat the two of them up.

"Thanks, man," Cal whispered with a smile as he disappeared.

"Help yourself?" Bob said with his hand out, looking like he was still holding a coffee in it as he walked up the metal steps and closed the door behind him.

Bob pulled the curtain on a small window, letting in a few slivers of light, making the trailer look like a scene from an old black-and-white Hitchcock film. The window was so high up nobody would be able to see in, but the light was strong enough so that they could see one another and find places to sit. Bob did not want to risk running the truck early and turning the light on.

"Listen up," Bob said, sounding like his old high school football coach. "We managed to obtain a small plane that will be waiting for you at the airport in Negros. The Old Man knows a pilot who can take off without filing a flight plan. It was not cheap. It will take us several hours to get there today with the traffic. I got a friend to drive my motorhome back and I told Skinner I would share the driving with him, but he does not have a clue you two are stowaways back here, okay? I am going to have him pull the rig over just before the airport under the pretence of me needing to take a leak or wanting to check the tire pressure or something. Then I'll sneak back here and let you folks out. Stay low until we drive away. The plane you are looking for is baby blue with a white stripe along the side. It is a single-prop number MC1902. The pilot's name is Juan. Or wait a minute, maybe it was a white plane with a baby-blue stripe." Bob started looking for his notepad.

"And maybe his name's not Juan but José, the second most popular name down here," Cal said sarcastically.

"Hey, I think we've done pretty darn good under the circumstances, buddy!" Bob retorted. "The pilot has no idea who you are or where you're headed. He just knows that he isn't filing any flight plan before he takes off." Bob pulled a wad of cash out of his pocket as he spoke. "The deal is, you give him a thousand bucks before he turns the prop and another when he drops you off."

"Don't say 'drops us off,'" Laura said with a nervous smile. Bob and Cal laughed.

"There's a few extra hundred in there for you guys as well, in case you need some money," Bob said warmly as he handed the bills to Cal.

"I'll take care of that," Laura said, reaching over and taking the rolled bundle away from Cal and stuffing it in her bag.

"Where did you get this on such short notice?" Cal asked as a tear almost formed in the corner of his eye.

"The Old Man took up a collection and some of us just took a little less pay. He knows you're good for it," Bob said, patting Cal on the shoulder to shore him up. Cal was looking as though he was going to cry and Bob knew he could not let that happen in front of Laura.

"You think I should be feeling pretty guilty about now, huh?" Cal asked sheepishly.

"I don't know how you feel. You put in many good years with the Old Man. You felt you needed a break. He knows that or he wouldn't have done this."

"But if you told me you felt like fresh dog crap right about now, or the sludge that collects at the bottom of a septic tank, I wouldn't stop you from feeling that way," Laura said, doing her best impression of Bob and showing off her good-humoured side, which Cal thought had been pretty scarce thus far.

"Thanks for everything, man, you've been absolutely wonderful through this whole ordeal. I can't begin to tell you how much I appreciate it," Laura said. With enthusiasm, she threw her arms around the spherical Bob.

"Make sure little buddy over here and you get out alive. That will be all the thanks I need," Bob said. "You two hide here in the mini-bay until we get out of town. I am sure there will be spot checks looking for you guys and this baby will be one of the trucks they pull over for sure, but we are hoping they will also take the view that we would be crazy to try and sneak you out in this one. The car will be over top and I'm sure they won't make us move the car. Most people wouldn't even know there was a crawl space underneath unless they happen to have been part of a race crew." Bob slid open a steel trapdoor in the floor that revealed a small three-by-six-by-three-foot compartment that allowed mechanics to get underneath the race vehicles and work on them while they were being transported or if the weather was bad. One of the mechanical engineers had even put his hard-earned degree to work and installed a drain plug.

Now the tiny bay was nothing more than an extra storage compartment, usually full of ice and beer.

Cal climbed into the empty chamber and Laura squished in, half beside, half on top of Cal.

"Is it safe in here?" Laura asked, sounding a little nervous.

"Just don't lead him on," Bob teased.

"That's not what I meant," Laura replied sharply.

"Well, we only had one person fall through in the past year," Cal said, laughing.

Laura threw Bob a look.

"He's kidding," Bob said. "You're safer in there than you are out here. And you only have to stay in there until you feel us get up to highway speed after the spot check." Bob slid the trap door slowly over the two figures and saw the fear in Laura's eyes as the lid closed. Bob's big smile was the last thing she saw as darkness surrounded her and Cal.

Bob rolled the Stallion over the hatch, clamped it down and threw a tarp over it. "That should keep her safe."

✳ ✳ ✳

Tony and Ramon were at the roadblock on Highway 1 on the outskirts of La Paz overseeing inspections when Ramon noticed the big rig they were sure contained their suspects.

"Here it comes," Ramon said to Ramiros as the truck approached. The rig came to a grinding halt in front of the guards at the checkpoint. Ramon and Ramiros stepped out of their Jeep and strolled over to the cab.

"I don't know about the US of A," Ramiros said, stepping up to the driver's-side window, ignoring Skinner who was driving, and looking directly at Bob in the passenger seat, "but in Mexico, those who assist in the escape of a criminal get tried right alongside them, for the same crime."

"Wow! Is that so," Bob said calmly. "Someone would have to be a damn fool to do that then, wouldn't they?" Bob tried to conceal the smirk that was lurking just underneath his blank expression.

"A damn fool or a very good friend," Ramiros replied. "Have you seen your damn good friend lately?"

"Not since you and I danced at the pool party back in La Paz," Bob said with a smile on his face. The humour of the remark was not lost on Ramon. Ramiros noticed that Ramon was smiling at Bob's little jab.

Meanwhile, the officers who had checked the trailer reported to Ramiros that it was all clear.

"I told you no one was in the trailer. If Redman was in there, I would have known about it, right, Bob?" Skinner asked.

"Right," said Bob, staring straight at Skinner, looking as sincere as he could.

"If there was anyone back there I would know about it," Skinner said, looking at Ramiros. "And I'm telling you straight as an arrow there isn't anyone back there." Ramiros stepped down from the cab of the truck and he and Ramon walked back to their Jeep and watched the rig pull away.

"I know they're in one of these trucks," Ramiros said to Ramon with a frustrated sigh.

"They're all being searched and if they're in one, we'll find them," replied Ramon matter-of-factly.

"This is the crew he worked for and this is the crew he's leaving with. I can't see him leaving any other way," Ramiros said with the expression of a determined pit bull on his face.

"It scares me when you get that look," Ramon said as they pulled away and starting passing all the trucks in the convoy. Tony wanted to stay close to this band of gypsies but well out of sight.

✳ ✳ ✳

As soon as she felt the truck picking up speed, Laura slid the tiny lid to the bay open, slithered out from under the car and the tarp, and turned on a light.

"Leaving so soon? It was just getting cozy in here," Cal said as he came out and headed straight for the tiny fridge. Cal pulled out a beer and started to guzzle it down. "Would you like one? We've definitely earned it!" Cal said proudly.

"I think I will have something," Laura said as she walked over to the fridge.

"Hey, we finally see eye to eye," Cal said with a big smile.

"I hope I'll never be drunk enough that we see eye to eye on anything," Laura said, pulling out a can of Coke. "In fact I plan on never drinking again. It's not going to be easy, so it would be nice if you could respect that."

Cal finished his beer, took another from the fridge and walked away from Laura without saying a word.

"I'm sorry," Laura said as Cal turned off the light and perched on a cot in the back corner of the trailer. "I didn't mean that the way it came out. "You've been amazing through this whole ordeal." Laura waited for a response from Cal but none came.

"It's just that I shouldn't be here in the first place. It's like a bad dream that just will not end. And when I wake, even from a good night's sleep, I'm shrouded in this big dark cloud of worry."

"No, it's me who should be sorry. I owe you an apology for not showing a little more sympathy for the situation with your son. And unforgivably for drinking and driving with you on-board. I've just never spent a lot of time around someone who does not drink a lot lately and it's just become second nature to me. Therefore, I am the master and creator of this bad dream you are in. You somehow just ended up in my nightmare. I am truly sorry. I wish there were an easy fix for you. I've been constantly wondering how to get you out of this, but nothing comes up. I will do whatever I can. I won't bail on you, no matter what."

They sat in silence for a bit, Laura with her Coke and Cal with a Bud. Then Laura stood up and grabbed a blanket.

"Thanks for saying that. I am just tired now, this is not like me," she said, and with that, turned out the light and lay down in the dark for what seemed like an eternity.

Occasionally Laura would hear Cal go to the fridge for a beer. She figured he was either drowning himself in self-pity or just pouting. The next time Laura spoke to Cal was when the rig started to slow down a few hours later and she decided to wake him up. With her eyes now well-adjusted to the dark, she noticed Cal was now surrounded by empty beer cans as if he had been sitting around chatting with his old friends, and he gave Laura a hard time when she woke him up. She was completely perplexed as to why Cal had reverted to his old self at this particular stage of their ordeal, and after he had given such a heart-felt apology. It had seemed to Laura that he was turning a corner. She was very worried that he had gone back to his old ways at the crucial moment of what seemed like their imminent escape.

✳ ✳ ✳

Bob told Skinner he would grab them a few beers from the back of the truck when he'd finished draining the snake. This would give him an excuse to go into the trailer. Laura was propping Cal up when Bob stepped in. "I'm not interrupting anything, am I?" Bob asked.

"Don't be silly," Laura, said. "I'm just trying to get the drunken son of a bitch up. I think I said something that hurt his feelings so instead of accepting my apology he got hammered."

"Well, it must have been a large slice of humble pie he needed to muster up, because this guy doesn't get hurt that easily," Bob said, staring down at Cal.

"Knock it off, you two. I am not hurt and I am not comatose. I just felt like having a few beers. Not a big deal. What's up?" Cal asked sluggishly.

"Well, funny you should ask," Bob said. "We're just shy of the airport but it looks awfully quiet out there. I mean, it is a small airport and it is Monday afternoon but there is not a plane taking off or landing and it is still light out. I do not like the looks of that. I was hoping it would be just light enough by the time we got here for the plane to legally take off."

"If you two are done discussing the ideal conditions for takeoff, you'd best come have a look," Laura said, peering out the side window.

"What is it?" asked Cal as he stood up and came to Laura's side. "Aw fuck!" Cal screamed. Two vehicles filled with Mexican Feds were racing towards the truck.

"That Ramiros fella is coming this way," Bob said, looking out the other trailer window.

"Did you give him the envelope?"

"Sure did, but he said he had to bring you in anyway"

"Damn! Get out there and stall them while Laura and I get back in the hole," Cal said, grabbing Laura and slipping under the tarp. Bob took two beers from the fridge and locked the door behind him. He opened a beer, handed one to Skinner and then started to kick the tires of the truck. Skinner hopped out of the cab. "What's up, man?" Skinner asked, opening his beer.

"Your guess is as good as mine," Bob said, raising his can to Skinner in a silent cheer.

"Just happen to be having a little engine trouble by the airport, gentlemen?" Ramiros inquired politely through the open window of his Jeep as it came to a quick dusty stop beside the rig.

Bob gave Ramiros a pained look. "Thought I'd drain the weasel, grab us a few refreshments while we're stopped and check the tires. It's been a long ride, but looks like everything thing is A-okay, so if you want to finish that beer, Skins, we can vamoose," Bob said as he took the beer from Skinner. "But thanks for checking in with us."

"Not so fast, fellas!" Ramiros shouted as Bob and Skinner headed back to the cab.

"Sorry, forgot, no open beer in a moving vehicle." Bob guzzled his beer down, then, as macho as possible, crushed his empty can to half its size with one quick squeeze.

"How'd you like to open up the trailer so we can have ourselves another look around in there?" Ramiros asked bluntly.

Bob looked surprised. "Isn't much to see. One race car is pretty much the same as the next these days."

Ramiros snapped, "Cut the crap and open up all the doors this time so we can have a good look."

"You're like a fart in a car; you just aren't going to go away, are you?" Bob said, looking pissed off and staring directly into Ramiros's eyes.

The trailer flooded with light as all the doors swung open, including the two large doors at the rear. All six officers climbed in and started poking around.

Ramon soon noticed the clips holding the race truck in place were not done up and the tarp was hanging loosely over it, just barely covering the cab. "Hey, Ramiros," Ramon yelled, "over here."

"Damn! I could have sworn I clamped that down before we left town," Bob said, leaning toward the tarp.

"Step back," Ramiros ordered. He pulled out his gun and pointed it at Bob. "You've been enough help for one day."

"No need to get nasty," Bob said, stepping back.

"Looks like we got us a little sunken bay under here, what do you suppose might be in there?" Ramon said to Ramiros, a smile reaching across his face.

"If you really want to help, help me move this truck out of the way," Ramiros said to Bob. Ramiros, Ramon and Bob rolled the truck back a few feet, fully exposing the trapdoor.

Ramon cautiously leaned forward and slid the metal door aside while Ramiros and the rest of the officers trained their guns on the pit. The door opened, revealing only an empty space. The rest of the patrol, including Bob, looked on in astonishment.

Suddenly the tremendous roar of the Stallion's engine broke the silence. Fumes, smoke and fear filled the trailer within seconds and it took twice that long for anyone to realize what had happened.

The incredible forward thrust of the Stallion sent everyone scattering for his life, and the heavy canvas tarp tore off as if it were mere rice paper. Through the smoke, Ramiros and the others could barely see the figures of Cal and Laura as the powerful machine leaped from the trailer out into the freedom of the Baja dusk. The officers' shock soon changed to the realization that the objects of their pursuit, who, moments ago, were well within their clutches, were disappearing into the vastness of this majestic desert.

The car handled the landing from the back of the truck with ease and Cal spun it around to face the trailer.

"We're innocent!" Cal shouted at the indistinguishable silhouettes of Ramon and Ramiros, who were now standing at the lip of the trailer, looking down on the two fugitives. "We didn't take the money."

"Not according to the bumps on my head!" replied Ramiros, unloading a couple of rounds of ammo that ricocheted off the metal driver's cage. Cal switched gears and pushed his foot to the floor. Laura's head jerked back, hit the cage and stayed there as the tremendous thrust and power of the machine spewed a precipitous amount of Goodyear rubber into the environment, once again making it almost impossible to see.

"Put your bag on the floor and do up your seat belt!" Cal yelled at Laura as the truck vibrated wildly in a stationary position.

"What?" Laura yelled back.

"Do up your seat belt!" Cal hollered back again as he flicked two silver toggle switches on the dash. The twin turbo boosters kicked in and flames shot out the back, turning the tips of the chrome tailpipes red as the spire impaled itself in the unknown vastness, leaving Ramiros and the rest of the Feds in a state of shock.

Ramiros looked at Ramon "We're going to lose them."

"I knew I should have ordered the Turbo option when the new vehicles came out this year," Ramon muttered, but no one heard him as they all scampered for their Jeeps. Tony pushed down hard on the gas pedal and the Jeep responded beautifully. It was going as fast as it had ever gone off-road and still it felt like they were just watching Cal and Laura disappear in the burning-red sunset, leaving only a wondrous, golden plume of Baja dust behind.

CHAPTER TWENTY

"The scenery's nice but do you have any idea where we're going from here?" Laura asked Cal.

"Due north, to the border and beyond," Cal said hesitantly.

Suddenly Laura found herself gasping for air.

"Are you going to be sick?" Cal asked.

"No, I think I swallowed a bug," she replied.

"Probably just a flying cockroach," Cal said nonchalantly.

"*Now* I'm going to be sick for sure," Laura said, sticking her head out the window. Or rather pulling aside the rubber net where the window used to be. A bullet caromed off the side of the car. Cal had slowed down a bit after their original getaway, not realizing the police had maintained their pursuit at full speed. Laura pulled her head back in. "Actually, it didn't taste that bad."

"You get used to them," Cal said.

"How far do we have to go to get to the border?" she asked, changing the subject.

"About five hundred miles or so," Cal replied, "but what I'm really worried about is what we do when we get there."

"Get where?" asked Laura.

"Tijuana," Cal said looking over at her. "We can get lost there."

Laura reached into her bag and pulled out a bandanna. "Five hundred miles," she repeated. Frowning, she wrapped the bandanna around her face, bank-robber style.

"That'll really scare 'em, pilgrim," Cal said in his overused and very poor John Wayne imitation.

"Funny, but I've had enough unplanned meals for one day, thank you."

The mountainous, rocky terrain had forced Cal to slow down and turn the vehicle towards the town of Negros, which they had no choice but to drive through. Cal took a quick look back and saw Ramiros and Ramon had gained ground on them. He chastised himself aloud for not paying more attention.

The supercharger on the Stallion was great, but it was only recommended for use for quick starts, passing or an extra boost near the finish line. The trouble with the turbo was that it was an unsustainable speed. The Stallion became very hard to control at that high speed and the fuel consumption meant they'd have to refuel in no time and, eventually, revert to a regular speed. Cal hoped to maintain their current advantage over the Feds until he could hit the open desert again.

As the Stallion entered the town, Cal noticed a crowd of a hundred or so people gathered in the main square, which was also the only street leading in and out of this tiny little enclave. They had to reduce their speed almost to a crawl. Laura glanced over at Cal and noticed his hands were sweaty and shaking. Cal's face was wrenched and twisted and tiny beads of perspiration were running down the lines in his face, lines that seemed to have become longer and deeper even in the few days since Laura had first met him. "What's wrong?" Laura asked delicately.

"Nothing's wrong," Cal snapped. "I can't just ram the car

through the crowd, there are too many people. Somebody will get killed!"

"Well, you can't slow down too much or they'll catch us." There was a moment's silence between them, and Laura gently placed her left hand on Cal's face. "It's okay. I understand. I know what happened."

"What do you mean?" Cal took a quick look into Laura's eyes. "Who told you—Randy?" he asked.

"It doesn't matter. It's no big deal. Everyone pretty much knows the story. You're more hero than bum, you should be proud of yourself. I'm proud of you for what you did and I'm proud of you for getting behind the wheel of this thing," Laura said, leaning over and kissing Cal's cheek.

"She's not a thing, her name is the Stallion. I've been calling her that since way back when I first started driving for the Old Man and we just kept naming every new car ever since. This is the best one we have ever built. If I'd been driving her, we would have won." Cal smiled back at Laura as he flicked on the full set of lights with several motions of his index finger, completely overpowering the beautiful evening light and illuminating the crowd with the harshness of ten thousand watts of pure tungsten. Cal pounded on the horn, gripped the wheel tightly and pushed down on the pedal just a little harder. This time Laura was anticipating the thrust. Feeling the rapid increase in speed under her, she gripped Cal's knee tightly with her left hand and grabbed the built-in roll-grip above her door with her right.

"Thank you for saying that," Cal hollered over the roar of the engine looking focused, staring straight ahead.

As the car picked up speed, the startled crowd scattered, exposing a priest and some young children who Laura surmised were the centre of attention and the reason for this gathering.

"And so, children of God, I bestow upon you His blessing in the name of the Father, the Son and the Holy Spirit," were the priest's last words before he noticed the speeding car and darted off to the side of the road.

"I've changed my mind," Laura said nervously. "Slow down before you kill someone and really get us into trouble."

Cal hit the horn hard again and all the kids scattered, except one in the middle who had a stick and was about to swing at a piñata hanging from the lamppost in the middle of the island in the main square. Cal was about to slam on the brakes when someone ran out and snatched the unsuspecting kid from harm's way just as he swung, nailing the candy dispenser with all his force.

Candies and small toys flew in complete disorder, in every direction as the Stallion passed underneath, a few of them landing on Laura's lap. The crowd, over a hundred thick by this point had rushed back to the fallen piñata, closely mimicking chickens at feeding time oblivious to or refusing to move out of the way for the smaller and slower moving police car.

An exasperated Ramiros stepped out of the Jeep, which with its lights still flashing come to a complete stop. The Stallion's dust rising over the heads of the massive cluster of the candy-crazed children. "Now what do we do?" Ramon asked Ramiros, who was still sitting in the driver's seat, looking completely perplexed. "We would not have caught up to him anyway, as soon as they got on the other side of town past the ridge, they would have hit the open desert again and lost us. We'll need a plan, and they won't get far without gas so we can start with that in mind"

"Judging by the direction they headed out of here, my guess is they'll take the old mining road, which will likely include a pit stop at Mike's." Ramiros bent down and looked inside at Ramon with a big grin on his face. "What do you think?"

"Not a lot of choices out here for gas, that's for sure," Ramon said, smiling back. "That would almost seem like a sure bet."

✳ ✳ ✳

Laura looked behind her as the Stallion cruised at a comfortable speed along the first paved highway they had been on since they escaped from the rig. "Now this is more like it," she said, getting comfortable. "And the Feds are nowhere in sight."

"Don't get too comfy," Cal warned, looking back to ensure there were indeed no Feds behind them. He made an abrupt right turn off the main highway onto an old mining road.

"Smallest off-ramp I've ever been on. I didn't even see the sign," Laura said, bouncing around in her seat.

"There's only one place I can refuel this thing this far south and hopefully not get caught, and that place would be Mike's Sky Ranch."

"Ah yes, the infamous Mike's Sky Ranch, the inner sanctum of the Baja racers, off limits to women. Remind me again why it is so special. I've forgotten, never having been allowed to go there," Laura said sarcastically.

"A Grand Tradition," Cal said with assurance.

"Grand Tradition," repeated Laura.

"Yeah, it's the original halfway point of the race. Back in the sixties and seventies any driver who made it that far had a lot to celebrate. Some of the racers would celebrate for a few days before rejoining the race. Back when it was not so much about winning as it was just being in it."

"That's it?" Laura asked, looking stunned.

"That's it? Geez, woman, after you've been racing for twelve hours straight, been beaten up by a few cacti, and you're hotter than the hubs of hell during the day and colder than a well-digger's ass by night! What would feel better than a dunk in a hot tub, a hot meal with a cold beer and then tellin' stories all night long around the fire with a few friends? Besides, I think the ban on females during the race was lifted years ago. Not even sure why Mike had that on in the first place." Cal looked as if he had just told her the scientific meaning of the universe.

"You call that tradition?" retorted Laura. "Tradition is Christmas, Thanksgiving, seeing the *Rocky Horror Picture Show* at midnight on Halloween. Those are traditions. I will even concede the Super Bowl, the World Series or the Stanley Cup, but *Mike's?*" As Laura finished her dissertation on what was a real tradition the two-way radio interrupted them.

"Baja here to Mexico's most wanted, can you read me, over," came Bob's voice. Cal and Laura were both speechless. "Hey, can you guys hear me? Over."

Cal picked up the handset. "Mexico's most wanted here. Sorry we didn't get to say goodbye, but we had to leave in a hurry."

"Perfectly understandable, little buddy. How's it going? Are you in the clear? Which way are you heading? Do you need any fuel?" Bob's voice came bellowing back into the Stallion.

"Hello, you two, I don't mean to be rude and interrupt, but you guys are on an open frequency," Laura said, looking at Cal with a grin.

"Good point there," Bob conceded.

"What serious racer is retired now, but still plays a significant role in the life of the racers down here?" Cal asked into the two-way.

"Jesus, this is no time to be playing a game," Bob replied.

"It's not a game this time, Bobby, and it isn't for beers, so you'd better get it right. And that's a big ten-four on the fuel as well," Cal spoke back.

"I can handle the fuel. I'm having a little trouble on the exact locale of where to hook up."

"Think of tradition!" Laura piped up. "Bonding with the fellers, when you're as cold as a well-digger's ass, over."

"Aha! I'm there. I've got it!" Bob yelped.

"You got that?" squeaked Laura in surprise.

"What would your best ETA be?" Cal asked. "In the unfortunate event that there is no fuel available there. It is, after all, after the race. I've never been there *after* a race."

"I'll need at least till midday tomorrow. The roads I have to take to get there are not quite as direct as the route you're taking, and I'm driving in a somewhat slower vehicle but we are carrying a full load of fuel so if there isn't any there we've got you covered. You'll probably get there sometime tonight, I imagine?"

"I guess I can kill that much time."

✷ ✷ ✷

"Drive careful, over and out," Bob said to Cal and Laura, putting the mic back in its cradle and looking over at Skinner, who was giving him a completely bewildered look.

"What kind of trouble are you getting us into now? We were lucky they let us go back there without skinning us alive! Or throwing us in the slammer," Skinner barked at Bob. "That was a complete and total breach of twenty years of friendship."

"I know, I'm sorry, but I couldn't risk telling you and, honestly, once we got through the spot-check I thought we were clear, just drop them off at the airport and you would not have even known. We will fuel them up quickly tomorrow and be in and out of there like a three-peckered goat. It'll be a piece a cake, trust me," Bob said with his double-dimpled devilish grin. "Are you getting tired? Would you like me to drive?" he asked solicitously, trying to change the subject.

"Looks like you guessed right," Ramon said to Ramiros, turning down the volume on the shortwave radio to cut the static noise. "We'll just sneak in tonight while they're sleeping and—"

Ramiros interrupted Ramon. "First, you can't just sneak into the Sky Ranch at night, they'll see us coming for miles, and second, we need to send for backup. We know they'll be lying low there until midday tomorrow anyway so there's no hurry."

"I think we should call for backup to meet us there, hide out in the hills until that guy shows up with the gas. As soon as they hook the car up to the gas pump, we'll swoop in. That way, they won't be able to go anywhere and we'll get all of them," Ramon said, waving his arms madly. "This time we won't miss."

Anthony looked at him in amazement. He had never seen his serene partner that animated before. "I guess we could use the backup, and anyway they'd see us coming from a mile and a half away if we tried to go in tonight. Unless we sneak in on foot, in which case you're right, they might get away. I'm sure they'll have someone standing guard," Anthony conceded as he picked up the two-way to call for backup.

"Tomorrow we'll be ready and well equipped for the big show-down and we'll have the sun on our side. I like it."

"I like it too," Anthony said. "Still, I can't help wondering why they gave us this money back. He says in the letter it fell into the woman's bag by mistake. They wish it had never happened and swear they never intentionally took a dime. I don't know. The captain says we still have to bring them in. I would like to pay that guy back for the hit on the head, but I'd be happy to let it go after that.

This money thing is troubling me, Ramon. I did not know we had that much money in the safe, but apparently, there it was. Would they not have given the whole amount back if they had taken it by mistake? Alternatively, would they play us for fools and think we would let them go if they gave back part of it? I don't know, but something is not sitting right with me."

"I think it'll all work itself out tomorrow when we catch them. That's what we must do to get to the bottom of this." Ramon put his hands behind his head, clasped his fingers and laid his head back against the headrest. He closed his eyes.

CHAPTER TWENTY-ONE

"So this is it?" Laura said a few hours later, laughing a little as they approached the large, sprawling neo-seventies ranch-style structure that had appeared before them a few miles earlier as a speck on the horizon. "Mike's Sky Ranch conveniently located in the middle of nowhere. The sacred sanctuary where miners with cold asses go to bond and have a good time."

The dogs quieted down as soon as they recognized Cal, but they were not quite as receptive to Laura and would not let her out of the Stallion until Cal had spent time making a personal introduction.

"By the way, that's a well-digger's ass! Not a miner's. And be nice or you'll hurt Mike's feelings, he is very proud of this place and his reputation," Cal said as the pair entered the massive open room with worn-thin-but-wide-and-polished-to-a-beautiful-shine knotted hardwood floors. The large pine beams stretched across a towering cathedral ceiling, begging every first-time entrant to look up and admire them. The walls adorned with pictures of racers and celebrities, other people connected to the race, spanning nearly two, and half decades; it looked like a still documentary of the history of the race. The collection of photos was so comprehensive and varied in its chronicling of this infamous event that if you imagined a TV camera focusing on one picture at a time in chronological order along with Morgan Freeman narrating you would have a wonderful Discovery Channel documentary.

Laura could feel the warmth of the magnificent fireplace and the charm of the log-and-stone structure.

"We don't usually get too many visitors this soon after the race!" a jovial and boisterous voice bellowed out from another room, not concerned in the least that someone had entered the premises unannounced this late at night. "So to whom do I owe the pleasure of their company?" Mike came out to meet the pair from the comfort of the Story Room.

"Sorry, Mike, I didn't dare radio ahead to let you know we were coming for fear of letting our whereabouts be known."

Mike had been relaxing by the fire in one of the big overstuffed chairs, with a drink and a newly chosen book from the Sky Ranch's massive library. Mike prided himself on not only finding lost and rare gems at the book auctions that he loved to attend but also on keeping a tiny section well stocked with recent and flavour-of-the-month offerings. The Sky Ranch was not your typical B&B, in fact most people likely wouldn't classify it as a B&B at all. Mike never advertised and you would not find it in any directories or listings. The patrons of the Sky Ranch came from word of mouth or were returning devotees.

The Sky Ranch was not your typical inn and definitely not a spa, although Mike was proud of his gardens with the giant hot tub surrounded by two-hundred-year-old cardoon cacti, some reaching as high as sixty feet. Those who stayed there on a regular basis were those who came down to do some off-road adventuring, or just to enjoy the serenity of the place without any of the splash or expense of some of the other places offering "the true desert getaway experience." Every night there was a spectacular show of lights courtesy of the universe. The average temperature was a perfect 25 to 35 Celsius during the day and a very pleasant 20 to 15 degrees at night. Those who stayed there loved it and most returned whenever they could to explore the vast undeveloped wonders that surrounded it, or just to totally relax and absorb all the natural Zenlike qualities of the place, hoping to carry a little bit of it home with them when they had to leave.

"I thought this was going to be my first night to myself in a week. Hell, damn, Jesus Christ, Cal Redman," Mike said, pushing back his thick curly black hair that was just starting to go grey. "What the hey are you doing here this time of night and with such a fine-looking woman?" Mike enveloped the two of them in a big warm embrace.

"I don't mean to question your methods," said Cal, "but why didn't you come out to see who it was. We could have been anyone."

"Well, for starters, just anyone wouldn't have gotten two feet out of their ride if the dogs didn't recognize 'em. And if they did manage to get by the dogs, I'm pretty handy with my shotguns. It's just the way we do things around here. Hell, I don't even lock the doors at night, in case someone gets lost on their journey, we will welcome them in. Usually they can afford to pay for the room and a meal."

"Speaking of journeys, our journey is becoming a very long and interesting story, my man, and I'd love to explain it all to you but if you don't mind, Laura and I would love to have a quick bite, shower and hit the sack. Is that okay?"

"Fine by me, but there's not much left over. I had a full house this year, was cleaned right out, of everything that was good anyway. Haven't had time to restock yet, but I'm sure I can fix you up with something decent, especially a cold beer," Mike said as he headed off into the kitchen. "I didn't think I was going to see you this year," Mike hollered back from the kitchen. "Rumour has it you've become Baja's most wanted or something."

"Yeah, it's gotten very weird, Mike. It's like one bad dream after another and sometimes I'm not sure I am ever going to wake up from it."

"You know what? I am sorry if this seems rude, but I can hardly keep my head up right now. Where can I sleep?" Laura asked Cal quietly.

"I take it all the rooms are empty?" Cal asked Mike.

"Now that the race is over, the late-fall hunting kicks in. But it's an empty house tonight, so take any room you want," Mike replied.

"They each have their own shower, too," Cal added.

"Thanks," Laura said, turning toward the hall. "Is there one you recommend?"

"I like them all but the ones on the right have a view of the gardens," Mike said.

"I'm looking forward to a good night's sleep," said Laura. "Something tells me tomorrow's going to be a long hard day again."

"It may well be, but I'll have a treat for you tomorrow, regardless," Cal said sweetly.

"A treat, what kind of treat? Like I'll wake up and we'll be in Kansas?" Laura said, disappearing into a room.

"We'll definitely have a Mike's-style breakfast waiting for you in the morning anyway. That should get you through anything tomorrow throws your way," Mike added as Laura closed the door.

Cal headed into the kitchen, grabbed a beer and helped Mike make up a snack before the two of them headed to the Story Room. Cal was anxious to bring Mike up-to-date on his life and Mike knew that this was one story that would be Baja folklore for years to come. They talked well past midnight.

"You get yourself a good night's sleep," Mike said to Cal as the two of them realized almost simultaneously that the hours had passed quickly and Cal was getting wiggly-eyed. It was time for bed. "I'll stand watch till sunrise, but the dogs will pick up on anyone coming within a quarter mile of this place. Just one of the few things I like about this place is you can see someone coming for about a day and half."

"Hey, man, thanks. Sure you don't mind?" Cal said with a sigh of relief. "I don't want to get you into any kind of trouble. You still have to live and work down here long after we're safe back home."

"Do I have any choice?" Mike asked with a smile.

"No," Cal said, shaking Mike's hand and giving him a brief but heartfelt hug.

"I'll put on a pot of my famous coffee and I'll be just fine reading on the porch until you get your lazy ass out of bed." Mike paused just before he left for the kitchen. "You're really sleeping in another room tonight?"

"Afraid so, señor," Cal replied as he headed down the hall towards his room.

"Damn shame, a goddamn shame," Cal could hear Mike saying as he walked into the kitchen shaking his head in disbelief.

✺　✺　✺

After breakfast, Mike made a fresh pot of coffee and suggested that Cal and Laura take a cup and relax in the hot tub. He would clean up while they waited for Bob to get there with the fuel. "Well, you know I'd fill you up myself but we ran out of the high octane a day or so ago. I think I might have half a drum left over on the stage truck trailer, but other than a bit of regular for my truck, I can't be much help getting you on your way sooner."

"What are you saying? Just clam up on the apologies," insisted Cal. "You've gone beyond the call of duty already. I just hope that Bob hasn't run into any snags and will be here anytime now with the Stallion's special blend, and then we'll be on our way, and no one will be any the wiser. It'll be just like we were never here."

✻ ✻ ✻

"Now this is more like the trip I had envisioned coming down here," Laura said, settling her back against the wall of the hot tub, luxurious warm water surrounding her. "I'd love to come back here when I can relax and truly enjoy this place. The view is absolutely breathtaking."

"So what you're saying is that you'd like to make this a tradition?"

"No! I definitely did not say that, or even imply that," Laura said with a friendly grin.

"Here, let me help. Lean back and close your eyes," Cal said.

"Not on your life," Laura said, but the look on her face suggested different.

"This is better than sex and you won't feel guilty after," said Cal. "It's Mooshoo Yeeitsue."

"Never heard of it," Laura said, leaning back and closing her eyes, feeling a little more trusting. Cal took hold of one of her feet and began to massage it very gently but firmly as the surging water bubbled around her body and the warm Mexican morning sun beat down on her face.

"I'm sorry I was so quick to judge this place without having ever come here. It's not at all what I expected," Laura said as she opened her eyes and looked around again at the giant cacti and beautiful gardens and trellises that surrounded the hot tub. "Mike is an absolutely wonderful person, not at all what I expected."

"Gee willies, gay nephews that I actually get along well with and well-read, intelligent friends. Sorry I had to shatter your image of me!" Cal said, half-laughing as he continued to put Laura in a state of complete relaxation with his massage technique.

Part of the beauty of Mike's Sky Ranch was the Sierra Nevada mountains off in the distance, which provided a spectacular view any time of day. However, they also provided shelter for Ramiros and his officers, who had set up camp just out of sight a few hours earlier.

✳ ✳ ✳

"Shall we go in?" Ramon asked.

"No. If we go now they'll see us coming far too early. If we wait, the sun will swing around and they won't see our dust until we're already there. Also we'll wait until they start filling up the car, they'll be focused on that and won't be able to get away as quickly," Ramiros replied. Putting down his binoculars, he asked, "Do you think Alessandra would like it if I massaged her feet in a hot tub?"

"You don't own a hot tub," Ramon replied.

"I meant if we went away somewhere, where they had one." Ramiros shot Ramon a look before he lifted the binoculars to his eyes again.

At the same time, he noticed Bob and Skinner were fast approaching up the long laneway to the Sky Ranch.

✳ ✳ ✳

"Did you see that?" Bob asked Skinner.

"See what?" grumbled Skinner, not at all happy with Bob for roping him into helping Cal and Laura. He had barely spoken two words to Bob since the incident at the airport.

"It looks like the sun's reflecting off a piece of glass up in the hills over there," Bob replied, pointing right at the spot where Anthony and Ramon were.

This time, both Bob and Skinner saw the sun sparkle off the officers' binoculars.

"Holy shit!" said Bob. "Someone is right up on that ridge watching! What are we going to do?"

"No fuckin' idea what *you're* going to be doing. I'm not going to be doing anything, you're on your own on this one, compadre."

* * *

As Cal continued massaging Laura's feet, she said, "You are certainly an enigma. I would never have taken you for a guy who studied ancient Japanese relaxation techniques." Laura replied with her eyes closed in total relaxation mood.

"That's good because you'd be right," said Cal. "I just made this up."

"Really? Then where did you learn to do this?" asked Laura with her eyes open now. "On second thought, I don't want to know. Who cares. It feels good and that's all I need to know," said Laura, resuming her position. "So I'll just pretend it's Mooshoo-whatever and enjoy it while it lasts."

Cal smiled at her with his big boyish grin.

No sooner had Laura closed her eyes again than they both heard the big semi come to a squeaky stop. Within seconds, Bob was in the middle of the ranch, huffing and puffing. "Hey! Where is everybody? The jig is up. Come out, come out, wherever you are!" The sound of Bob's voice came bellowing through the open French doors, thumping through the peaceful tranquility of the Japanese garden, overpowering the sound of the whirlpool jets and completely disrupting Laura's relaxing foot massage.

"We're out here, buddy," Cal answered, sounding completely dejected by Bob's arrival.

"I was looking forward to seeing you again," Laura said to Bob as he came through the doors, "but your timing stinks."

"Smelly as it may be, little lady, somebody's been watching you guys from the ridge over there," Bob said, indicating the direction from which the flash came with a slight tilt of his head, so as not to give away that he knew they were being watched. "And I don't think they are going to be content to sit and watch any longer knowing that we're here with the fuel. Better hurry up and get your warm and bubbly asses out of there and into something less comfortable. I have a plan but we have to hurry."

Parked at the north side of the house was an old 1950s flat-bed tractor-trailer. The bed professionally rigged as a sound stage. Complete with scaffolding for lights and speakers, for bands to play on. Mike sometimes had concerts at his resort, everything from classical to Mexican traditional to rock. Many musical celebrities had passed by Mike's. Often he would talk them into putting on a concert, which would attract the locals as well as overnight or weekend visitors. He liked the activity and most of the concerts generated some extra cash too. The stage was on the trailer so he could move it around to wherever he wanted it.

Skinner, Mike and Bob had just put a couple extra barrels of fuel and the pump on the trailer with the help of a tractor when Bob noticed a plume of dust in the not-so-far distance; then he noticed dust from three directions.

The dust was coming from the police trucks as they raced down the ridges onto the flatlands. They were now only a few miles or so from Mike's.

Bob and Skinner had the gas on the flatbed and were in the cab as Cal and Laura made a dash for the Stallion. Laura saw the dust trail from the police cars moving closer. "I told you they would figure it out," Laura said as they hopped in the car. "What are we going to do now?"

"I think we're going to gas up the Stallion and then drive like hell for as long as I can," Cal said as he drove the car around to the side of the house where the truck was.

"The truck is moving," said Laura, surprised. "How do they think we're going to put fuel into the Stallion if they're moving?"

"I think that's the whole idea," Cal said. "I've got to pull up on the flatbed and they'll drive around until we're fuelled up, and then we're on the road again. There is no way we would have time to fill up in the usual way before the Feds get here. That was probably their plan. Catch us unawares with a nozzle up the Stallion's ass."

"That's what I love about you. You have such an eloquent way of phrasing things."

A look of fright crossed Laura's face when she saw Bob climb out of the cab of the truck and make his way to the back of the flatbed to release the drive-up ramps with the truck almost at full speed, which these days was not much. Laura's thoughts where whirling around her head so fast she could not keep them organized. They were a jumble of everything from jumping out of the car and surrendering—at least she would be alive, she thought—to seeing her son, to hoping this was all a bad dream and that she would wake up soon. She even bit down hard on her lip just to make sure she really was awake.

The truck rocked wildly and Bob fell against a stereo bolted to a metal rack, accidentally turning it on. "Middle of the Road" by the Pretenders came blasting over the loudspeakers.

Cal saw the look of horror on Laura's face and tried to reassure her. "Don't worry," Cal said. "We've rehearsed this a thousand times. We thought we would try it in one of the races if we were in a tight one and wanted to keep moving while filling up."

"Really?" Laura asked hopefully.

"Well, we tried it once at a race in Texas but it didn't go well so we put it back on the practice list."

Bob stood at the ready by one of the gas barrels with the make-shift hand pump and nozzle in his hand. Cal lined the Stallion up with the ramp as the Feds raced towards them. He pushed the pedal down hard to the floor and steadied one hand on the wheel, the other on the shifter. Laura closed her eyes. When she opened them again the Stallion had come to a very abrupt stop resting on the back of the flatbed. "Fill 'er up," Cal said to Bob, his smile as wide as a barn door.

"Would you like your oil checked with that, sir?" Bob said, smiling back until they heard a bullet ricochet off one of the metal bars near his head. The Feds had stopped chasing and decided to try shooting. A few bullets came precariously close but the truck was moving away too fast.

Bob left the nozzle in the car still being fuelled and wobbled over to a nearby contraption and pushed a button. The diesel generator fired up right away and smoke from the fog machine started billowing out. Because the truck was moving, his strategy did not have quite the desired effect but it did make it a little harder for the police to see them. Bob raced back and finished filling up the Stallion. Now completely encased by the fake fog Bob could barely see the car or Cal and Laura. Extremely pleased with himself that he had had the wherewithal to think of this added bit of trickery, Bob grabbed Cal's head and pulled it in to his chest in a kind of man-hug gesture.

The Feds had retreated to their Jeeps and started chasing again, only this time they were firing their guns as well.

"Hey, I can't thank you enough, man, for everything you've done," Cal said to Bob. "I'm sorry I—"

Bob cut him off. "Yeah and look at you. You are kind of racing again. Man, am I jealous. I'd trade places with Laura in a minute if I could."

Laura started to unbuckle her seat belt. "All you had to do was ask."

"Hey, you take good care of him out there. As pathetic as it sounds, he's all the family I've got left," Bob said.

"Not a good time to get all maudlin, with the Feds chasing us," Cal said, reaching out and putting a hand on his shoulder.

✳ ✳ ✳

Ramiros had split up his crew so that one Jeep would flank each side of the truck, with him and Ramon behind in the middle.

"You're not thinking of going up that thing yourself, are you?" Ramon asked hesitantly.

"I was," Ramiros said with a wild, excited look on his face. "We could block him in up there. They would have to surrender then!"

"Forget about it, man," Ramon said, looking at him sternly. "We can barely see the truck."

Just as Ramon uttered those words, there was a lull in the dust and the two officers could see that their targets were about ready to exit the back of the truck.

"Open fire!" Ramiros cried into his radio handset. "But watch the crossfire. I can't afford to lose any of you." Another shot ricocheted off the Stallion, causing Laura to duck and cringe.

"Okay, you guys are out of here," Bob said, pulling the fuel nozzle out, spilling gas everywhere.

"Hey, hold on a sec, I almost forgot something," Bob added as he raced back to the front of the trailer with bullets fired by the

Feds narrowly missing him. Bob grabbed a gym bag full of stuff and placed it on Laura's lap. "Here, some stuff that might come in handy." Bob gave Laura a kiss. He reached over and shook Cal's hand. "Hey, man, next time we meet it'll be at Harry's Bar, and we'll be sitting pier side having a few oysters and a cold one watching the sunset."

Just then, another of the Feds' shots hit the back of the car.

"Get your asses outta here," Bob urged. He ran to the front of the car and, using all the strength he could muster, pushed the Stallion back to the edge of the ramp.

"Bye-bye!" Bob said, waving. He gave one final push that saw the car go rolling backwards down the ramp.

Just as the Stallion hit the ground, Cal spun it around, shooting past Ramiros and Ramon, who had managed to get themselves closer to the truck. Cal once again found himself driving the Stallion as fast as he could—not for fun, not to win a race, but to rescue himself and Laura from what would surely be a difficult and trying experience, even if they could eventually prove their innocence. He instinctively knew that surrendering under these circumstances to these officers was not an option he particularly favoured.

Ramiros quickly turned his Jeep away from the truck and circled around to continue the chase with Cal and Laura. "Okay, everyone, turn around and follow the car. Forget the truck for now!" Ramon said into the radio.

One of the officers in another Jeep fired off a last shot as his vehicle came to a stop. He hit one of the fuel cans on the back of the trailer. The explosion and the blaze were instant and stunning, the sound deafening.

Hearing the explosion, Laura looked back only to see a pillar of flames shooting from the back of the truck as it slowly came to a rolling halt.

"Oh my God! Stop the car. We have to go back!" Laura screamed.

"Are you crazy?" Cal exclaimed, now driving at the safest top speed he could reach. "We can't go back there. They're so pissed right now, they'll shoot us before they'll ask any questions."

"What about Bob? We can't leave him there to die."

"Our lives won't be worth a rusty bag of nails if we turn back. Bob will be fine," Cal said, taking Laura's hand. "He was raised on a farm up in Canada, corn- and breastfed. Bob will outlive the two of us." They exchanged small smiles as Cal bore down into his seat and pressed even harder on the gas pedal. More sand and dust spewed from behind the Stallion, making it hard for Ramiros and Ramon to see them.

Laura reached into her bag and pulled out a large bottle of fingernail-polish remover.

Cal looked over with a puzzled expression on his face. "When in perilous trouble, do your nails. Is this in some kind of female survival manual so you'll look good when you die?" Cal asked, incredulous.

"Never mind the wisecracks. If you want to get out of here alive, do what you do best and drive this damn thing and let me worry about the rest."

"Yes sir, no problem, sir," Cal responded with a salute.

Laura reached into the bag that Bob had given them and took out a full bottle of tequila.

"How did you know that would be in there?" Cal asked.

"Do bears shit in the woods?" Laura replied without looking at Cal. She was busy pouring some of the tequila onto her bandanna, then she refilled the difference with her nail-polish remover. She stuffed half of the bandanna into the bottle.

"Got a light?" Laura turned to Cal with a devilish grin on her face. Cal, never having seen this side of Laura, was confused and gave her a look of total scepticism. He reached into his shirt pocket and handed her his lighter without question.

"I've got an even better suggestion if you're up to what I think you are."

"And what's that?" Laura said, sounding suspicious.

"Pour out half the bottle and fill it with fuel."

"And how do you propose that?"

Cal undid the plastic mesh from his driver's-side window frame, then leaned out, pulled out the safety pin on his side of the hood, and suggested Laura do the same. Then Cal popped the hood latch.

"Okay. Now drain half the bottle, lean through the window and lift the hood of the engine. When you look inside, you will see a clamp holding the fuel hose to a filter and just beside that, you will see a small release valve. Undo the flip, open the little black valve but first hold the mouth of the bottle to the valve opening. You'll spill some but don't panic, the bottle will fill up pretty quick. If you open the valve too much we'll come to a grinding halt. Make sure most of the fuel is getting through to the engine. When the bottle is full, close the valve and re-clamp the hood as quickly as you can. Got it?

Laura was still looking at Cal with her big brown eyes in bewilderment a few moments later when a bullet ricocheted off the dashboard in front of her, snapping her back to reality.

"Um, sure, okay, I can do that."

A few moments later Laura brought herself back in and sat smiling at Cal, holding a bottle full of fuel and alcohol.

"Okay, slow down," she suggested.

"What?" Cal asked.

"Just trust me and slow down a bit. Let them get a little closer," Laura said as she lit the end of the bandanna.

The pursuing Jeeps gained quickly as Cal took his foot off the pedal. Laura stuck her head out the window and tossed the Molotov cocktail at the closest Jeep. The concoction hit the Jeep's front grill and exploded instantly.

"YES!" Laura screamed as she watched the Jeep go up in flames.

The burning truck swerved and rammed into one of the other Jeeps, knocking it headlong into a giant cactus and bringing both vehicles to an abrupt stop. All occupants abandoned the vehicles quickly and the one on fire blew up, leaving only Ramon and Ramiros in the chase.

Cal stared in amazement at Laura, who was grinning from ear to ear. She could not believe the total mayhem she had created. She was even more surprised that she could have even conceived of such an idea.

"Well, my dear, I am truly impressed," Cal said.

Laura stopped admiring her own handiwork and settled back into her seat.

Then Cal noticed Laura's face had changed to a look of complete fright. "Has this thing got wings?" Laura asked.

"She's fast but she can't fly. Why do you ask? They're never going to catch us on the ground now," Cal said, confidently.

"How about when we're lying dead at the bottom of that canyon up ahead," Laura replied sharply.

Cal turned his attention back to the front of the Stallion instead of admiring Laura's handiwork behind them and suddenly noticed the canyon. A small one as far as canyons went, maybe ten feet wide, but still a canyon.

"Oh shit! We could be screwed here. Pardon my Spanish," Cal excused himself, looking at Laura. "We'll never make it over that."

"Don't turn chickenshit on me now, Redman. If anybody can get this thing over that piddly little pothole it's you," Laura said, trying to sound brave.

"I might be able to get us over alive, but you'll be in a wheelchair in a Mexican prison for the rest of your life."

"Three years ago you would have jumped this just for the hell of it, from what I hear. If you make this jump, I mean with us still alive and the car still running, I'll give you a foot massage," Laura blurted out.

"That's great but I probably won't have any feet left to appreciate it," Cal said a little nervously as the Stallion approached the edge of the canyon.

"It's a promise, if we both make it in one piece," Laura said, tightening up her harness.

Cal looked for the shortest gap and spotted a small mound of dirt off to his left. He figured if he hit the mound at just the right angle and flicked the turbo switch at the same time, with a bit of luck, they might just make the jump.

One of Ramon's bullets careened off the side of the Stallion as it left the ground.

"Our only chance to ditch these guys is here!" Cal flicked the turbo switch and the flames shot out the back. The Stallion's front wheels hit the tiny mound of dirt and propelled them up with a rocket-like force.

Laura grasped Cal's arm with one hand while her other hand gripped the roll bar so tight it would have had to be pried off with a crowbar. She closed her eyes and started to recite the Lord's Prayer.

✳ ✳ ✳

"I can't believe they're actually trying to jump that! This just proves they must be as guilty as hell. No way else would they risk their lives like this as opposed to surrendering and proving their innocence," Ramon said to Ramiros as he turned the Jeep hard to avoid going over the edge himself. Ramon brought the Jeep to a sliding sideways stop several feet from the lip of the drop and the two watched in amazement as the Stallion leaped over the canyon.

"Not really," Ramiros replied without taking his eyes off the Stallion.

"It's kind of like one of those witch hunts they had in the medieval days."

"What do you mean?" Ramon said, scratching his head and realizing he had been holding his breath as he watched the Stallion miraculously fly through the air.

"You know, if the priests or government suspected someone of being a witch they would put them on trial by tying them to a big wooden chair and then submersing them in a pond for several minutes. If the person lived, they would be convicted of being a witch and burned alive at the stake. However, if they died they were presumed innocent and given a proper burial. I don't know what to believe."

Ramiros finished his story just as the Stallion pounded down safely on the other side of the canyon, a mere twenty feet away, but it may as well have been miles.

"Yahoo!" they heard Cal holler as he high-fived Laura, who only just now had both eyes wide open.

The officers watched, dejected at having come so close to catching them. Now could only sit and watch as the Stallion righted itself and picked up speed.

The last thing the officers saw of the pair that day was Laura leaning over and planting a kiss of appreciation on Cal's right cheek. The Stallion faded into a tiny speck in the glaring sun.

"Damn! So are you saying they should burn alive at the stake now when we catch them?" Ramon said, slamming his fist down on the hood of their Jeep, putting an apple-size dent in it.

"No, I'm saying they are in a no-win situation. I know they are guilty of something but I'm not sure what. The situation does not seem to be as clear as it should be, Ramon. There's something fishy going on, but our job is just to bring them in and let the higher-ups take care of the rest. Let's go see what happened back at the ranch, make sure the other officers are all right. Come on, my friend," Ramiros said, putting his arm around Ramon's shoulders as the pair stood staring off into the deep blue, beautiful mid-afternoon Baja sky. "They have a long way to go yet. Don't worry, we'll find them."

CHAPTER TWENTY-TWO

Cal was very tired and losing his ability to focus, having been buried for some time now underneath the Stallion, trying to fix an array of parts that had been loosened or damaged by their heroic jump over the canyon. Despite only having the limited tool kit that accompanied the Stallion at his disposal, Cal had found a way to fix what might have become some serious mechanical issues in the future.

He poked his head out periodically to try to explain to Laura what he was working on and tell Laura what he could use; miraculously Laura would find something in her bag or come up with some random item lying about that would work. Now the batteries in the flashlight were getting low and the light was getting dimmer, but Cal thought it best to save the batteries in case of an emergency. He was tired and starting to lose his focus. A small transistor radio played softly beside him, crackly static interspersed with distinct Latin rhythms. It was time to pack it in and enjoy what was left of this tranquil night. Cal thought it might be their last, at least for the next little while. Something was still bothering Cal about what had actually happened back at the police station and why he and

Laura were still recipients of all this attention. Especially after he had given the money back.

Laura had been standing for a long time near the open fire, which Cal insisted stay very small and well hidden behind a large protruding boulder; the fire was not much more than a couple of twigs burning, and would have been barely able to make toast. Still Laura insisted on some form of heat and light, she had nothing in her bag that was warm, and she had not camped out like this, staring up at the stars, since she could remember. This time of year in the Baja, the temperature can drop from the mid-20s to barely above zero within hours of the sun going down.

When Cal looked out from underneath the Stallion to pro- nounce it in good running order and to say that he was finally calling it quits for the night, he could not see Laura anywhere. He eased himself out and headed over to a large cluster of boulders divided by a lightly worn path partially lit by their poor excuse for a campfire. He quickly calculated that they were probably not on a main trail, but that this was a path if seldom used, and they should best get moving. Cal quietly and nervously called Laura's name, but heard nothing back. When he finally spotted her, he saw that she was standing on an overhang, a small ridge that allowed its oc- cupants to survey the vast empty beauty of the Baja and the billions of stars that lit it up at night. Laura was looking pensive. "Careful, you might get whatever it is you're wishing for," Cal said, trying to inject some humour into what he sensed to be a sad moment.

"I'd forgotten how beautiful it is out here at night. Just look out there. There must be a hundred billion stars and they are all so bright. It makes you feel so small, lost and insignificant."

"It's nights like tonight that are the reason I love coming down here," Cal said as he eased up beside her.

"A lot of people have the Baja all wrong. It's not just about the racing. You nailed it when you said 'look at those stars,' billions of them, thousands of light years away yet they look close enough that you feel if you walked a few hundred feet in any direction, you could reach up and touch one. You just do not see stars like this back home, or anywhere else that I have been."

"So, like Albuquerque?"

"Funny, but when you see a sky like tonight's it truly makes you wonder how guys like Stephen Hawking can even sleep at night, trying to make sense of it all and then put it into layman's terms so that the rest of us neophytes can make some sense of it as well."

"You're absolutely right though, that's the trouble with discovering new things. The more you learn the more you realize how little you know. It can be very discouraging—almost enough to make a person not want to discover or take on new challenges at all. Interesting train of thought, I hope that doesn't keep you awake at night." Cal shuffled his feet a bit; he realized they were both just trying to make conversation but silly stuff was coming out. The pair were standing close enough that their arms touched lightly. Neither one moved away. "Laura, I'm truly sorry. I guess I've never apologized for getting you into this mess, have I? I've realized in the past few days that I've been on my own for such a long time, I really haven't given much thought to how the things I do affect others. I've become completely self-absorbed."

"That's okay. I'm too lazy to carry around a grudge for long."

Cal gave Laura a bewildered grin that broke into a full-out smile of appreciation for how she was trying to make light of what had become an extremely serious situation.

"Seriously, this has turned into something way more catastrophic then even I could have imagined, and I've found myself in trouble down here before."

"So the rumours go," Laura said light-heartedly.

"Well, I've always managed to talk myself out of whatever mess I was in or it just blew over, but I can't believe this thing has gotten so out of control. I do not know what to say except I will do everything in my power to make sure you get out of here safe and unharmed, I can promise you that. And then find a way to make it up to you. I didn't really pull over. I weaved off the road. I shouldn't have been drinking and trying to put out a fire." Cal smiled appreciatively at Laura. "Well, actually, Laura, I was a damned selfish asshole. I should not have been so careless with someone else's life. I've gotten away with drinking and driving pretty much my complete adult life, I've never given it a second thought. I hadn't realized it was getting so out of control. I've been on a slow descent into hell, one that I didn't notice until now. So I'm really sorry I almost took you with me, and got us into this. We're going to get out of here and back home safely. I promise you."

"Shit happens. I learned that the hard way. Getting back is the least of my worries," Laura said sadly, realizing what a cathartic moment this was for Cal.

"I don't understand. I know it won't be easy but we'll make it."

"Remember when I said everything in the world I owned was in here?" Laura said, lifting up her bag. "Well, here is the first half." Laura took a large Ziploc baggie out, unlocked it, and spread its contents—ashes—out into the still night air. The breeze was so calm the ashes almost fell straight down.

"I risked my life for Shake'n Bake and now you're throwing it away?"

"Not exactly. Now how does that saying go? Ashes to ashes, earth-to-earth, dust to dust? Goodbye, Marty, darling, I love you. You will live on in my heart forever," Laura said softly as tears started rolling slowly down her wind-reddened cheeks.

"Not bad. Have you done this before?" Cal said lightly, trying to break the seriousness of the moment but then realizing Laura was truly sad.

"I was going to do this in private but it's good for me that you're here. This is what Marty wanted. I finally got my shit together enough to bring myself to do it. After Marty's death, I just fell apart and the doctors handed out opiates like jujubes. It didn't take long for me to get hooked. It was easier to get drunk and party with my friends than it was to buckle down and raise my little boy and make a living on my own. Imagine me, type-A Laura, falling apart."

"It could happen to anyone. No one is impervious to fate. Some people are just luckier than others, that's all it is. I have concluded it is very random, everything has to be random or nothing is, so it works for me if I think nothing happens for a reason. The main thing is that you recognized you had a problem and you are dealing with it—what more can anyone do? One thing racing has taught me is that you can't always control what happens to you, but you can control how you deal with it."

"My alcoholic mom left my alcoholic father and me for a richer alcoholic asshole when I was only three, and all she said to me the day she left was to take good care of him. I spent the next fifteen years of my life raising a human being who was kind and gentle but a dreamer." Laura paused again and wiped her eyes with a tissue. "Everything I have, I got by myself, no handouts and no fairy godmothers. That was my lot."

"You don't have to tell me this if you don't want to. Regardless of what happened to you, you've turned out pretty darn good as far as I can tell." Cal put his arm around Laura and gave her a sincere hug.

"That's okay. It actually gets a little better, that was the hard, traumatic part," Laura said, and gave her nose a swipe with a tissue. Then she continued. "I came home from school one day when I was about fifteen expecting to see dad passed out drunk, as usual, on our lumpy old couch that never seemed to bother him but instead I found him handcuffed to his bed.

"He said to me, 'You're going to hear a lot of cussing and screaming and I don't care how stinky it gets in here or what I say, don't undo these cuffs for one week, or longer if I ask. Promise me right here and now or leave this house and go stay with your grandma.' I was so shocked I had no idea what to say. So there we were, two incandescent lights learning how to shine in the tiny confines of our own inconsequential atmosphere and we actually made it through the first week, and so we agreed on a second, with bathroom privileges (only because I couldn't stand the stink or cleaning him up anymore) which he honoured. He'd made up his mind to quit drinking and he knew this was the only way," Laura finished with a deep breath.

"And how is he doing today?" Cal asked sympathetically.

"He died six years later. He had done excessive damage to his body by then, but we had a wonderful six years, I know some kids do not even get that. Then I go and do the same thing to my child. Here's the other half of why I needed to get my bag back." Laura pulled a picture from her bag. "M. J., little Marty Junior. If I want him back, I have to be clean and sober for at least a year and hold a steady job, thus the writing gig with *Off Road Magazine*, which I now happen to love anyway and, after going through all that shit with my dad, I realized that no one intentionally wastes their life. But way too many look back on a life wasted. And I was determined to not be one of those people." Laura held the tears back as she showed Cal her picture of M. J.

"Pretty handsome fella, with his race cap and jacket on. He takes after his old man. I'd say he's worth whatever struggle you're going through," Cal said, sounding as sincere as he had ever sounded.

"Marty's parents still think I'm an unfit mother and my getting busted down here will give them all the ammunition they need to keep that court order in force. I only have a few days before I have to report in and show my stuff. Everything was looking good until this happened."

Cal stepped in front of Laura, put his arms around her tight and pulled her head in to his chest as she sobbed uncontrollably for a few minutes. When she stopped, she tilted her head up only a few inches from Cal's face. They stared at each other intently for what seem to Laura an eternity, then they released each other and moved apart slowly.

"Look out at the stars," Cal gently suggested. She looked at him quizzically, then shifted her head and gazed at the shimmering ocean of light.

"Now picture yourself in the middle of that vastness: immortal, and in perfect health, never having to do anything to sustain yourself, your total existence provided for, but you are all alone." Cal spoke softly in a monotone voice. "No one to talk to, no one to share your life with, you're all alone. You float in a state of perfection forever and ever, but all alone. Would you wish for that?"

"No," Laura replied sadly. "That would be a horrible existence."

"Well, that's what you were feeling when you lost Marty. That, my darling, is what life is all about. Sharing our lives with others leaves us vulnerable too much pain, heartbreak, it can threaten our very existence and test everything we ever believed in, but if you eliminate all others from your life, it might seem perfect, but it would essentially have no meaning, no purpose. Having no obstacles to overcome simply means you are not moving. Having no arguments simply means you have no one to argue with, and as much as I love racing, even I have come to realize, in the greater scheme of things it is purposeless, inconsequential to the soul or the betterment of humankind as, with most human pursuits, like people who climb Mount Everest and die. What the heck was that for?"

Laura looked at Cal gratefully and stroked the side of his face. "You are definitely more philosophical than the philistine I imagined. You are quite a puzzle Mr. Redman."

"Well, that's the main reason I've not gone back to racing. I'm grappling with questions like this all the time now. I just didn't feel I could talk to Bob about it this way. He's such a meat-and-potatoes guy most of the time."

Cal moved away slowly. "I've got her fixed . . . the Stallion, so let's put a few more miles behind us tonight. We might even make it as far as Momma Espinata's," Cal said as he kicked sand over Marty's ashes so they would blend into the landscape better.

"I suspect you and Bob think very much the same way. That is why you have been friends for so long. I think if you opened up to him the way you have to me tonight you might be surprised. I know he feels the same about you. I am sure Bob wanted to open up a bit as well, but he feels you are a gristle-and-ribs kind of person too. If he is okay, God willing, the first chance you get the two of you should head for a quiet place, and just start talking without any pretence or macho crap. You might be surprised how much alike you are."

Cal heard every word Laura said, as he headed back toward the fire to put it out, and was thoughtfully mulling it over. Especially the God-willing part got Cal thinking about the gas can explosion back at Mike's. He wondered how Bob and Skinner were doing.

"Hey, are you missing a small bank packet, a little brown envelope?" Laura asked.

"No. Why, what's up?" Cal responded, still focused on putting out the fire.

"There's one here in my bag," Laura said, taking a small brown envelope out of her bag and passing it to Cal. They moved to the Stallion and Cal sat down in the driver's seat. Turning on one of the overhead lights, he began to examine the contents carefully.

"The packet is from a bank in Tijuana and it has a locker key in it. It looks like it fits a bus station or airport locker or something like that," Cal said, holding the key up.

"Actually it looks more like a safety deposit box key and that would explain why it's in a bank envelope. It is probably from a bank, presumably the bank that's on the envelope."

"But how did it find its way into my bag?" Laura asked, looking perplexed.

"The only explanation I can come up with is that it must have been in the safe at the jailhouse and ended up in your bag with the money. When I put the money back, it likely stayed in the bottom of the bag. I certainly never noticed it."

Cal's legs were still outside the car and Laura squatted down and rested her elbow on one of Cal's legs and her head in her hand. "This key must be something very important. Maybe that's why they want us so badly," Laura said wearily, thinking this whole thing was just becoming too much for her. "They must know we didn't take any more of the money than what we gave back?"

"I'll bet the key is definitely what they're after, but I think they think we have more of the money as well. I still think we were set up. Something else must have happened after we escaped," Cal said, slowly lifting his legs, careful not to let Laura's head drop. "But they desperately want this key."

"Why did you take away my pillow?" Laura asked, standing up.

"We'd better get going if we're going to put some serious mileage between us and them. I am sure they will start looking for us at the first sign of daybreak. We'll have to find shelter by then." Cal started the engine, invading the perfection of Mother Nature's silence with the twist of a key. As he pressed down on the pedal he sent millions of molecules of sand and a dozen little Stone Age-looking reptiles that had taken what they thought was secure refuge under the car, scurrying away in all directions.

✳ ✳ ✳

A hundred miles south and, just as tired, Ramiros and Ramon sat in the Jeep in front of Ramiro's house. "They'll probably drive all night tonight and rest all day tomorrow. We should do the same," Ramon suggested.

"No, I think we should start to get in sync with them," Ramiros put forth. "I think we'll get a good night's sleep, meet tomorrow around midday. I plan to drive all day as well as tomorrow night, so sleep as long as you like tonight, my friend. Somebody will spot them soon."

"I'll call before I come by," Ramon said as he pulled away, looking sluggish.

Ramiros stood statuesque for a moment as he watched Ramon drive away, then turned and faced his house: his sanctuary.

The Ramiros home was modest but beautifully gardened and well maintained. By the rest of the neighbourhood's standards, this house was a standout, yet everyone knew they were welcome, and often came by for tea and a chat or a BBQ. Alessandra always made sure the candles in the cast-iron holders that lined the walkway were tall and she lit them for Anthony's return every night. He would blow them out one by one on his short but heavenly walk to the front door. Anthony liked that his house always looked so nice when he came home. It made him strong. It was these small gestures and her attention to detail that he truly appreciated about Alessandra—and the fact that his wife was incredibly loving and beautiful. He knew he was the envy of all his male friends. His neighbours constantly teased him about his blowing out of the candles every night and asked how did he manage to get any sleep with such a beautiful wife and when was the first baby coming, but that was the way of his hood, and these things were always said with kindness, no malice or disrespect was intended.

Life is good, Ramiros thought, blowing out each candle as he walked by it, then stepping into his house. Well—life *was* good until these two Americans came along. He just wanted to catch them and get everything back to normal. He was quiet, knowing Alessandra would be asleep and he was careful not to wake her as he slid into bed and draped one arm lightly along her side, letting it come to rest on her hip as he did every night.

"Did you catch them, I hope?" Alessandra asked in a low, gravelly, sleepy voice.

"Not today, but we're getting close. It won't be long; they have to run out of luck sometime," Ramiros said, gently running his hand along Alessandra's silky-smooth skin until it came to rest firmly cupping one of her beautifully formed firm breasts. He felt her nipple rise between his fingers and he pulled himself tight to Alessandra's back, making his body a perfect fit with hers.

"What will happen to them if you catch them?" Alessandra asked, slowly coming back to life from her short sleep.

"That's up to the courts to decide. My job is to catch them. And why are you so curious about them all of a sudden, I thought you were sleepy?" Ramiros joked as he kissed the back of her neck while slowly sliding his hand down from her breast to the lower part of her stomach. He loved to feel her there, especially right where her hair met her thighs. He loved the curves, and the feel of her bones, hair, and flesh. Anthony gently ran his hands down the inside of her thighs. He knew the weight of his hands felt nice on her; he could feel her moving ever so slowly.

Alessandra moaned and pushed her ass hard into Ramiros. She reached behind her body to grip him firmly in her hand and smiled, enjoying feeling him grow.

"I'm tired of practising," Alessandra whispered as she turned her neck so they could kiss. "I want to get to work on the real thing."

"I want it to be perfect, when the time is right," Ramiros said softly. "And when will that be, honey?" Alessandra asked, moaning even louder now as she moved her body to let him in.

"When I make captain, and catching these two should help speed that up," Ramiros whispered back while pushing in hard.

"Then we better make sure you're in a good frame of mind, Detective Anthony Ramiros." Alessandra pulled herself away and rolled over gently on to her other side to face Anthony. He loved the way she kissed. He loved staring into the vast depths of her eyes while being inside her at the same time. He loved tracing her body with his finger, and how she felt and moved, he knew he loved her completely. He was sure they would love each other for the rest of their lives and he knew he was a very lucky man to feel that way. He also wanted a baby as much as Alessandra did but he wanted to make sure they could afford a good life for the child. He did not want every day to be a struggle the way his parents had started out. Then Anthony had to close his eyes, the passion was too great, it was like looking deep into her soul, he felt like he was going to drown as he pushed slowly but harder in. After a few more thrusts, he cupped her tiny firm buttocks with his right hand and pushed her up so he could go even deeper. Alessandra was breathing hard now, her mouth open, kissing him gently, both arms wrapped tightly around him as if she would fall if she let go. Anthony opened his eyes again just before his release and sensed the love that existed between them. Anthony collapsed slowly onto Alessandra as he gently slid his hand out from under her. He carefully rolled back to his side of the bed, taking his full weight off her. Alessandra lay quiet and still. Anthony kissed her on the lips, then gently snuggled his head beside her shoulder on the pillow. Alessandra clasped his hand in hers, and the two drifted off to sleep completely enjoying the moment, knowing it might be a while before they were together again.

CHAPTER TWENTY-THREE

Cal glanced over at Laura, whose head was bobbing lightly up and down, like a wine cork drifting lazily on a lake on a still summer's evening. The morning sun, just heeding the rooster's call, cast a hard light on the far side of Laura's face, illuminating her fine features with sharp, exacting angles that would have made most women look as severe as the Wicked Witch of the West. Even then, tired, dusty, exhausted and with her hair looking like she just arrived home from a night out, Cal marvelled at how beautiful she was. Even though Cal had exonerated himself a smidgen last night with his heartfelt apology and by letting Laura discover the softer and more profound side of his personality, particularly his quest for understanding some of the more esoteric, mystifying questions of the universe and the part that we as humans play in it—even so, Cal was still Cal.

Laura's head rolled gently to the left and she caught Cal staring at her as her eyes slowly opened.

As beautiful as Cal found Laura's face, he discovered the long dark shadow that had formed in Laura's cleavage to be even more enchanting. The image was striking, the inside of Laura's right breast completely in the dark, framed by her white blouse, with only a few strands of her thick hair lying limp across the open area beautifully contrasted by the left side, which was favoured by the soft morning sunlight. This showed every dimple and blemish, with the shape and light changing every time Laura took a breath, in and out, up and down. Cal found it hard to shift his gaze as he pondered the artistic merits of this pose. He wished he could capture the image in a photograph or painting. Then Cal realized Laura had busted him—but turning away sharply at this point would draw even more attention to his lecherous behaviour so he just kept staring at her.

The two gazed at each other in silence for what seemed like an eternity and at that moment Cal could think of nothing else but stopping the Stallion and taking Laura in his arms. Laura sensed that Cal's stare was more passionate then intrusive, and not wanting to make him feel awkward, she effortlessly broke into a broad smile and a long stretch. Although she did not know exactly where Cal had been staring, she could feel the wind going down her blouse. She lightly tugged the sweatshirt that had come loose around her shoulders and gave a little shiver as she tied the sleeves together tighter around her neck and pulled the garment down lower, to give the appearance that she was just chilly. The top, she could tell without looking down, covered up any areas that Cal may have found captivating, and she was pretty sure she'd managed this without making Cal feel like he had, in fact, just been busted.

❋ ❋ ❋

"Next to the stars at night, the thing I like best about Mexico is the light," Laura said. "It seems to be like no other place on earth. The way it just catches the edges of things and lights them up softly, it's almost surreal. You want to stop and stare at it, or if I could, paint it."

"I was just thinking the same thing," Cal said, clearing his throat and smiling back at Laura.

"Speaking of sun, I was hoping we would be at Momma Espinata's by now but we still have a few minutes to go before we clear that ridge over there and then we'll be just a minute or two from the orphanage. As beautiful a morning as it is to go for a drive in the desert, this baby creates a plume of dust you can see for miles. I hope those guys took the night off and are a long way behind us or they'll be on top of us like a bear on a berry bush when we stop."

"God, I haven't seen Momma for years. I met her a few times when I was down this way with Marty. How is her orphanage doing? She is such an amazing woman. I always thought I would like to write a book or try my hand at writing a screenplay about her someday. Her life is incredible and she has accomplished so much. She has dedicated her life to those children. She is the Mother Teresa of Mexico," Laura said.

"She's doing fine, I think. The orphanage was full to capacity and low on funds, as usual, the last time I talked to her, but I guess we will find out soon enough. Next stop—Rosarita." Moments later Cal was manoeuvring the Stallion through some tricky terrain up the ridge and onto the main street of a village. Cal only had to stay on the main road for less than a quarter mile but still he was in plain view and he knew that was not a good idea in the daylight. Cal was extremely relieved when he pulled out of sight, in behind Momma Espinata's house, and into the big barn without incident.

As Cal concentrated on hiding the Stallion as best he could, Laura contemplated how one person's fate could have such an immense impact on someone's life and how that *one* life could have such a positive impact on the lives of hundreds or even thousands of others.

If not for the love and fortitude of Momma's grandparents, she would not exist today, nor would her famous orphanage. Laura remembered the stories she had heard, and imagined Momma's grandfather as a young prince, heir to the throne of Spain, stepping off the boat onto the shores of the mysterious land that was conquered Mexico. The story went that, thinking this would be one of his last great journeys as an impetuous youth with his schoolmates; Prince Edgar Espinata embarked on the freshman adventure of his life, but not with the outcome anyone expected.

Within days of his arrival, he fell madly in love with Élan Inez and the two became inseparable. Edgar soon disobeyed his family's wishes and destroyed his father's greatest dream (that his son would one day be king) by abdicating the throne to stay in Mexico and marry Élan.

"How dare he marry a mere Mexican peasant?" Those cutting words, the last words a saddened Edgar would ever hear from his angry father, rang in Edgar's head until the day he died. Undaunted and in complete bliss, Edgar and Élan settled in Rosarita, a small patch of land on a ridge overlooking the beautiful Baja Valley.

Living a sparse life in a two-room adobe house, they set up shop. They rode a single donkey, their only means of transportation at the time. They started the region's first chili pepper farm and raised three children who in turn had many children of their own, one of the grandchildren included Maria Espinata, who would become a saint within her lifetime. All the grandchildren kept their grandparents' name in their last names.

Laura thought of how a small town must have soon sprung up around the efforts of that one family in the middle of nowhere. The chili peppers, a gas station, the small museum, the restaurant and then the orphanage; Rosarita, seemingly destitute and barren. Yet a strangely enigmatic and magical place. Rosarita is nothing more than the result of hard work, love and devotion, like a single organism, completely in harmony with its surroundings, and self-sufficient, with no other town in a hundred miles.

Cal looked over at Laura. He could tell she was deep in thought. "Whatcha thinking?"

"Promise not to laugh?" Laura said thoughtfully.

"Scout's honour," Cal said, taking a deep breath, relaxing after being on the road for so long.

"Yeah, I bet you weren't even a Scout."

"Actually, I was, so in this case it means something." Cal turned to Laura and smiled.

"I was thinking about what would have happened to this space in the middle of nowhere if Momma's grandfather hadn't abdicated the throne and married her grandmother. We'd probably just be driving through more open desert right now instead of being able to stop in this beautiful oasis, all because of the efforts of two people in love."

Cal stared at Laura.

Feeling a little dejected, Laura pouted. "You 'Scout's honoured' me that you wouldn't laugh."

"I'm not going to laugh," Cal said. "It's just that I've been driving at almost breakneck speed for the past few hours, we finally get here, I park the sucker and you hit me with this completely nonsensical commentary, when all I desire is one of Momma's tacos, an ice-cold beer and twelve hours of sleep!"

"No fear of you ever becoming a hopeless romantic, is there?" Laura said as they left the car and walked over to the main house.

Momma lived with one of her daughters and her brother in the old adobe bungalow. The main house, lovingly landscaped with Momma's rose gardens, was one of the prettiest houses in town. The town had several buildings, including its only restaurant, which had surprisingly good food because it was mostly run by Momma's daughters: the one she lived with and the other one, who was married but still helped out at the restaurant and orphanage. They also ran the town's only gas station, which did about 50 percent of its annual business during the week of the Baja 1000. Besides the orphanage and the museum there was the chili-pepper-farming operation, which employed the orphans who were old enough to work and half of the town's available bodies during harvest, also offering temporary work for migrant harvesters from nearby towns.

Momma's house was by no means fancy but it was well kept and comfortable, with its oversized couches and chairs placed strategically for the best views through the floor-to-ceiling French doors that opened wide onto her terrace and beautiful garden. The living room is kept cool with tiled floors and post-and-beam construction. There were plenty of doors and windows to allow for airflow. The two large ceiling fans that Momma kept constantly running. You could almost picture the house featured in *Architectural Digest*. Momma kept the house pretty much as her grandfather had built it and which her parents had added to over the years. Being of Spanish aristocracy, if he did not have a lot of money when he abdicated his princedom, he certainly kept his good taste and sense of design.

After shooing the curious children away, Momma welcomed Cal and Laura into her house and led them to the main room, the one she was most proud of, because, from it you could see her gardens, and it was the coolest room in the house. Without even thinking about it and even though there was an abundance of other options, Cal and Laura sat close together on the couch, which did not escape Momma's notice.

"It's starting to feel like a small town of its own around right here in this house," Cal said, commenting on the dramatic increase in the number of children at the orphanage. "I don't recall you ever having this many kids!"

"It was only a matter of time," Momma responded, with a sad look in her eyes, "before the death and destruction from the drug trade would outweigh the positive effects it had on the local economy. The Narcos are becoming very strong in Mexico and it seems there is nothing anyone can do to stop them. I've had to turn away children for the first time since we opened. Almost all the kids here are casualties of drug-related incidents; we're stretched to the limit every month; we struggle to pay the bills now. It's like never before. The Baja 1000 could not have come at a more appropriate time this year. We sold out of gas on a few occasions this year, but luckily for us there was a much better delivery system in place and the gas was replenished very quickly. The restaurant was busy every day, the girls run off their feet for a week. We rented out overnight parking spaces to many of those big RVs for the first time this year and that helped. Those people were a little demanding at times, but ultimately they spent a lot of money. Just filling their gas tanks was wonderful for us. And they ate a lot at the restaurant."

"Here, let me give you a small donation. I came through here on my way south in such a hurry one night, we never had time to stop and say hello," Cal said, pulling out some of the cash Bob had given him.

"No, I won't hear of it," Momma said. "Bob called here to see if you had come by. He told us what happened but was worried our phones were tapped so he could not say much. I only told him I had not seen you or heard from you. You're going to need every penny you have until you're safely north of the border." Momma paused and took a sip of her tea. "Once you're there, mail us down all the money you want," she said with a grin. "It wasn't that long ago that between the crops, the restaurant and the gas bar, museum and chili peppers we made more than enough to take care of things. Now there are so many kids, and we can't grow enough to feed them, and buying food is getting so expensive."

There was an awkward moment of silence as they absorbed the sadness of Momma's plight and wondered what they could possibly do in the future to help.

"Sorry to hear things have become so bad down here, Momma, but," Cal said, clearing his throat and almost feeling guilty about asking his next question, "how did Bob sound?"

"As I said, he did not say much, but he sounded okay. He was very concerned about you."

"I hate to ask you this, I realize I may be getting you into some trouble, but do you know of anyone who might be able to help us get across the border?"

"No need to feel ashamed for asking, my friend," Momma said, leaning over in her rocker to touch Cal's hand. "You are in a tough spot and no one deserves our help down here in God's suburbs more than you.

"I have a friend who is an ex-racer, he didn't do too well so you probably never met him, but he now lives with his adorable and—I believe— trustworthy wife. She's a very well respected professor at the university there and he's a good mechanic. I'll call him tomorrow. I'm sure he'll help you if he can," Momma said. "You get your sleep now. We can talk more, is later this evening ok? Or if you do not budge, I will let you sleep right through the night. Are you hungry; would you like something before your nap?"

"Actually, I wouldn't mind saying hi to Emilio before I conk out. Is he around?" Cal asked. "I'm sure he's wondering why I didn't stop in this year."

"Yes, I believe he is. I saw him the other day. He's gone through a growth spurt this year and has become such a tall, handsome boy."

"I'm going to go and visit Emilio," Cal said to Laura. "Would you like to come?"

"Is that the boy you hit?" Laura asked.

"Yeah, I sort of take care of him," Cal said. "And I like to visit him whenever I can."

"Sort of take care of him!" Momma scoffed. "He's being too modest! Cal made sure his race insurance paid for all his medical bills and he is personally paying for him to go to a very good private school."

"Really!" Laura smiled at Cal.

"Well," added Momma, "you'd better take the back way and stay well hidden. Being seen by too many townspeople would not be wise. The race is over now. You will stand out walking down the street."

✳ ✳ ✳

On the other side of town just off the highway Cal and Laura approached the door of another typical Rosarita house: small, traditional adobe. The first thing Laura noticed was the house had small but well attended gardens, which seemed to be a theme throughout the town. The house was kept in good repair. She thought of how industrious these people must be to work hard all day, probably six or seven days a week to make ends meet and still have time to look after their house and garden. "Hello! Anybody home?" Cal hollered in through the screen as he knocked.

Emilio's father came to the door.

"Ah, Senior Redman, Emilio was hoping to see you but we didn't think we would this trip, not after what Momma told us about your spot of trouble. Emilio is home from school for a few days and will be very happy to see you. Emilio! Señor Cal has come for a visit." Emilio came running to the door and threw his arms around Cal.

"Hey man, I missed you! I'd never come down here and not stop in to see you," Cal said, giving Emilio a big hug.

Elaine, Emilio's mom, appeared. "Would you like something cold to drink?" she asked. Elaine paused for a second, looking at Laura. "And who do we have here?" she asked.

"This is Señorita Laura. She has been my travelling amigo for the past few days. Sorry! Laura, this is Jorge and Elaine and, as you've probably guessed by now, this is my pride and joy, Emilio."

"Nice to meet you all," Laura said, sticking out her hand to shake Emilio's but Emilio lent over and gave Laura a small hug instead. Everyone smiled at Emilio's warmth.

"Come, sit down. Tell us all about this big adventure we've been hearing about, and tell us if there is anything we can do to help," Elaine said, leading everyone into the living room. Emilio took Laura by the hand and led her in.

"Well, first I want to hear how well this young man is doing in high school. I hope you're still getting top marks, Emilio," Cal said.

※ ※ ※

Meanwhile, some time ago, back at the ranch . . . Bob looked up from where he lay and could only see blue sky with the odd puffy white cloud floating by as the smoke and flames dissipated from the exploding gas can. He thought he was dreaming.

But as the humming in his ears slowly subsided and he started hearing normally again, he quickly realized where he was and regained his coherency enough to remember what was happening.

Everything was in slow motion and it seemed like an eternity to Bob, but Mike had come to his side within minutes of hearing the explosion.

As Mike placed his arms around Bob and helped him sit up straight, Bob shook his head from side to side rapidly to help clear his brain of all the extraneous noise.

"Are you okay? Can you hear me?" Mike asked.

"I think I'm fine," Bob replied, moving his mouth around in odd shapes just to make sure it was working okay.

One by one Bob tested all his limbs to make sure they still worked too.

"I think I'm good," Bob said, putting his arm around Mike's shoulder.

"Let's try standing me upright, shall we?" Bob said with a hint of optimism.

As Mike struggled to help Bob to his feet a sudden look of worry appeared on Bob's face.

"Are you okay?" Mike uttered hesitantly.

"I think I'm fine, a little dirtier and worse for wear than I was an hour ago, but where is Skinner? Is he okay?"

"I believe Skinner to be his old self. He was walking back to the house dusting himself off, saying something about getting a cold beer and sinking into the hot tub. He was also uttering a lot of profanities and superlatives somewhat connected to your name and asked me to check on you."

"Yep, that sounds like him. I guess I best leave him alone to simmer in the hot tub a bit."

"Very wise idea," Mike said as the two of them stood slowly upright.

As Bob and Mike surveyed the ranch it looked liked a war-torn village in a small third-world country. An image you might see on the evening news. The explosion had blown the scaffolding off the truck trailer, and it was lying in pieces everywhere, along with the giant speakers and various other particles of debris. There was still plenty of black smoke and flame coming from the gas can, and it wafted slowly around the ranch. In the distance black smoke was still emanating from the burning police Jeep. However, there was no sign of the police anywhere.

"I don't know for sure, but from what I could see through the binoculars I think Bonnie and Clyde made yet another getaway," Mike said as he helped Bob hobble slowly back to the house.

"Well, I guess I'm just too small a fish for them to fry, or that Anthony guy is starting to like me." Bob grinned.

"I think it's more like he hopes you learned a lesson here today and will keep out of this. They didn't even come over to see if you guys were okay?"

"I don't know, Mike, there seems to be an awful lot of attention being paid to these two for what I understand has happened. And since Cal even gave back that money, you'd think they would drop the hunt. But maybe this guy just holds a grudge, ya know, for knocking him out and stuff, but it sounds to me like the captain fudged most of it up to get some extra cash, so they could just call it a draw and move on."

"I think there is more going on here than meets the eye. But whatever it is, I sure hope Cal and Laura can make it back to the US while someone else gets to the bottom of this."

"In the meantime," Bob added, "I'll call Momma and give her the heads-up they might be headed her way. That would be the only safe haven for them between here and the border . . . as far as I know."

"I think a very cold beer and a seat on the back deck is in order," Mike said as the pair entered the house.

"That and we need to keep an eye on Skinner, make sure he hasn't opened your gun case and is not tactically planning a way to shoot me and make it look like an accident."

"He'll be fine after a good soaking in the tub, just tell him he'll finally have some exciting stories to tell his wife and kids when he gets home."

"Yeah, who would have thought of the bookish Skinner signing up to help two fugitives escape from Mexico. That alone will put this Baja in the history books."

Bob smirked. "Let's grab those beers and make sure he hasn't drowned."

CHAPTER TWENTY-FOUR

The early-morning sun illuminated the beautiful stained glass windows of the humble but spotless and charming classic adobe interior of St. Boniface Church. Alessandra started her bimonthly confession to the padre. "Forgive me, Padre, for I have sinned. I know someone who has stolen money and I'm not quite sure what to do about it."

"This person is close to you? Someone you love?"

"Yes, and it was a very large sum of money. This person would surely go to jail, but I know the money this person took was in itself obtained through less than honourable means although the person that took the money would put it to good use," Alessandra continued.

"The amount of money and how they would use it is irrelevant, my child. You know this. To steal is not wrong simply because you take something that belongs to another. It is wrong because it takes something from you. It takes your truth! The heart of the person who steals will no longer be true and no matter what that person does with the money it shall forever be covered in a sinful tarnish that no amount of polishing will remove. I have known you since you were a little girl. I know your heart is pure and if you listen to it, it will tell you what to do. Peace be with you, my child," the padre said, closing the sliding door.

* * *

Anthony was also up earlier than he had anticipated and decided he would make breakfast for himself and Alessandra before heading out to pick up Ramon and pursue their prey. When Alessandra walked in, he was in a good mood. Wearing nothing but his boxers and a T-shirt, he was preparing scrambled eggs and dancing to the music on the radio.

"Here, let me do that," Alessandra said as she took the bowl and mixer from him. Ramiros passed her the bowl and then, placing his hands gently on Alessandra's hips, started dancing with her.

"And where did you get to so early this morning?" Ramiros asked, half singing. "I thought maybe the market, but I don't see you carrying anything."

"I was at church," Alessandra said a little tentatively.

"Church today? Why today and why so early?" Ramiros asked, looking puzzled.

"I went to see the padre. Here, come sit down. I've got something I have to tell you." Alessandra sounded more serious than Anthony had ever heard her.

"Are you pregnant?" Ramiros asked. "It's okay if you are . . . I'm just—"

"No, no, not that. I wish it were that simple," Alessandra said, putting the now well-beaten eggs into the frying pan and trying to avoid looking directly at Anthony.

"What could be more complicated than you being pregnant right now?" Anthony asked, looking a little more serious.

"Well, you know how you think you don't want us to have a baby until you've made captain or, as you keep saying, 'win the lottery'?" Alessandra busied herself setting the table, still avoiding eye contact. "What will happen to that couple that you're chasing if you catch them?"

"*When* I catch them, they will probably be brought in, then the rest is up to the judge. If the colonel catches them, I doubt they'll make it in alive."

"Do you know how much was in the safe?" Alessandra asked innocently, now putting the food on the table.

"No. It was the captain and the colonel's special-project money but the papers said one hundred thousand US. What is this all about, why are you so interested in these people and this money? What does it have to do with you going to church this morning?" Anthony asked, digging wholeheartedly into his eggs. Alessandra poured him some coffee and pulled up one of the sturdy wooden kitchen chairs that Anthony had built, and sat beside him.

"Well, I sped up the lottery part of us having a baby." Alessandra took a big gulp of air and a sip of Anthony's coffee.

"You don't drink coffee," he said, looking confused.

"I took the money from the safe," Alessandra said, looking Anthony in the eyes without flinching.

"What do you mean, you took the money from the safe?" Anthony asked, choking on his eggs.

"I know, I know. I honestly don't know what came over me," Alessandra said, looking sad and taking Anthony's hand. "Don't say anything just yet. Let me explain what happened . . . I brought your dinner as usual, found you both unconscious and tied up and washed the blood off you just as I explained earlier. The part I left out was that before I did all that, I went into the captain's office to call for help and also to try to find the keys to the cell and that's when I noticed that the safe was open, and I looked inside, I can't even explain why, I just was curious. I saw all that money and suddenly without any thought I just started shoving it into my bag, put it in the car, and then I had to go to the nearest restaurant to call Ramon because the lines were cut. So I quickly came home and hid the money as well. I had absolutely no idea how much money was in there or why I did that."

"Why didn't you tell me sooner? We almost killed them for nothing!" Tony exclaimed, looking Alessandra sternly in the eyes. Tony noticed a single tear starting down Alessandra's left cheek and then one on the other. He wiped them away with a gentle single stroke of his hand, and softened his gaze upon her.

"I thought that they would just get away and that would be the last we would hear of it and then, later, I would make up some story as to how I got the money. I had not really thought that far ahead. All I could see was you and me and a little Tony, in a beautiful new house, living near the ocean." Alessandra put her head down on Anthony's lap and started to cry heavily.

Anthony rubbed her back gently, and then pulled her to him, squeezing her hard. "I love our little house. I don't need to live near the ocean. Oh, my dear Alessandra, what have you done? I have to think of what to do now. We have to do something quick before any harm comes to them. I am not sure what to say or do right now. You have put my career and our life in jeopardy. I can't believe the woman I have been married to all these years, the woman I love, could do such a thing. I feel like I don't even know you. But I have to try and get word out to save this couple from any more harm."

"Please forgive me, Anthony, I know it was a terrible sin!" Alessandra cried.

"I understand . . . but it's the Redman guy and that woman you need to ask for forgiveness. I was going to eat and pick up Ramon—I have to go get him right away. The colonel was going to come by the station today, and we were going to head north. I suspect the fugitives are resting by day and driving at night so now we will just keep driving and searching for them. Hopefully we can find them before any harm comes to them. This is going to be hard to explain to everyone but at least all the money will be back and, so far, no harm has come to those two.

"I am pretty sure he will be really pissed but as long as he gets all the money back and what they already gave back is returned as well, the colonel will hopefully stay calm and just call off the search. I am not sure where the money is from or why it was in our safe, but I hope he is so happy to have his money back he will let this thing go. Where have you put the money?"

"Under the loose floorboard under the bed," Alessandra admitted, sniffling a bit. "I love you too much and now it's caused so much pain. I hope this will not hurt your chances of being a captain. But I just couldn't live with this any longer, especially if anything had happened to those two," Alessandra said with a painful moan as she lifted her head to look up at the one person she had come to know as the perfect man. "How did I get to be so lucky to find you? I hope you can forgive me?"

Tony bent over and kissed her gently on the lips. "We have known each other since we were little kids, my dream has always been to be with you, for as long as I can remember. I could never imagine you doing anything like this. Still. I know you took the money only thinking of it being good for us, but this would always have been tainted money and no good would have come from it. I know how much you love me to have done this, but I love you even more for telling me about it now. I'm the lucky one. I just have to get over the shock. I will be okay, and I think everyone will be okay. I may have to wait a long time now to make captain but hopefully if we explain the situation and give all the money back, things will be okay in time."

CHAPTER TWENTY-FIVE

The colonel and the captain listened intently as Sergeant Ramiros told his story. Anthony stood tall, strong, and tried his best to make light of the situation, emphasizing that no real harm had been done, and they could simply call off the search, the whole event would go away and somehow they would just have to get word to the fugitives that they were free to leave the country.

A little hush money and an apology to the fugitives would probably smooth things over. "Although I still owe him something for hitting me over the head," Ramiros added, trying to keep the atmosphere light, but he could see the colonel was furious.

"You're sure no one else knows?" asked the colonel.

"I'm sure she wouldn't have told a soul. She is not proud of what she has done," was his reply, defending his wife devoutly.

"And what did she say about the key?" the colonel asked. "Nothing about the key in a small brown envelope? She said nothing at all about a small key?"

"I swear, she just told me about the money. What does a key have to do with this?" Tony asked with genuine concern.

"Nothing, nothing at all," the colonel said, sounding more

relaxed as he walked slowly around behind Anthony. "Let's have a drink to celebrate," the colonel suggested—and then in one swift motion he took his pistol out of its holster and hit Anthony across the back of the head. Anthony dropped to the floor, out cold. "Lock him up for now and we'll deal with him later," the colonel ordered the captain, as he headed out the door. "We will have to make it look like he was in on the robbery, fake an accident later. But right now I have more pressing matters."

✳ ✳ ✳

The colonel was extremely kind, polite and understanding, Alessandra thought, after she had just put them all through so much trouble.

"Are you sure you don't want anything to drink?" Alessandra said, still sounding worried.

"No thanks, Mrs. Ramiros, Anthony already explained what happened. I just need to know if there was anyone—anyone else at all—that you talked to about the money." The colonel stared deep into her eyes as if he wanted to see into her very soul. Alessandra felt a cold chill crawl slowly up her spine and she had to look away from him. Her demeanour changed so that even the colonel noticed.

"It's a simple question, Mrs. Ramiros," the colonel said, trying to sound a little less intense.

"I already told you, no one else knows. It is not something I would go around telling anyone. Every single dollar is still in the bag! Come see for yourself," Alessandra said with a little hesitation, sensing something had changed, but she headed off to the bedroom to get the money, hoping the colonel would just take it and leave now.

"I hope this won't affect Anthony's job. I swear he had nothing to do with it. I only just told him this morning and he insisted on going to tell you right away." Alessandra's voice came out muffled from underneath the bed. What Alessandra did not know was that the colonel had reached into the open closet door and pulled out one of Ramiros's baseball bats. From her vantage point, all she could see was the colonel's highly polished steel-toed black leather shoes.

"Oh, don't worry about Anthony, he's very secure right now," he said with a touch of glee in his voice. Alessandra pushed herself out from under the bed and rolled over on her side to get up. But before she had rolled over all the way the colonel, using the fat round end of the bat, pushed Alessandra's left shoulder down to the floor, then stood straddled over her and pinned her to the floor even harder. He roughly placed his left foot on her other shoulder, causing her to gasp in pain.

"Don't scream or even make any sound at all or I will hurt you even more." The colonel's tone was no longer friendly.

Alessandra was stunned. She stared in disbelief and horror as the colonel looked down at her. He grabbed the bag from Alessandra's hands. "Don't move," he said as he riffled through the money without counting it.

"It's all there, I told you."

"What about the key, the little tiny packet with the key in it. *Where is it?*" The colonel's reluctance to believe Alessandra was unceasing. Never before in her life had Alessandra experienced such aggression. The colonel shifted and set one foot down hard on each of her wrists, forcing them tight against the hard wood floor.

"I am running out of patience, dear, so tell me, what happened to the key?" the colonel asked in a soft voice. He took off his belt and lightly dragged the buckle across Alessandra's face.

Terrified and crying, Alessandra pleaded with the colonel to believe that she knew nothing of the key.

CHAPTER TWENTY-SIX

True to her word, Momma did not wake Cal and Laura. Neither of them stirred in their beds. After they'd returned from visiting Emilio they'd had a small dinner before tucking in for the night. Momma thought it best to let them sleep as long as they needed. She would prepare them a bag of food and send them on their way whenever they woke.

The dust settled around Officer Miguel's cruiser as it came to a complete stop at Momma Espinata's Restaurant. He brought the two-way radio speaker to his mouth: "Officer Miguel here, calling in my usual break, over."

"All's quiet on the Baja front, Miguel, enjoy your break," came the reply from Roberta, the dispatcher. Miguel walked into Momma's Restaurant as he had done a thousand times before, sat down in the same bench seat he always sat in and felt very much at home; as he should. He was married to Lucy, the youngest of Momma's daughters.

"Hey, what's good today, sis?" Officer Miguel asked his sister in-law Maria, whose turn it was to be working the early-morning shift.

As affordable as Momma's was, unless you were from elsewhere, passing through, you likely did not go to Momma's for
breakfast. Not many of the locals could afford to eat in restaurants
at all. Other than during the Baja 1000, brunch was not a happening time in Rosarita's only cantina.

With its tacos menu named after all the historically famous
racers—the Marty Supreme, the Redman Spicy Deluxe, the Iron
Man four-for-the-price-of-three special—Momma's restaurant
was a regular tourist stop during the Baja. The place was always
spotless and the food was fresh and delicious. Any of the orphans
who were old enough and still in Momma's care, usually worked
a short stint at the restaurant. Many of the regulars who made the
winter trek down to the Bay of LA or farther down to La Paz or
Cabos San Lucas liked to make a point of stopping there.

"You ask the same thing every day, Miguel, and every day I give
you the same answer. I swear to God my sister married the most
boring person in the world. If it was not for Lucy taking pity on
you, I think you would have been just as happy married to a cactus. Take her away from here. Give her a life. Why don't you take
her on a real vacation someday? You keep promising her, but you
never go! Everything is good here, as you know. Would you like
the same boring egg sandwich with ketchup and a coffee or are you
going to surprise me today?" Maria asked. Already knowing the
answer, she opened the egg carton, plopped two eggs on the grill,
put the toast in the toaster and had the coffee poured all before
Miguel had uttered a single word.

"I guess I'll have the usual," Miguel said. "I'd hate to throw
you off your day."

✳ ✳ ✳

Meanwhile, at Momma's house, Cal and Laura were getting ready to leave. "Wow, best sleep I have had in days. You're always so generous, Momma, I'm sure they'll canonize you one day," Cal said, giving Momma a big hug.

"Not too soon, I hope. I believe you have to be dead before they do that!" She gave Cal and Laura each a big kiss. "I took the liberty of gassing up your car last night. I thought it best under the cover of darkness. I let one of the older boys drive it over to the pumps. He was in heaven. He wants to be a racer now!"

"How can we repay you for your kindness and all the good you do for these children?" Laura asked.

"Come for a longer visit in happier times. It has not been the same since they put in the paved highway. I have a new saying now: 'Rough roads bring good people, and new roads bring all kinds.'" There was sadness in Momma's eyes. "Here's the address and a map to my friend Andreas's place. He knows you are coming and he knows not to talk to anyone about it. He does not know the details, but he can be trusted. Please, let me know when you've made it home safe," Momma, implored as she watched the two of them walk to the barn. "God is with you," she called out as they rounded the house and disappeared from her sight.

Officer Miguel was relieving himself, looking out the tiny window of the washroom when he saw Cal and Laura open the barn doors. He glanced at them casually for a moment, thinking they were just regular tourists who'd spent a night at Momma's, but when they swung the barn doors wide open, exposing the Stallion, Miguel knew instantly that he had the fugitives right in front of him.

"Hey, wait right there!" Miguel hollered through the open window, forgetting he was still emptying himself into the urinal.

Cal looked over his shoulder and saw Miguel's head sticking out the bathroom window.

"Damn, it's showtime again already. Let's get the hell out of here!" Cal said to Laura as they pushed the rickety doors through the dirt to open them wide enough to let the Stallion pass.

"I'm a police officer and I order you to stop right there," Miguel called to them again as he fumbled with his zipper. A second later, Miguel was running as fast as he could, drawing the handgun from its holster. He had to run through the restaurant and around to the back. Miguel knelt down on one knee, half hidden behind one of the porch posts. "Hold it right there or I'll fire!" Miguel uttered the order with his hand shaking wildly. He had never drawn his firearm in action before.

Cal had his right leg raised ready to hop into the Stallion through the open driver's-side window when he heard the shot and felt the excruciating pain of the burning bullet up near his thigh. He fell hard, twisting in agony in the dirt as Laura rushed around to see what had happened.

No sooner had Miguel fired the shot than he felt the excruciating pain of a solid quarter-inch cast-iron frying pan making contact with the right side of his head and that was the last thing he remembered before regaining consciousness a few hours later.

✳ ✳ ✳

"You're going to have to drive, I've been hit," Cal managed to relay to Laura as he crawled around to the passenger side.

"I write about these cars. I don't drive them."

"Get your beautiful sweet ass in that driver's seat, and just drive like you've never driven before, baby. I will help you, just feel her, the Stallion will let you know what to do," Cal said, pointing to the driver's seat. "And get us the hell out of here as quick as you can, or you won't be writing about anything for quite a while." Cal had not yet realized that the person who fired the shot was immobilized. He also was not sure whether there were other offi-cers nearby. Cal pulled himself up into the passenger seat, moaning in pain. Laura hopped behind the wheel, but then noticed Maria had rushed over to help get Cal into his seat.

"I've bought you guys some time but you better get out of here quick," Maria said, smiling at the worried-looking pair.

"You are going to be in so much trouble, Maria," Laura said, strapping herself in behind the wheel, studying the complicated instrument panel.

"Don't let it scare you, you won't have to know what 90 per-cent of those readings mean," Cal said, grimacing. "Just turn the key, put it in gear and drive it like a normal stick for now. I'll ex-plain everything else you need to know as we go.

"Thanks for saving our butts," Laura said to Maria as she started up the Stallion. "You'd better get out of here before I run you over."

"I'll be fine. Please don't worry about me. He's married to my sister. And she definitely wears the overalls in that house. What is he going to say? May God be with you," Maria said, making the sign of the cross.

"And with you," responded Laura with trepidation as she inched the Stallion forward. She had heard it umpteen times be-fore; but the sheer noise of the engine frightened her. Laura felt the power of the vehicle the second she slipped it into gear and as she pushed down on the gas pedal, it leaped forward like a racehorse hearing the bell and seeing the gates fly open.

Laura flew out of the old barn-board structure leaving behind a cloud of smoke, dust, straw and hopefully her fear.

"Now I know where it gets its handle," Laura thought aloud. As terrified as she was, she knew she had to overcome her fear of driving a machine like the Stallion. In fact, she suddenly realized she had never felt so exhilarated in her life. Instinctively, Laura knew her mission was to drive as hard and fast as she could and get them into the safety of the vast uncharted desert pronto, hopefully not killing either of them in the process.

"Which way do I go?" Laura asked without taking her eyes off the road, gripping the wheel.

Gritting his teeth, barely able to speak, Cal pointed, directing Laura straight ahead. "North," he mumbled. "Just keep her going north, stick to the desert and try not to be seen. I have the address of Momma's friend Andreas in the bag Momma gave us." Then he passed out.

CHAPTER TWENTY-SEVEN

Alessandra Elizabeth Ramiros woke up to a severe pounding in her head and the sound of the telephone ringing. Barely conscious and unaware as to why she was lying on her bedroom floor, she tried to sit up. The overwhelming pain had her dropping back down immediately. She noticed that her face was numb and there was blood everywhere. She tried hard to remember what had happened. Then Alessandra managed to tug hard enough on the cord of the phone to bring it crashing down to the floor, and luckily for her, close enough that she could reach it.

✴ ✴ ✴

A short time later Anthony and Ramon were striding down the halls of Salvatierra General Hospital in La Paz.

"I'll kill that son of a bitch, the fucking bastard! He is dead! He is dead! Ramon, I swear on my mother's grave, he will not see another sunrise!" Anthony was spewing, fuming with rage.

Ramon had never in his entire relationship with Tony seen him in such a rage, or seen him walk so fast. He found it difficult to keep pace. "She's going to be all right, Tony, calm down," Ramon was reassuring Anthony as they entered Alessandra's room. "She's in the best possible hands in almost all of Mexico now."

As soon as Alessandra saw Anthony, she burst into tears.

"God, I'm so sorry," Alessandra said out of the right side of her partially stitched-up mouth.

"Shhhh. Rest now, my darling, the doctor said you're going to be okay," Ramiros said, holding her as tight as he could without hurting her.

"Can you stop him before he finds that couple?" Alessandra asked feebly, trying to hug Ramiros back.

"Don't worry about them, you just get some sleep," Ramon added from the foot of her bed.

"Anthony, as soon as I had taken the money home I knew I had made a big mistake. I have never seen so much money in one place. I just thought a lifetime of savings for us; a lifetime right here in my hands."

"If they had just paid their fine and left it at that, none of this would have happened. Your heart was filled with good intentions, you could not have seen this was going to happen and I know you meant them no harm. Try not to worry. Ramon and I will find them in time." Ramiros was doing his best to comfort his wife while he himself was still struggling to understand what Alessandra had been thinking.

"But what I don't understand is, if they didn't take the money, why didn't they just turn themselves in?" Alessandra asked, as she tried to take a sip of water through the straw that Ramiros held up to her mouth.

"Why?" Ramon exclaimed. "Look what happened to you! Guilty or not, Redman's a seasoned gringo. He knew something wasn't right. But he also knew they had something more valuable than the money or the colonel wouldn't have kept after them with such determination. We have to find out what that is," Ramon said, looking at Anthony. "There's something going on that we don't understand yet. Something that's going on way up high, or he wouldn't have done this to us," Anthony added, rubbing the bump on his head from the colonel's pistol. "They must have some kind of protection from very high up."

"You two had better get out of here and find them before the colonel does, don't worry about me—I'll be fine, but I could never live with myself if anything ever happened to them."

Anthony gave Alessandra a kiss on the cheek and squeezed her hand gently. "I love you. I'll see you in a day or so."

"I love you, too, and don't worry, Nana's on her way over. She'll stay here with me as long as you're gone."

"Come on, we have to go!" Ramon tapped Anthony gently on the shoulder as he turned to leave.

"I'll call you as soon as I can," Anthony said as he hugged and kissed Alessandra goodbye one more time before he headed out the door.

Ramiros left the room as slowly as he could, he did not take his eyes off Alessandra until he and Ramon were completely out of the room.

Ramon said, "You know my dad went to school with Judge Socorro. I have talked to him already and explained what happened. He said not to worry, and to find the two Americans if we can. But he also he would let you stay free, to try and get to the bottom of this. It sounded fishy to him as well. You and Alessandra have been charged as accomplices in this robbery by the captain so he could keep you locked up for some reason. Socorro believes my side of the story for now, so we've bought some time, but we better find those two and make sure we keep them alive until we get to the bottom of this, or we could be in a whole heap of worse trouble ourselves. We need them alive as much as they need us right now."

✳ ✳ ✳

Cal lay motionless; the only sign of life the barely audible moans Laura heard him emit occasionally. He was sweating profusely.

Laura had been surprised at her own strength as she hauled Cal from the car to the makeshift bed she had set up for him near the fire. She had always wondered if it were true that in an emergency or crisis a person could become stronger, even think more quickly and more clearly then they did under normal conditions. Now she knew it was true.

Laura took the Swiss Army knife she had found in the toolbox of the Stallion out of the fire and prayed for the strength to do what she knew she had to do next. She hoped that the knife would be sterile enough and that she would not kill Cal in the process. Laura sharpened the knife one more time against the flattest stone she could find, and cleaned it off with the newly opened bottle of tequila. She laid the knife blade back in the fire, then undid Cal's belt buckle and zipper and pulled his jeans down past the bullet that had lodged itself in his inner right thigh.

Laura had decided to drive all day. She felt they were far enough into the desert that they'd be safe from being spotted, and she wanted to put as much distance between them and Rosarita as she possibly could.

She figured that no one knew exactly where they were headed, only that they were likely trying to get out of the country.

Her only encounter with another human all day had been convincing a very confused but friendly farmer to let her buy some gas from him. After filling up from his large storage tank, she paid him well and was on her way again. She thought she had covered up Cal quite cleverly, making it look like he was trying to sleep during the gas-up. It was now completely dark out and she had felt comfortable enough to stop and attend to Cal as best she could.

She was savvy enough at this point in the adventure to realize a hospital was not an option. She was also exhausted.

Laura caught herself gazing at Cal—fixated on how muscular his thighs were. There Cal was in the middle of the Baja desert, miles from nowhere, sweating like a roasting pig, near death and all she could think about was why this scene was not happening under different circumstances.

She gave her head a big shake and yelled, "Laura, focus!" She took the tequila bottle and poured some into the hole where the bullet had entered Cal's body. She hoped and prayed that the bullet was still somewhere near the surface and would be easy to get out.

Cal thrust himself violently upward with a scream before settling back down again, moaning. "Here, drink this," Laura said, holding Cal's head up and dribbling some tequila down his throat. Cal sputtered and coughed some of it back up in Laura's face. "That's the thanks I get for finally condoning your having as much to drink as you want?" she teased, trying to distract him from the pain she was about to inflict on him.

"Here, have another drink. I think this is going to hurt you more than it'll hurt me or something like that," Laura said, pouring as much of the "anaesthetic" as she could into Cal.

"I think you should spend some quality time with Bob when we get back. That's if he's still alive," Laura went on, mostly to distract herself from the upcoming task. She knew that Cal could not hear her and even if he could, he would not comprehend or remember a single word she said. She could vent to him all she wanted now and never have to pay for it later. Tempting though that was, she needed to calibrate all of her attention on getting the bullet out of his thigh.

Laura lifted the knife from the fire, cooled it down a bit, and sterilized it again with the tequila. Squinting and taking a deep breath, she dug the knife deep into one side of the bullet hole. She had no clue what she was doing except from what she had learned in the few first-aid classes she had take as a Girl Guide. Laura had been the only person who knew how to apply a proper Band-Aid or splint for Marty's crew, if anyone needed help before a proper medic arrived. Laura just assumed she would have to dig this bullet out. After a few short seconds of digging around that seemed much longer, Laura felt the knife strike the bullet. It was not as deep as she had first feared—it had entered Cal's body off to the side—a couple of inches more and it would have missed him altogether. Laura exhaled a sigh of relief. She twisted the blade to the side a bit and went deeper, her teeth clenched with concentration. When the blade was beside the bullet, she applied pressure against it and pulled the knife back up, drawing the bullet with it. Cal gasped, his whole body tightened. Laura noticed that the veins in Cal's neck now stood out like a wire fence.

As soon as Laura could see the top of the bullet, she dropped the knife, leaned over and pulled the bullet the rest of the way out with her teeth, just taking away the pressure from the edge of the knife. She felt Cal's body relax almost immediately.

The taste of warm blood, meaty flesh and the bullet sent shivers down Laura's spine. It took everything she had to keep herself from vomiting. She spit the menacing bullet into the sand and poured a tiny bit of tequila over the open wound, dampened Cal's dry lips and wiped his forehead with a few more drops of Momma's liquid gold. Cal now lay completely still. She thought for a moment that she might have killed him.

After a few moments, she could hear him breathing deeply. Tearing off a large section of her T-shirt, Laura created a bespoke bandage, marvelling for a few seconds at her own virtuosity. She cleaned the wound one more time with some antiseptic from a tiny medical kit she'd finally found in the Stallion and put some of the gauze over the opening. She then tied the torn piece of T-shirt around it to hold it in place. Not bad, she thought, before pulling Cal's jeans back up. She hoped that she had made all the right decisions. She could not think of anything else now except that she had to keep on driving. She hoped she could figure out the map and find Momma's friend's house. Getting Cal there as soon as she could would now become her focus.

"Okay, folks," Laura said to herself out loud again, as if addressing a small busker show crowd, "Laura will once again attempt the amazing lifeless-body manoeuvre." She took a long drink of water, then, placing her arms under Cal's, she dragged him as carefully as she could and spent several minutes struggling to strap him into the passenger seat of the Stallion. Laura gathered up their belongings and tried her best to make it look as if no one had been there. Strapping herself into the driver's seat, Laura stared out at the vast emptiness and for the first time became acutely aware of just how alone and vulnerable she was right now. Laura felt a chill and gave a little shiver as a cool night breeze came up.

"I suspect there is no heater in this thing," she said jokingly in Cal's direction. Feeling a little more confident, she turned the key and pushed down hard on the pedal. The roaring, throaty sound of the engine excited her. Laura loosened her grip on the wheel a touch, shifted firmly into first, took a deep breath as she let the clutch out and felt the Stallion respond beautifully as they surged forward.

Laura understood for the first time the desire, the need of the racers to blast through the desert at full speed for twenty-four hours; it was exhilarating! She could not understand now why she never had the desire to drive one of these before. Soon she found an open path that looked like a back road carved out by farmers from years of use. Laura searched around for the switch and flicked on the huge bank of halogen lamps that adorned the front grille and roll bars of the Stallion; all at once, it looked like daylight for thirty feet in front of her. With all the extra light, she felt even more confident and pressed down even harder on the pedal. Again, she felt the power underneath her. Laura caught herself smiling and glanced over at the listless Cal as if to say, *Now I get it*. She headed precariously, bravely, into the dark and foreboding endless Baja night.

CHAPTER TWENTY-EIGHT

The atmosphere at Momma's house was somewhat less celebratory than when Cal and Laura had arrived.

"You're sure you wounded him before you 'tripped and knocked yourself out'?" the colonel asked Miguel, rechecking his story to make sure Miguel had his facts straight. The captain sat silently crouched on a stool near the door.

"I'm not sure where I hit him, but I saw him fall."

"Well, we're happy you called this in, this is a big break for us. Thank you, Officer, and I will make sure you receive some form of commendation for your efforts. Now get that nasty bump on your head looked after," the colonel said with a knowing grin—knowing that something was amiss with the whole story, but a least they had a lead as to how far away Cal and Laura might be.

"I'm on my way to see the doctor now," Miguel said as he let himself out.

The colonel refocused his gaze on Momma. "If you refuse to tell me where they were headed, Señora Espinata, I can make life extremely miserable for you and your lost children down here." The colonel waved one hand around in a small circle.

"You don't know what miserable is, Colonel. It does not get much worse than what some of these poor souls have already lived through. Besides, your kind has never given us a single peso," Momma said with a heavy sigh, resting back in her chair. "How much less could you possibly do for us? Should I go and find copies of the letters we have sent to your offices over the years, inviting you to come down here and see the good work that we do? We have been asking, almost begging for your financial aid and even a tiny portion of the millions of dollars that is confiscated or seized from the drug lords every year that we hear about, but nothing! Not one worthless peso ever found its way past your office to meet our meagre needs. Not even a kind response. Now you come looking for our help, to find someone who is not even a Mexican but who has personally helped us out more than the whole police force. *How dare you?*"

"You do good work here, Momma. Your reputation precedes you. It is growing quickly all over Mexico. Maybe I could find some of those precious pesos you so desperately need if you help us now," the colonel said. Appearing to be relaxed, he took a sip of his cold tea, leaned back and crossed his legs.

"From who; your new bosses, the drug lords themselves?" Momma said angrily

The colonel sat back up quick and straight as if he was going to hit Momma. She flinched in her chair. The colonel leaned in as close to Momma's face as he could without actually touching her. "Tell us where they are headed and no harm will come to you or your children."

Momma sat thoughtfully for a few moments and then she answered in a soft voice: "He said he had some friends in Los Algodones, just west of—"

"I know where Los Algodones is! That would mean ... they will likely cross into Yuma, Texas—not a bad choice. Thanks, Momma.

You've been a big help," the colonel said as he stood up to leave. The confused-looking captain stood at the same time.

As the colonel left Momma's house he put a few pesos in a small wooden collection box just outside Momma's door. Momma had set it up so the girls in the restaurant could tell customers about the orphanage and often after they had eaten, on their way out of town, they would stop over at Momma's house and drop in a few coins. The captain followed him by putting in a single peso and giving Momma a big fake smile.

"Thank you for your *generosity*," Momma said under her breath as she watched the colonel drive away in his brand-new, made-in-Mexico Lincoln Escalade into the quiet of the Baja night. She stood, leaning against her door for a few moments, to appreciate the beauty that surrounded her.

✳ ✳ ✳

"That's right. I believe they are headed for Tijuana," the colonel said into the two-way radio. "And we believe that the man may be wounded, so start checking all the hospitals, drugstores—anywhere they may have gone to get help or supplies."

"I'll call Verner. I think it's time we take him up on his offer to help," Carlo's voice came back at the colonel and the captain.

"Fine," snapped the colonel. He cut off the radio sharply, upset at the thought of Carlos getting Verner involved. He knew that would not show him in a good light and would not sit well with Verner. There would be no advancement for the colonel for a while now. Even if settled soon, he knew his career was in jeopardy. He knew he had to do something fast.

"I didn't hear Momma say they were headed for—"

The colonel cut off the captain before he could finish. "You imbecile, how the hell did you ever make it to captain?"

"I married your cousin Vanessa and—"

"Do you really think Momma would actually tell us the direction they were headed in?" the colonel sneered, his voice lush with contempt for Momma's goodness.

"You think Momma is lying?" the captain asked in his usual tone of meek compliance and confusion.

"No, I don't think she's lying, exactly. I think he has friends in Los Algodones," the colonel said calmly. "But I sure as hell don't think he's going to visit them on this trip. Even if he were, Momma would not have come right out and told us. Los Algodones is just far enough away that if we focused our search there they would likely have enough time to get over the border somewhere else and my guess is that somewhere else includes the crowds of Tijuana. They are still fugitives so even if the Americans find them, they have to hold them for us, but I would much rather catch them here. Also, if they have any clue what that key might be for, I'm sure they'll try to discover what is in that box before hightailing it back to the US."

"So now what?" the captain asked, his voice filled with anticipation.

"I think we should double back to San Felipe and take a plane to Tijuana. There is no sense in us driving all the way up, and I suppose Verner should be able to catch them now. With all the new sophisticated equipment they have on the US side those two will be sitting ducks out there in the desert," the colonel said, looking disappointed both at the prospect of not catching Cal and Laura himself and at having to face Verner.

CHAPTER TWENTY-NINE

"What's our mission, sir?" asked the pilot of the Apache helicopter, the most sophisticated helicopter in the world some would say. Although the Russian Havoc and the French Tiger are fierce attack weapons in their own right, the Apache has an impressive 520-kilometre flying range. Capable of 296 kilometres per hour, with 16 anti-aircraft missiles, 1,200 rounds of bullet fire and an astonishing array of other features and weapons of the seek-and-destroy type, this Apache housed more than enough weaponry for the upcoming task. Verner, in delightful anticipation, strapped himself into the pilot's seat.

"We're looking for two well-armed, very dangerous suspects in a recent high-profile robbery that took place down in Baja, Mexico. The two are carrying sensitive information. We are temporarily on loan to the Governor of Baja, Mexico, and this is a very hush-hush, classified mission, son," Verner said authoritatively. "Our mission is to find them and retrieve the stolen information or at the very least dispense of them in any way we can so that the information they are carrying does not fall into the wrong hands. I will brief you in greater detail once we are airborne." Verner was grinning from ear to ear as the nimble Apache lifted off. Now that he was in charge, Verner was confident that the two suspects would soon be apprehended.

"With all due respect, sir, if this baby can't find them and eradicate them, then they aren't out there," the pilot replied, sporting a grin that put Verner's to shame.

"They are reported to be heading towards Tijuana," said Verner. "But no one is sure where they are right now. There aren't that many clear routes, especially in the desert, that would easily lead them here, so let's start by covering the areas near the 101. I'm sure they'll be keeping that in their sights."

"South it is," the pilot responded, and then Verner's head kicked back just a little as the pilot plunged the chopper forward.

✼ ✼ ✼

Anthony and Ramon had pulled their Jeep over to listen to the broadcast between Carlos and the colonel. "Hmm, interesting. Tijuana, they said," Ramiros said aloud. "Why would they pick Tijuana when they could get out almost anywhere with that truck they're driving?" Ramon asked.

"They must have a reason for going there and I'd bet it has to do with whatever it is the colonel is looking for. I would bet my life on the fact that they stopped at Momma's on their way out, and she will know exactly what their plans are. She would supply a safe refuge for them, not to mention gas and food," Ramiros said.

"We're not that far from Momma's, we could drive over there," Ramon said, turning the Jeep around. "She may be able to shed some light on the situation."

✼ ✼ ✼

"I'm almost positive they headed for Los Algodones, Señor Ramiros," Momma said as she poured Anthony and Ramon their tea. Momma could tell that Tony and Ramon were not at all like the others. Momma hoped they were telling the truth—that they actually wanted to save Cal and Laura. But after so many years of scratching out a living, trying to save souls and seeing way too much of the worst of the worst in the Baja, Momma could not bring herself to believe anyone in a uniform would be trying to help Cal and Laura at this point. Even her own son-in-law Miguel she felt could not be trusted 100 percent. He seemed like a good soul and he loved her daughter but the claws of the drug lords pierced deep and they controlled their world with fierce tactics, so no one was safe from the wide cast of their net. As much as she wanted to trust the pair, Momma could not bring herself to divulge any specific information as to where Cal and Laura might be.

"For some reason, the colonel is convinced they're headed for Tijuana," Ramon interjected.

"Let the colonel think what he wants," Momma said, trying to hide her fear that she had inadvertently given something away to lead the colonel to Tijuana.

"Momma, my wife, Alessandra, is lying in a hospital bed tonight, having needed thirty or so stitches to her head and some serious bruises to numerous other parts of her body because of the colonel. He and his goons will stop at nothing to keep whatever their little conspiracy is from getting out to the public. That, I am sure, includes killing Señor Redman and his girlfriend. Ramon and I seek your help. We hope our atonement may not come too late. Alessandra and I could not live with ourselves if anything happened to them." Anthony sat quietly, trying not to stare at Momma, sipping his tea, hoping he had gained her confidence.

"I've told you everything I know, Sergeant. I believe that a bullet may have hit Cal so maybe they've gone to Tijuana for help."

Momma eyed the pair suspiciously to see if she could notice any trace of their reaction that would give away their intentions.

Anthony stood and walked towards the door, gesturing to Ramon to follow.

"Thank you for that bit of information, Momma. I understand your reluctance to tell us much. I only hope we can find them before the colonel does." Anthony put a few pesos in the collection box on his way out. Momma appreciated Anthony's gesture more than the colonel's, knowing it was coming from a completely different place.

"Thank you, Sergeant," Momma said, embarrassed at his generosity and almost feeling guilty for not being a little more forthcoming with information. She just was not sure enough of her instincts to trust the two men at this point. "You say the colonel is going to Tijuana anyway?"

"Yes, Momma, I'm sure it was nothing you said, he probably assumed you would lie to protect the fugitives. He has sent every available man and called in the border patrol to search any route they might take to get to there, so I implore you, Momma, if there is anything you can tell us that will help us to find them first, it will only help them."

"I see." Momma paused. "Maybe he did say Tijuana, maybe you should go there instead?" Momma was still reluctant but feeling somewhat better about leading Anthony in that direction now that she knew the colonel was heading there anyway. It would not do any harm and might do some good. She wished she knew for sure.

"Thanks, Momma," Tony said. "At least we know not to waste our time searching elsewhere." Tony handed Momma his card. "My office number is there. If you can think of anything else that might help us locate them first, please call right away and they can radio me." With that, Tony and Ramon left the orphanage.

✳ ✳ ✳

"These are sad times in the Baja, my dear," Momma said to her daughter Maria who had entered the room once the two men left. "You need to carry a big heart and a big gun." Momma hugged her fully grown daughter as if she was twelve years old again. "You showed so much courage today. I am so proud of you."

"What was poor Miguel to do, lock up his sister-in-law?" Maria hugged her momma back with the same emotion. "Lucy would have cut him off like that!" She snapped her fingers for emphasis. The pair laughed quietly, but only for a moment, thinking of the dangers that still lay ahead for Cal and Laura.

✳ ✳ ✳

Laura had the focus of a female lioness out hunting for the food she needed to sustain her family. Looking straight ahead, becoming more comfortable behind the wheel and not having to look down when she shifted gears, she was able to achieve much higher speeds. She heard nothing but the loud steady drone of the powerful engine. She felt the tires weaving and bobbing in the thick sand and found herself making the required sudden adjustments more smoothly and with more accuracy and confidence. She was driving the Stallion. Fully engaged, she could feel every vibration in the Stallion's engine as if she had a stethoscope attached to its heart. She was amazed at how she could feel the wheels twisting slightly this way and that, and how she could tell exactly how to correct the steering wheel to keep the Stallion running straight. They were headed north according to the compass attached to the dashboard. She knew that with that and the map, she would eventually be able to hone in on Tijuana and the family that would help them. For now, she just had to navigate what remained of the open desert ahead.

Laura reached over and touched Cal's forehead. He was still very hot, but he seemed to be resting comfortably, at least as comfortably as anyone could be, bouncing their way through the Baja as fast as Laura could drive.

With all the lights on, Laura could see as clear as daylight for about thirty feet, and then, with nothing to block the light on this beautiful, clear evening, she could see vaguely beyond for well past a hundred feet. Laura wondered why, after fifteen years of marriage to an off-road racer, she had had absolutely no desire to get behind the wheel of one of these magnificent machines. Now here she was, all alone—or for all intents and purposes alone—negotiating her way through the Baja desert at breakneck speed with nothing but her intellect and intuition to guide her, and loving every moment of it. Now at the intermediary age of—she did not even want think of it to herself—here she was driving the very thing she had had a love/hate relationship with most of her adult life and now she found herself moving decidedly to the loving-every-moment-of-it side.

Laura had always known her only competition for Marty was "the Machine." She had never once questioned Marty's fidelity and the record book would show that Marty had never once abused that trust. What would Marty think of her now? Well, at least she had finally scattered his ashes where he wanted to be. She hoped that he would be proud of her for accomplishing this much behind the wheel so far and proud of how she was rebounding from her emotional collapse. If there was a heaven and if Marty was there looking down, he would be proud of the way she was fighting to get their son back and her life on track again. She thought of Marty Jr., and of what she thought would be a good life ahead. She also thought that if Marty Sr. was watching and had any kind of pull up there this would be a good time for him to help. On the other hand, maybe he had been helping already in his own way; they had

had some unusually lucky breaks. Maybe he was grateful Laura had finally got around to spreading his ashes around in the Baja and her good luck had come from his way of saying thank you. She looked out the mesh window, up at the starlit sky for a moment, and whispered a thank-you to Marty.

Laura's trance was broken when she heard a big semi truck in the distance and noticed a paved road up ahead. She had the foresight to kill the lights. The Stallion scooted across the highway. She was angry with herself for allowing her thoughts to drift off, for not noticing how close she was to a major highway before she shut the lights off. She knew one mistake now could cost her and Cal their lives. After a few moments, Laura felt secure enough to turn half of the lights back on. As bright as the moon was, she noticed the difference immediately, and wondered from how far away someone could see the Stallion with the lights on. She wanted to turn all the lights off, but thought that was just as dangerous for obvious reasons. She went with the bare minimum of lights that seemed safe and got her head refocused on driving. As there was only one major highway in the Baja she concluded that this must be Highway 1 and if she stayed just far enough away from it they would not be easily spotted, and if she stayed just close enough to it, it would lead her straight into Tijuana.

She could barely see the outline of the road now as it disappeared off into the horizon, so she turned the Stallion northward and prayed if she just kept the highway to her left, she wouldn't have to worry about getting too far off track. Laura was very worried about Cal and knew he needed to get somewhere fast where he could have his leg properly cleaned up and be resting in a bed that was not moving.

✷ ✷ ✷

Verner was staring out at the surreal green-black desert with eyes glued to the night-vision equipment. The animals, rocks and cacti glowed eerily in the display as the chopper passed overhead, sending everything scurrying.

"What's that?" the pilot asked Verner.

"What's what?" Verner asked, lifting his head up.

"It looks like some lights just came on, moving straight towards us," the pilot answered, realizing those were the first words Verner had spoken to him since they had left Tijuana. Most passengers would have divulged their whole life story by now but not this man. The pilot could sense that his passenger was one very cold and unforgiving soul.

"Well, they're definitely lights, and you're right, they are definitely coming this way," Verner said, looking pleased. "Judging by how far off the highway they were, odds are it's a buggy. And out cruising at this time of night, with minimum lights on . . . Just for fun? I don't think so. Being seen is not what this person wants. Any bets it's our target?"

"I am not really a betting kind of guy, sir, but if I were, I'd tend to lean towards your theory, so I certainly wouldn't bet against it, if that's good enough for ya, sir."

Verner instructed the pilot not to turn on the running lights, which was illegal for any licensed pilot anywhere in the world, but especially illegal in the Baja because of the drug problem. Aircraft caught flying without running lights or identification would be shot down, or at the very least surrounded, when they landed, by the local authorities and the occupants arrested on the spot.

✵ ✵ ✵

Down on the ground, Laura heard a noise that seemed to be louder than the car engine but she could not see anything. *Great! Car trouble!* she thought. Cal mumbled something incoherent. Laura looked over to see how he was doing and put her right hand on his forehead to see if his temperature had come down any, but she feared it was getting worse. She was just thinking of stopping to wipe Cal down with the last bit of water she had left, when suddenly the searchlights of the chopper came on and lit up the inside of the Stallion like a microwave oven.

Laura heard a voice blasting through the loudspeakers of the Apache: "Stop your vehicle right now and no harm will come to you."

Laura froze for a moment, staring at Cal, in a panic. "What would he do in this situation?" she wondered. And she realized and appreciated for the first time just what a marvel Cal had accomplished to get them this far. She wasn't about to give up easily, not just yet.

"I repeat! Shut your vehicle off now! Come to a complete stop. Exit the vehicle with your hands up and no harm will come to you. You can't get away," the voice said as the chopper circled and came in close behind.

Laura slowed down as if she was stopping. Verner instructed the pilot to bring the chopper down. All Laura could see was a cloud of dust illuminated by the chopper's lights and she figured the people in the chopper could see even less. The second the chopper landed and its engine had been cut, she pushed the gas pedal to the floor as hard as she could. The Stallion roared and just spun in the sand. Realizing her mistake plus the fact that they were temporarily invisible, Laura eased off on the gas pedal a bit and the Stallion bolted forward. Laura could feel each wheel separately under her. She coaxed the Stallion somewhat magically through the dust cloud and felt open space again.

They flew forward with the same G–force as an amusement park roller coaster but this time Laura was ready for the rush and held the car steady. The Stallion was several hundred feet away from the chopper before the dust settled and Verner and the pilot realized what Laura had done.

"Well, that settles that. Let's just blow the little fuckers up," Verner said as the two men ran back to the chopper still in a lingering cloud of dust.

"What exactly do you mean, 'blow them up'?" asked the pilot nervously as the chopper lifted off.

Verner gave the pilot a bone-chilling look of disdain.

"There are no metaphors in use here, just do what I said." Verner spoke very slowly in choppy emphasized syllables. "Blow them the fuck up. As in, make them disappear," Verner ordered, giving the pilot a look at his crooked, not-so-happy grin as opposed to the toothy smile he had exposed when they first met. "Like they never existed, blow them up."

"I can make them disappear if you like, sir, but are you sure that's what you want? I do have to file a full report when we get back."

"You won't have your job long enough to file a report if you don't do as I say." Then Verner softened his voice. "What's really important here, son, is that the information they are carrying does not fall into the wrong hands. Trust me, son, you'll be a hero if we annihilate them. I will personally nominate you for a medal. And I'm sure there will be no end to the gratitude of certain Mexican officials." Verner settled into his seat, admiring the smile he had just put on the nervous face of the fresh young pilot. Verner was actually looking forward to this game of fox and hound. He missed the thrill of the chase, which he had not experienced in the past several years and this one did not pose much of a threat—no personal danger, and he was quite confident of the eventual outcome.

"Whatever you wish, sir. I have some neat shit on this baby that can certainly make them disappear," the pilot said as he let a few rounds of ammo go, blowing the heads off some cacti. "But may I suggest that I just try to disable them first?"

✳ ✳ ✳

It took all of Laura's energy and strength to keep the rubber side down and not let the Stallion flip over. She would never have imagined that she could drive anything this fast, never mind the Stallion, in the dead of night in the middle of the Mexican desert while a helicopter was cutting down everything around her with machine gun fire. She swerved side to side and weaved between the cacti, trying to avoid getting hit, but every once in a while a bullet careened off the side of the Stallion or made its way through and she would hear it clang inside.

"There's way too much interference down there for this light stuff, and I don't know who the hell is driving that thing, but man can they drive! I'm going to have to try something a little more substantial," the pilot said, flicking a switch that started a red light on the dashboard flashing. "That looks encouraging," Verner said with a sadistic grin. Within a few seconds, the red light had changed to a solid green. "Armed and ready, sir."

"Fire at will, pilot," Verner said, his gaze returning to the night-vision screen. Verner's face was perverse with anticipation. "I can't wait to see what this thing can really do."

Just before the pilot pushed the Fire button, Laura hit the highway and veered north at full speed, temporarily throwing the Apache off its rhythm. It did not take long for the chopper, tilting hard to the right, to get the Stallion back on target. Although he was well within striking range though, again the pilot did not push the button.

"What's wrong? Why don't you fire?" Verner was starting to sound annoyed again.

"I'll blow a hole in the highway the size of a swimming pool," the pilot responded. "But let me see if I can hit them with the light shit now and knock them out."

The pilot fired a few rounds of ammo. Laura heard the pinging of metal on metal and saw the sparks flying all around her as the bullets hit the Stallion. She looked at the dash and the ancillary turbo button. She bit her lower lip, grabbed the wheel tightly and flicked it on.

Her head slammed against the back of her seat and she hung on for dear life, holding the steering wheel in a death grip as the nitro kicked in. As long as she looked straight ahead, she was fine, but when she looked sideways out the window, everything was such a blur that it made her sick. As far as she could tell, the road was straight for the next few miles with no oncoming vehicle lights ahead so she just let the Stallion loose and aimed it straight.

The pilot was amazed at how quickly the Stallion pulled away.

"This is no time to be careful! If they get away, you'll be spending your days washing this thing not flying it, so fuck it—go ahead and install that swimming pool!" Verner was furious, watching the Stallion pull even farther away.

The pilot pushed the throttle forward hard and reset the rockets to ready position. As soon as the Stallion was in range, he depressed the fire trigger and the chopper's nose pushed up from the force of the release of the rockets.

Laura was looking at asphalt, stars and then asphalt again as the Stallion completed a perfect 360-degree flip from the force of the explosion. Verner and the driver could not believe what they had just witnessed. The pilot was set to hit the trigger again when the Stallion disappeared down a large dip in the highway and into a small valley. The chopper stayed low and followed the dip but had to pull up and veer off to the side quickly, narrowly missing an eighteen-wheeler transport truck that came up over the rise.

The truck driver rubbed his eyes and said aloud to himself, "Wow, man, I've got to quit taking these things. Them bugs are getting way too big." He reached over, plucked a plastic vial of pills off the dashboard and threw them out the window.

By the time the frazzled pilot regained stability and finessed the Stallion back in sight, it had just disappeared into a tunnel almost a mile long.

This also let Laura know they were getting close to Tijuana. The chopper pulled up hard and the pilot pushed it to its limits to beat the Stallion to the other side.

Within a few feet of entering the tunnel, Laura turned off the nitro and slammed down hard on the brakes, then sat for a moment regaining her composure. She was never one for heavy sweating, not even when she worked out, but she noticed her hands were completely soaked and there was perspiration dripping from her forehead. She wiped off her hands on her jeans and drew her right arm across her brow to clear away the moisture. When enough time had passed that she could be sure the chopper would have reached the other end of the tunnel a mile or so away, she threw the Stallion into reverse, backed out of the tunnel and cut back into the desert with no lights on.

The only thing Laura was cognizant of at this point was the pounding of her heart. Then she noticed the bright lights of Tijuana shimmering way off in the distance. Laura knew she was taking a big risk. She concluded that although it was a big gamble, with her lights out she would have to go slower but would stand a better chance of getting away. She estimated the chopper would wait at the other end for at least a minute or two, before assuming she'd either stayed in the tunnel or done what she was doing, which was trying to slip quietly back into the desert. While the chopper hovered in anticipation, Laura stepped hard on the gas and prayed for a miracle as the Stallion picked up speed. The full moon gave her just enough light to make out shapes and see where the ground was relatively flat. She focused on trying not to hit anything big, and on keeping the Stallion upright and moving northwest, towards the city lights that were getting closer by the second. She also knew she was running out of desert and would soon have to start driving on the streets that were beginning to appear in the distance.

When she felt she had escaped far enough into the desert, Laura brought the Stallion to a halt. She could see the lights from the new suburbs that were above the valley that led into Tijuana. She knew she was now getting close to the house of the friends that Momma had suggested they go to. She also felt that if she could get the Stallion into the heavily populated area, they would be safer than they were right now, as a sitting duck.

Laura looked again at the map Momma had provided. She prayed she could find the house before their assailants caught up to them again.

Laura took a quick look behind her, almost afraid of what she would see, but the Apache was still hovering at the opening of the north end of the tunnel. With a giant sigh of relief, Laura wiped her hands and brow again, swallowed the few remaining drops of water in the canteen and pressed down confidently on the gas pedal. Her plan—she grinned—if she could call it that, having had little time to formulate one, was to keep going straight into the desert with Tijuana and the suburb to the north until it looked like she had completely bypassed them. Then she would head north and circle around, coming into the suburbs from the east. It would be the long way in, but hopefully the most unexpected and the safest. She knew by the time Verner and the pilot figured out she wasn't coming out the north end of the tunnel and in fact wasn't even in it anymore, they would have to start looking for her all over again, with no clue of which way she might have gone. If anything, she figured this would buy enough time to get her and Cal to a crowd-ed area where it would be too difficult to blow them up.

＊ ＊ ＊

On the other side of the tunnel, the chopper hovered near the opening with its lights off, just out of sight. The pilot and Verner saw headlights approaching and their bodies tensed in anticipa-tion. The pilot readied himself and his ammunition. Turning on his lights, he dropped the chopper into position. Then just before he pushed the Fire button, he realized he was aiming at a large motor home.

"Fuck, fuck, fuck, fuck, fuck!" Verner bellowed, slamming his fist down hard on the dash. "They must have doubled back! How could I have been so stupid?" he said, looking at the dumbfounded expression on the pilot's face.

Inside the motor home, sixty-one-year-old Mr. Kalkaska from Minnesota was complaining profusely to his wife, Edna, about how rude some of the drivers were down here, using such bright high beams. Even though he had flicked his off and on several times to remind them to turn theirs down, they had refused.

CHAPTER THIRTY

At a stoplight in a small suburb overlooking Tijuana, two muscle cars full of bored teenagers killing time on an unusually warm November evening, were revving their engines getting ready to race when the Stallion roared past them. They all looked on in total shock.

Laura slowed down so she could read the street names. She studied the map intently and found the cul-de-sac she was looking for. She carefully turned on to it, fearful of seeing a chopper waiting around every corner. Laura spotted the safe house, pulled the limping, gasping-for-air, sore and bullet-riddled Stallion past an old but mint condition pickup truck and went straight into the garage, fingers crossed that, miraculously, this was the right place of refuge.

Hands twitching, Laura shut off the engine and breathed a sigh of relief. Even if she had the wrong house, the chopper was nowhere in sight and she prayed she had at least found a much needed temporary safe haven. Then a dark-haired man of medium stature came running through the house door that led into the garage and pushed the button that closed the garage door behind her, shutting out her fear and angst with it, at least for now. Intuitively Laura knew she had navigated her way safely to Momma's friends. Placing her head in the palms of her hands she started shaking profusely, releasing all the pent-up emotions she had accumulated over the past few days; they came pouring out of her like Niagara Falls. The reality of what had just transpired was sinking in, the severity of their situation and the remote odds they had of getting out of this—whatever mess it was—and the miracle that they were still alive all came to a unified point and she sobbed uncontrollably without any thought as to where she was or who was watching.

After a few moments, Laura heard a chopper hovering outside. She stopped crying and held her breath as its powerful searchlights flashed through the seams in the garage door, tracking back and forth.

✳ ✳ ✳

"I am Andreas," the man whispered but loud enough for Laura to hear him.

"You are safe here." Andreas crouched as small as he could make himself in the far corner. He held an index finger to his lips to indicate to Laura to be as quiet as possible. Everyone in Tijuana was quite familiar with helicopters flying overhead. Andreas was not sure what new vision technology this chopper outside might have, but he knew that some of them were equipped with heat and motion sensors that could pick up moving shapes inside buildings. He knew they were very sophisticated and hoped that he and Laura had gone quiet quickly enough so as not to have been picked up. He was worried the heat from the Stallion might give them away.

Then as suddenly as it had appeared the chopper moved on.

When Andreas felt sure the immediate danger had disappeared, he went over to Laura.

"I'm Laura. Cal's been shot in the leg. I've extracted the bullet but we need to get him some medical attention, I think?" Laura said, looking nervous.

"Louisa, my wife is a professor of psychiatry and so she has plenty of medical training. Momma got the message to us Cal may have been hit by a bullet. The room is all set up. Hopefully there is no infection and she can tend to him," Andreas said as he helped Laura carry Cal into the house. They settled him into a bed. Louisa had bought whatever she thought she might need from the drugstore without raising any suspicion. Louisa went to work on Cal right away, removing the blood-soaked, dirty dressing and looking at the wound.

Within an hour, Louisa was praising Laura's handiwork and nursing skills. "You may have another calling," Louisa joked. "Seriously, I do think you saved his life, well done."

Laura updated her gracious hosts as to the full extent of her and Cal's situation. She also took the strange key out of her purse and showed it to Andreas, on the off chance that he might know what it could be to, and he agreed it was likely for a safety deposit box.

Cal seemed to be resting comfortably and they grew more hopeful as time passed that he would not need a doctor, at least not right away.

Laura cleaned herself up, and even though another bedroom was made ready for her, she settled into a big comfortable chair beside Cal.

"I'll just keep an eye on him for a little while before I go to bed," said Laura, but by the time Louisa had returned with another cup of tea for her, Laura had nodded off to sleep herself. Louisa placed the tea quietly down on the nightstand beside her and tip-toed out of the room.

Laura was in a deep sleep brought on by pure exhaustion,

oblivious to Cal's moaning and tossing and turning. Cal mired in his recurring nightmarish hallucinatory dream: *The car Cal and Bob are driving swerves to miss a little boy chasing a soccer ball, the car flips over.* And even stranger things happen from there. It was never exactly the same dream twice but it always contained some of the same elements. Cal bolted straight up in bed, drenched in a cold sweat. As he regained his composure and his breathing returned to normal, he looked around the strange room. At first he was terrified that they had been captured and he was in a hospital bed, but then he saw Laura asleep beside him in the old chair. Cal lay back down slowly, reached over and rested his hand gently on Laura's and, looking around the comfortable room, surmised that they must be in a safe place. He slowly drifted back to sleep and heard neither Andreas nor Louisa coming in and out through the night to check on them.

✳ ✳ ✳

In the morning, when Andreas quietly opened the door to the spare room to check on his guests he found Laura asleep beside Cal, lying on top of the covers. He gently laid a blanket over her and closed the door as quietly and slowly as he could and went back to the kitchen where Louisa was making breakfast.

"They are both still sound asleep," Andreas informed his wife as he picked up the phone to call Momma and let her know in code, assuming her phone was tapped, that the duo had arrived late and exhausted but alive and not to stay on the line more than a few seconds so they could not trace the call.

"They'll probably sleep for the full day," Andreas said to Louisa as she set out their food, "so I think I'll go into town and see if I can find out what this key Laura gave me is for. It is obviously for a bank deposit box or locker. I'll see what I can find out."

"We have no idea what those people will do, someone may be watching, so you make sure to be very careful. Do not take any chances. Promise me if something isn't right you will just come home?" Louisa begged. Andreas shot her a confident but understanding smile as he left the house.

✳ ✳ ✳

After the third bank, a now tired and increasingly frightened Andreas found the safety deposit box that matched up with the key. He removed the single item, an envelope containing two folded pieces of paper, and headed back home. He was positive no one had followed him.

Laura woke late in the day, and after checking on Cal, padded groggily off in search of her hosts. Louisa was nowhere to be found, but Laura caught up with Andreas in the garage, where he was wedged under the Stallion with his tools beside him on the ground. "There must be an angel up there with a lot of pull watching over you two. Judging by the number of bullet holes in your car, you are very lucky to be alive and at the very least you're lucky this damned thing even made it here," Andreas said as he heard Laura's footsteps and pushed himself out from underneath the Stallion.

"Don't ever repeat this to anyone, but at times I really felt someone else was driving," Laura said shyly while Andreas stuck his hands in a nearby can of grease remover and then wiped them off.

"There are enough bullet holes in this thing to call it air-conditioning, and not one came close to hitting you?" Andreas' cheerful manner was evident and Laura knew immediately why Momma had chosen his and Louisa's home as a safe haven for her and Cal.

"At first, I didn't think they were trying to kill us," Laura said. "I thought maybe they just wanted to disable the car, but then they started shooting some really big stuff down on us and right into the car, and I thought for sure our lives were over." Laura looked at the pictures on the wall above Andrea's meticulously neat workbench.

"Well, they sure shortened the lifespan of the famous Stallion by a few years, but I'm pretty sure we can keep it running at a high performance level long enough to get you two to safety," Andreas said, drying his hands and moving towards Laura so he could see which pictures she was looking at.

"Were you a mechanic for a race team?" Laura asked.

"I was a racer," Andreas said proudly, not even noticing Laura's misconception.

"I'm sorry, I—" Laura started.

"That's okay," Andreas interrupted. "No Mexican has ever won the race. In fact, there are very few Mexican racers. Some years we don't even have a single entry."

"Maybe you will be the first," Laura said sincerely.

"Maybe I could have been, but my racing days are over. Louisa has been making reference to the kid word a lot lately," Andreas said bitter-sweetly.

"I know what you mean, now that I've actually driven one of these cars at high speed for quite a distance I get the thrill. However, it's no substitute for a family," Laura said. "I can attest to that firsthand."

"Speaking of family, I have something here I'd love to show you. I was a big fan of Marty's—he was so nice and had a picture taken with me. I was very sad when I heard he'd passed away." Leaning over his bench and taking one of the many pictures off the wall, Andreas handed it to Laura, saying, "You should have this." Laura moved it in close to her face and read the inscription: *All best wishes, and good luck to my new friend and worthy competitor Andreas. Marty.* A tear came to Laura's eyes when she read his name.

"What's the matter? You do not like the picture. You can leave it if you like," Andreas said.

"No! I love it, but I decided a short while ago I have to start living in the present, and stop dragging the past around with me. I have been working hard at learning to let go," Laura said as she handed the picture back to Andreas. "Maybe someday if I'm ever allowed back into this beautiful country, I'll come by and pick it up but mostly I've been putting things away."

"Any time you want it, it's yours. Speaking of coming back, we have to get you out first. Come on, let's go inside and go over a little plan I've devised."

✳ ✳ ✳

Andreas, Louisa and Laura were sitting around the kitchen table discussing the contents of the envelope and the escape plan that Andreas had come up with when the door to Cal's room opened and he wobbled and hopped on one leg into the light of the kitchen. Louisa was the first to see him and rushed over to help guide him to the table.

"Ah, Señor Redman, it is good to see you up and about. This is a very good sign. Please, come join us," Andreas said as he went to the sideboard and opened a bottle of tequila. "Welcome back to the land of the living." He poured out two shots and placed one in front of Cal. "This is worth celebrating."

"No, thanks," said a groggy Cal. "but I'd love some of that tea you're having." Cal looked at Laura, about to say hi to her and thank her for getting them there safely. He caught her smiling at him. It was an ephemeral smile, but it pulled hard and twisted at his heart. In that second, Laura's bright, warm smile made Cal think of the two of them, sitting by a fire, quiet, just enjoying each other with no drama, with no worry of being separated, nothing to fear. He could see how happy Laura was that he was alive. Cal hoped it was a vision of the future, a premonition. "Any trouble on the way here—was it hard trying to find the place? I do not remember a thing much past Mommas. I remember I heard a shot, and then this burning pain in my leg. I guess I passed out. How was the journey? We obviously made it, thank God." Cal fired questions at Laura as Louisa poured the tea.

"Not much happened," Laura replied. "Finding the place was the easy part. Before that, it was smooth sailing until I had to take the bullet out of you in the middle of the desert and then this super-powered futuristic helicopter showed up and started blasting the hell out of everything! The car looks like a colander; there are so many holes in it. Then a missile hit right behind us and we did a complete ass-over-tea-kettle. I outsmarted them in a tunnel and, oh yeah, I won a drag race with some teenagers here in town. Then Louisa took over and she did an amazing job cleaning out the wound and stitching you up."

Cal looked at everyone and laughed. "She's shitting me, right?"

All three faces stared blankly at Cal and when nobody said anything, Cal smiled at Laura with a smile to rival any movie star's.

"I've patched up the Stallion as best I could, but you can still see what Laura got you through, not to mention she got you here alive," Andreas finished. He slung back his drink.

"Sounds like I owe you my life?" Cal said, looking at Laura.

"You do, and I'll never let you forget it," Laura replied with a wide devilish grin.

"So, Cal, we were just working on a plan to get you guys out of here," Andreas said almost apologetically. "Sorry to break up the group hug but the Feds are everywhere. You two are a hot item of concern. I would have serious trouble trying to sneak you across the border even in the back of my uncle's septic truck never mind in a regular one, but I think I have come up with a good plan. It's a little outrageous and more than a little dangerous but if you think you're well enough to travel, it might work."

"I don't know how long I've been out of it," Cal said, "and no offence intended, but come hell or high water, we are leaving here tomorrow if we can. When I thought of getting out through Tijuana, I had no idea that they would still be after us with this much enthusiasm. What the heck do we have that they want so much?" Cal took a sip of his tea. "I certainly don't mean to sound ungrateful. I am so grateful for everything you have done but we do need to start moving again. Just to keep you out of danger as well, I'm sure someone noticed us coming in here and I'm sure that info will find its way back to the Feds sooner or later."

"Yes, thanks a ton. I don't know what we would have done without all your help and kindness," Laura added.

"Hopefully after tomorrow you can send us word from someplace safe. Oh, as to why they are still after you with such a vengeance, here is the envelope that was in the safety deposit box. I believe I have some answers for you." Andreas slipped Cal the packet.

Cal pulled out the contents and laid them on the table. There was a book with names and dollar figures beside each name in it, and another piece of paper with several account numbers on it—all held at the same bank. For each account, instead of a name, there was a security code to allow access to the account.

Andreas continued, "My brother said they do this all the time so no one can access the account even if they have fake ID. With the codes, you push in the code and that allows you the access to the money. This is where my brother came in handy. He is very well-known and respected. After much discussion, persuasion and reminding him how much Momma adores you, I got him to call the bank manager and read them the codes and after some persuasion on his part, they agreed to have the money ready for pickup tomorrow. You will still have to punch in the codes, but the money will be ready."

"Do you recognize any of these names?" Cal asked Andreas as he slipped him the list.

"Hmmm, Vita is likely Carlos Vita, governor of California Baja Sur. And Molina is a very powerful colonel in the army," Andreas said.

"I recognize the captain's name from the jail," offered Cal, "but the others I have no idea."

"Judging by the amounts of money printed beside their names, they're key players in something big. My guess would be drug trafficking," Andreas replied, handing the info back to Cal.

"What are the numbers on the other sheet?" Laura asked.

"Probably their accounts," Cal suggested.

"You are correct," Andreas affirmed. "The accounts are with the Banco Nord Mexico, one of the larger and more legitimate banks in Tijuana. Therefore, even these people would not be able to get away with anything too suspicious. So they have to play by the book, which is why they need these numbers, for now anyway."

"Well, this certainly makes things a little more interesting," Laura said, leaning back in her chair. "I'm sure they could figure out how to retrieve the money sooner or later without the actual numbers on hand, with those kinds of names attached to this operation, but no wonder they want us dead. If this information got into the wrong hands it could damage a lot of careers."

There was a moment's silence while everyone mulled over Laura's comments. "But I guess this could possibly give us a bit of a bargaining chip as well?" she added.

"It could," conceded Andreas.

"Yes, but one I'd rather play alive from the other side of the border," Cal slipped in.

"That's why I'd like to lay out the plan my brother Jose, who is in banking, and I came up with to get you guys back into the US. He is very smart and, it seems, a lot more creative than I give him credit for. So yesterday while you two were lounging about all day"—everyone smiled at Andreas for trying to defuse the severity of the situation by throwing in a bit of humour—"I took the liberty of going to all the banks and establishing where the bank was and then Jose did his thing. I have concocted a plan that I think you should at least consider." Andreas leaned over the table, unfolded a well-worn piece of paper and spread it out so that all gathered could see it clearly.

"I'll make some more tea," Louisa said, getting up from the table and gathering up the dishes. "I get nervous every time I hear this."

"I can't wait to hear it again," Laura said. "It is very risky, but a great idea."

"Well, this all sounds great, but first I have to ask: Laura, why do you want to do this? Don't you just want to get out of Dodge alive and get back to Marty Jr., and hand in what I am assuming will be a very interesting story and move on to the next chapter of your life?" Andreas asked, looking up at Laura.

"Yes, I do, very much. I am very torn right now, but I have given this some thought. For the little time I have had to think about this . . . I am not sure. But if there is a chance we are going to make it back to the US safely, knowing where this money has likely come from, assuming it is not from legitimate means of any kind, this is a life-changing amount of money. Better we have it on us, instead of leaving it here for the drug lords and a few corrupt government officials and police officers to spend." Laura paused for a moment, and took a sip of her tea. "I really have not thought it through much beyond that, but maybe we could put it to some good use. After what we have been through the past few days I feel maybe this money is meant to be ours. Even more important, if we get caught but have the money safely hidden somewhere, we could surely use it as a bargaining tool. Don't you think?"

"Well," added Cal, "the money in our hands versus just some pieces of paper and some names is certainly a much bigger weight on the bargaining table. That part makes perfect sense. I guess. Okay, next item on the table. It has been very nice of you to help Laura and me so far, taking us in and fixing my wound, and finding out about the money, and without even hearing the plan yet—why are you two doing this? What's in it for you?"

Louisa and Andreas looked lovingly at each other for a minute and then Louisa spoke up.

"Andreas and I are about to start a family, a little late in life by most of our friends' standards, but we are very excited. We have not had much time to discuss this, but right away it just felt like the right thing to do because for us we are hoping that life might be different for our children." Louisa smiled over at Andreas as she spoke.

"Life can be very difficult here. Not so much for us, we have a good situation, but there is so much corruption, a lot of people live under a blanket of fear, people feel helpless to change things here. We have been supporters of Momma's for some time now, we love the work that she does and her life's path." Louisa's eyes started to well up, as if she was going to cry, and Andreas took over speaking.

"When Momma called and asked if we could help in any way, we were not sure how, but it soon became clear what we could do. You know, Cal and Laura, there is so much more to Mexico than most people read about in the news or see on TV. Most of us are a very hard-working honest, proud people. If not for the corruption and drugs, Mexico could be a great country again, just as it used to be. Not the one we have today. Yes, we are happy to help. To do our little bit, and in the end maybe someone will be exposed, maybe someone will go to jail. We want to do what we can to help, if this means a step toward making our home a better place."

CHAPTER THIRTY-ONE

After some time going over the plans, Laura helped Cal back to their room.

"The other bonus to Andreas's plan is I get some new clothes out of the deal. Louisa is going to town tomorrow to shop for them. I wish I could go, but I know it would be too risky."

After she made sure Cal was comfortable in the chair, she snatched the nightgown that Louisa had lent her and disappeared into the adjoining bathroom. She came out a short time later and took a seat at a small writing desk beside the bed. She turned on the old brass desk lamp and started writing something by hand on a sheet of paper.

"While you've been slacking off, sleeping your life away, I've been over here working my buns off trying to finish the article I'm supposed to have written." Laura held up about twenty lined pages of written material, dangled them in front of Cal's nose for a second with a tongue-in-cheek look, then set about writing some more. Cal managed his way out of the chair and hobbled over to Laura. "You wrote all that, neglecting me while I lay here dying beside you?" Cal teased.

Laura smiled back at Cal as he went into the bathroom to change for bed. A few minutes later, Cal emerged wearing nothing but his underwear, a T-shirt and an old string mop on his head that made him look like he had long graying dreadlocks. Surprisingly only slightly off-key, he started singing Bob Marley's "In My Single Bed."

Cal gyrated as best he could with his damaged leg to his own off-rhythm chant over to where Laura was sitting, flinging the mop on his head back and forth, gesturing for Laura to come dance with him. Laura looked over her shoulder and tried very hard to hold back the laughter but could not. She eventually succumbed to the moment, abandoned her project to dance with Cal. He gently placed his hands on Laura's hips and moved her body closer to his. He did this mostly because he could barely move, never mind dance.

"Is this another rare Japanese healing technique?" Laura asked.

"No, man," Cal said. "It 'tis a Rasta-man technique," he went on in his best fake Rasta voice. "I'm making this one up as I go. It's called 'honesty man, putting myself out there.'" They danced without saying a word for a few seconds. "But the real question is, do you like my hair?"

Laura laughed. "Yes, the length is fine but I prefer you as a brunette, the grey makes you look too old."

"Mmm, you smell almost as good as morning coffee," Cal said softly into Laura's ear.

"I'll take that as a compliment," Laura said, moving even more comfortably into Cal's grip, mostly to help prop him up as he wobbled a lot but she also enjoyed holding him tight. "You seem to have recovered very quickly."

"Recovery time is incredibly important to an off-road racer's reputation. Our lives depend on it," Cal said, brushing his lips against her neck.

"That's right! You are a racer. Does this mean you can help me with my article now?" Laura asked, half in jest.

"'The Baja 1000 motor heads seek thrills, recognition and excitement, but not necessarily in that order, in the impoverished land of the desperate, but hopeful Mexican people. Surrounded by . . .' There, does that sound like a good start for your article?" Cal asked returning his attention to the soft warm skin behind Laura's ear.

"Enough cynicism for one night, you've just managed to get me interested in this racer's-quick-recovery thing you mentioned." Laura said softly, brushing her lips gently across Cal's neck and onto the lower part of his ear.

Still dancing slowly, without any music and without speaking, Cal kissed Laura gently on the back of her neck, waiting to see what her reaction would be. Then, looking her in the eye, he untied the lace that held her nightgown in place. They moved apart ever so slightly; neither one wanting to let go, but creating just enough space so that the silk gown that covered her body fell, hugging her tightly as it slipped to the floor as if it wasn't sure it should slip off or not. Laura helped the gown drop more quickly, without using her hands, moving her body.

"Do you really think Andreas's plan will work, can the Stallion can do what he wants it to?"

"I don't know if the Stallion can do what Andreas is suggesting but I know what I can do," Cal replied. He leaned over to turn off the light and led Laura now naked and shy into the bed.

"It's been a few years since I've been with a man," she whispered. "I'm—I'm a little nervous, I think, I'm not sure how I'll be . . ."

"It's been a few years since I've been with a woman I have really wanted to be with."

Laura stopped apologizing for the unknown, putting her arms around Cal's neck. Gently she trailed her fingernails along his thick, broad shoulders.

"Would you like to just lie together until we fall asleep?" Cal whispered, kissing her gently on the lips. "I'm sure I could struggle through a night of that if you felt more comfortable."

"Hell, are you crazy?" Laura replied, pulling Cal in tighter. "I've waited three goddamn years for this. I'm sure as hell not going to sleep through it. Besides we could be dead in a few more hours."

"And if we're not?" Cal asked quietly.

Laura paused for a few seconds before answering.

"Let's enjoy the short few short hours we have left here and if we make it back home alive we'll ask ourselves what happens next then. Deal?"

"Deal," Cal said as he let Laura pull his T-shirt up over his head, and then he laid his head back down on the pillow as Laura leaned in very slowly and gently to kiss him.

CHAPTER THIRTY-TWO

When Cal and Laura woke they were both exhausted. There is no feeling more euphoric and closer to heaven on earth than those first few days spent together when neither lover wants to leave the nest except maybe to go foraging for sustenance but, in this case, it was a mix of lust and being scared to death of what the next twenty-four hours might bring. With any luck at all they could be back in the US by this evening. Was last night the last time Laura would make love to Cal? Would she ever see him again? Would she ever see her son again? She vacillated between enjoying every second and her natural propensity for worrying about tomorrow. Destiny's hand could be smacking her on the ass right now. According to Andreas and his brother's plan there was a high risk she would be in prison by nightfall or possibly even dead.

Laura and Cal were still unaware of the change in their situation. They had no idea that they now had an ally in Anthony Ramiros. As far as they knew, they were wanted dead or alive by all sides. Why not, she thought—if there ever was a time or reason to live life with abandon, this was as good as any. Laura glanced down at her watch and then over at Cal who had just drifted off into that fuzzy-in-the-head place again, not quite sleeping but not awake. Hmmm, only seven thirty, Laura thought. What the hell. She rolled over to Cal, draped her arm over him and put her hand on his chest. Then gently, but making sure her breasts were quite firmly pressed against his back she snuggled in tight to the same form as Cal, making sure there was no room for doubt in Cal's cranium of her intentions. Laura, are you nuts, what has gotten into you? she wondered as she started to nibble on Cal's left earlobe and probe the back of his neck one more time with her free hand.

"Are you serious?" Cal mumbled. "Aren't you hungry?"

"We have time before breakfast if you're up for it. It could be our last," she said as she ran her left hand down his torso to see what the response would be. There was a slight moan from Cal, but in true Cal fashion it did not take him long to respond to Laura's touch. He rolled over, put his arms around her and drew her in close.

"If you're going to put it that way, there is no logical argument. I just hope you're wrong."

"I think you were right-on about your racer-recovery theory," Laura said before she breathed him in, put her lips gently on his, closed her eyes, and as slowly as she could, began to savor what she knew she had been missing for the past few years. As she took all the pleasure she could from Cal her only wish now was that they could just stay like this forever.

✻ ✻ ✻

While Cal and Laura lay blissfully enjoying what could be their last few hours alive, the tension in the atmosphere and the burst of action on the other side of town were completely different. The colonel and the captain were busy implementing what they thought was a brilliant plan for taking care of the elusive fugitives;

their clever plan at this point was simply to kill them. High atop the Field of Dreams in a lookout tower, the two sat comfortably in chairs with guns and binoculars at the ready. Knowing for sure now that their prey were somewhere here in Tijuana, they had every possible officer on the lookout for them.

The Field of Dreams is an empty strip of land approximately a quarter of a mile wide that runs the full length of the city of Tijuana along the northern border. Its sole purpose is to separate Mexico from the US. It's protected by a ten-foot wall on both the US and Mexican sides. Every evening just after the sun sets, hundreds of Mexican Nationals find a way over the wall and dash across the quarter-mile dust bowl, trying to reach the Promised Land. Every night most if not all of them get caught. Verner was busy commanding his troops at the customs station to pull over and thoroughly check any vehicle with enough room to hide two people. He had doubled security at all of the checkpoints along the US border and had tripled the air surveillance and roaming ground crews along any of the strips that would have allowed access into the US. However, he remained committed to the thought that the pair would try to sneak back into the US from Tijuana, disguised somehow. With no car or truck going unchecked, the lineups and traffic jams were horrendous, but Verner was vigilant and not giving up. He was frightened for his career, family and security. Everything he had planned for, meticulously and slowly amassing a significant stash of illegal and ill-gotten bounty of cash for a very comfortable retirement over the last five years was in jeopardy, so now he had a personal grudge to settle.

The colonel figured because all the field patrolling was done by the US, Cal and Laura's plan would be to disguise themselves as Mexican hopefuls, climb the wall with a crowd and get caught as quickly as possible on the US side. Once inside the holding tank they would then effectively plead their case and be home free.

There was no way the colonel was going to let this happen.

The colonel had his own plan. The walls planted with Special Forces officers ordered to shoot the fugitives on sight. The colonel had also arranged for officers to be disguised as local civilians, their sole objective to blend in with all the other El Dorado-ites, find Cal and Laura, shoot them dead and then (simply) disappear as quickly as possible into the crowd.

There were now full door-to-door searches. Any place that could be a possible hiding place for Cal, Laura and the car were searched. Along with roadblocks established on all roads that led out of the city, all that was left was for the captain and the colonel to do was sit back and wait in hopes that one of these plans would snare the pair. In addition, just in case they would get a shot, the pair were armed with the latest in hand-held missile weaponry that the US had to offer.

"I know they're around here somewhere. I can feel them," the captain said, lifting the binoculars to his eyes for the hundredth time that hour, scanning the wall. Just below and to his left the captain noticed that a small construction crew had started work on repairing a portion of the wall but he soon maneuvered his gaze to the city streets directly behind the crew, where the view of beautiful women was much more appealing.

"It's a good thing he only knocked you on the head when he escaped," replied the colonel, never missing a good opportunity to remind the captain whose fault it was they were in this mess in the first place, "or he might have done some serious damage."

As the day wore on and lunchtime came and went, the colonel was becoming less confident that they had a chance at catching them today. The colonel had nothing to do now but think of all the permutations that could come from this situation. He was extremely worried, aware of the fact that if this dragged on for days it would work to Cal and Laura's advantage. There was no way they could justify keeping up these kind of army-like search tactics for the two without raising more and more suspicion and scrutiny from the government and media. And if they did get back to the US he knew this would not go away quietly then. No, he needed those two dealt with in a very harsh, quick and permanent manner. The colonel was very confident that he could get Ramon, Anthony and his lovely wife to fade into obscurity. What really worried him was that even with all his connections and power, without the pass codes even he would have trouble getting at the money without raising many questions and drawing a lot of attention. The captain and the colonel were becoming more discouraged, and very grumpy with each other, to the point where the colonel was just about to climb down and go for a short walk to stretch his legs and give his eyes a rest from looking through the binoculars.

Just then, both men heard the familiar loud throaty rumble of the Stallion way off in the distance. At first, it was barely audible under the constant bustle and noise that was Tijuana, but the Stallion had a distinct sound. Even among its peers, it was unique: a throaty sound that Bob had worked on tirelessly for months, rebuilding the muffler and exhaust system repeatedly until he got it just right. Now it was getting louder and more distinct; headed their direction.

The colonel grabbed his binoculars and soon spotted the Stallion coming at full speed down the long, steep hill of Route 1 that bypassed the heart of the city and went as directly as it could to the border. The car would have to pass by the wall right below where the colonel and the captain where stationed.

"Attention all units, and I mean ALL OFFICERS who can hear this message. This is Captain Gonzalez speaking. Suspect vehicle has been spotted coming down Route 1 hill. I repeat, ROUTE 1 HILL. Use any and all force available to you to render this vehicle useless, and shoot on sight."

Within seconds, police cars and troops flooded in from every direction. The captain and the colonel watched from the tower, pleased with the response and the reaction time of the troops.

The Stallion moved at breakneck speed down the main highway and along the edge of the city. Suddenly the Stallion veered off onto a narrow side street. There were several cruisers in close pursuit and gaining. The car made another sharp turn, this time into an even narrower alley with all the cruisers following in its wake. The Stallion came to an unexpected complete stop. With tires smoking and screeching, it reversed at full speed, smashed through the first two cruisers, which barely had time to stop themselves and had the others making emergency exits into alleyways and climbing up on narrow sidewalks. It was total mayhem on the streets as innocent pedestrians scattered in all directions.

Back on the main street and in the clear, the Stallion continued its journey towards the wall as fast as it could, having just eliminated half the cars pursuing it. The colonel and the captain watched the whole event from the tower, tempers flaring as they witnessed firsthand the havoc the fugitives were wreaking on their cruisers and men, never mind the city and innocent residents.

"What the hell are they up to?" the colonel wondered out loud when he noticed that the construction crew had placed two metal ramps against the wall. The colonel quickly got on the private radio to Verner: "The son of a bitch is going to attempt to go over the fucking wall. Have all your men ready on the other side. I'll see if I can get some roadblocks set up to the wall."

Captain Gonzalez, hearing the colonel's plan, immediately got on the radio and called for all available officers in cars to set up roadblocks leading to the wall near the ramp. He also ordered any officers near the wall to go and take the ramps down, but he could see that the Stallion was travelling too fast and was only minutes away from reaching its desired destination.

"I need solid roadblocks on all the streets leading over to the wall near Third immediately." At the same time, Verner ordered his men out in the field to gather near that section of the wall where it looked like they were going to jump, but he knew it would take a while for them to get into their gear and drive over in the Jeeps.

Just before the Stallion reached a very makeshift roadblock that had been quickly assembled by the local police a very familiar semi-truck cab came barreling off a side street in front of them.

With one arm in a homemade sling, dangling loose enough so that he could work the stick shift, Baja Bob was driving the power unit as fast as he could. His old pal Skinner was along for the finale, riding shotgun and hanging on for dear life, strapped in as tight as he could get the seat belt to go.

"Baja Bob to Mexico's most wanted," crackled Bob's voice through the speaker of the CB in the Stallion. "Who was the first ex-racer to get his ass booted out of Mexico for good for crashing through a police barricade to help two fugitives escape? Over." The big rig drove through a hail of bullets and, crashing into the cruisers, pushed them out of the way for the Stallion to make its way through, tight on Bob's ass. Bob slowed down and gave a triumphant blast of the air horn in salute as the Stallion roared past.

The Stallion hit the sturdy but makeshift ramps at full speed as everyone in the vicinity watched in disbelief at the ingenious and gutsy move by the driver. The car was barely over the wall when both ramps were sent twirling off to the sides and came crashing to the sidewalk quickly scattering the bewildered crowds that had gathered.

The colonel and the captain fired a few rounds of ammo from their handguns, but the Stallion was travelling far too fast for them to hit and it shot over the wall like a rocket. It seemed to be airborne and in slow motion for at least a full minute.

Bob gave Skinner a high-five as he put the cab in park and witnessed the ass end of the Stallion catapult out of sight and hopefully, safely onto the Field of Dreams.

The colonel and the captain also witnessed the event but the colonel, not ready to concede any form of defeat just yet, reached behind him and lifted a small bazooka into position on his shoulder.

The Stallion had made an incredible leap, had gone even farther in the air then anyone would have expected when they concocted this hare-brained idea, but after bouncing around profusely for several seconds it sadly came to a sudden halt at the halfway point in the Field. It was the last jump that this incarnation of the Stallion would ever make. It lay still, bent, broken, twisted and smoking, with some smoke rising from the engine. The Stallion had finally broken a leg but it had accomplished what it set out to do, and that was draw a large crowd. Its occupants would now end up in the hands of the US government with a chance to explain their situation to what they hoped would be sympathetic ears.

"This won't be a Field of Dreams for those two tonight," the colonel said to the captain, just as he was about to pull the trigger on the ominous M72 rocket launcher which he now had straddled securely over his shoulder with its sights trained dead centre on the stationary Stallion. The colonel was set to pull the trigger when he heard a voice.

The words "Steady there, Rambo," rang hard in his ear and the colonel's face registered fear as the pressure of a cold metal gun barrel pressed hard against his temple. The colonel and the Capitan were so focused on the car and with all the noise and racket below they were totally oblivious to the fact that someone had climbed into the lookout booth. The colonel looked up slowly to see that Ramiros was the man holding the gun. Turning slowly, he saw Ramon holding a gun to the captain's head.

"You even think of pulling that trigger and you're a dead man," Ramiros emphasized. The colonel slowly put the bazooka down and all four men watched from the tower as the US patrol cars picked up the alive but shaken occupants of the Stallion and then they headed back to Verner's office.

Ramiros, Ramon, the colonel and the captain arrived at the office shortly after the patrol officers and were immediately ushered in, only to find Verner looking perplexed, staring at Louisa and Andreas. "Who the hell are these two?" Verner shouted in an uncontrollable rage at the colonel and the captain, before he realized the two were being held at gunpoint.

✳ ✳ ✳

In a much more tranquil setting on a quiet tree-lined street on the other side of Tijuana, a professionally dressed Laura, looking great in an outfit that she had borrowed from Louisa, calmly walked out of the bank with three oversized black leather duffle bags bulging at her side. The chaos and commotion engulfing the streets of Tijuana near the border crossing created the perfect distraction. Laura hopped into the old brown pickup truck that Andreas had given them and put the three bags between them. The bags took up most of the floor space. Laura looked over her shoulder again as Cal pulled away slowly, still not seeing any signs that they were being followed. Cal, hesitating, unable to believe they might just have pulled this off, also looked around for any signs that they were being followed. He saw none.

"Well?" asked Cal.

"Well, what?" Laura said. "I didn't stop to count it, though they wanted me to. Andreas's brother must be extremely high up in the industry. They had it all in these bags, ready to go. I just slapped down the name Andrea's brother told us to use on a few sheets of paper. They have the amounts on them copies are in the bag. There is one shit-load of money here." Laura smiled. "It weighs a ton."

"Would you listen to that? A little good sex and a bit of disposable income and all of a sudden she's a potty mouth! What next, some smutty ink, a little tat on the small of your back?" Cal grinned as he leaned over and gave Laura a kiss on the lips that he held just a little too long for someone driving. The truck swerved, but Cal focused his attention back on the road before he caused another accident.

"Stay focused, cowboy, the last thing we need to do is draw attention to ourselves after going through all this trouble. Would you like me to look at the documents to see how much money we have?"

"Um, let me think," Cal said pensively, taking his hand off the stick shift long enough to rub his chin, as if he was checking the length of his stubble. After a minute, he gave Laura a quick glance. "I think not right now. I think I would like to wait until we are somewhere safe, and can maybe relax a bit. I think I will get too nervous and think about it too much if I know. I don't want to jinx this. How about you?"

Laura smiled. "You racers are so superstitious, but now if I look and something bad happens, then I'll be to blame so I guess we wait." She placed her hand gently on Cal's left thigh and gave a tiny rub where she had taken the bullet out. "How are you feeling now?"

"Well, I won't be entering the Boston marathon anytime soon and I'm glad we're on open highway, I wouldn't be able to drive this thing all day in rush hour traffic, but I believe it's on the mend. The pain comes and goes but there is no sign of infection. You missed your calling; you should have been a nurse."

"Doctor." Laura smiled.

"Okay, doc, I'd like to find us a nice five-star hotel room and an ice-cold bottle of champagne and you can spend the rest of day tending to your patient." Cal grinned at Laura.

"That does sound wonderfully tempting but I'm sure getting as far away from this place as possible today, even over the border would be a much smarter course of action." Laura grinned back. "If Andreas's plan worked then he and Louisa have surely been caught by now and the cops will know we're still out here. Either way I'm sure they'll be back to looking for us as soon as they discover we weren't driving the Stallion, and God knows what has transpired. So as much as I love your idea of whiling the day away in carnal bliss, I strongly suggest we don't press our luck, but please hold that thought for a future day."

Having reached the highway heading east without any roadblocks or trouble, Cal and Laura could only assume that at least the decoy part of Andreas's plan had worked and all hands were busy trying to figure out what just happened. Question was, had it bought them enough time to get safely away from Tijuana?

Cal sped up to just over the speed limit and smiled at the open road that lay ahead.

"God, I hope everyone is all right. I wonder why we have not seen or heard any cops out looking for us. It seems too quiet to be true. What the heck is going on back there?" Laura said softly as she began to relax a bit herself.

"Well, I told Andreas I would not call him until we were safely over the border. And that's if he's not in jail. I'm not even sure what they could charge him with, at this point. Unless we get caught, of course. If we do he told me to make him and Louisa our first phone call. I'm sure once they discover who Andreas and Louisa are, they will be over at their house in no time, tapping the lines. I would like to know what the heck is going on back there. This is way too spooky quiet. Not at all what I expected. I think our cover is good, but not even *one* police car?" Cal half mumbled as he rode along with a big grin on his face, constantly checking his mirror for any sign that they were being tailed. He looked at Laura and noticed she had gone from somewhat happy to looking a little down.

"What is it?" Cal asked hesitantly.

"What's what?"

"You're looking a little sad over there."

"Sorry, now that I have a minute to think, I was just missing M. J. Hoping he is okay, and not worrying too much. I think I sounded pretty calm when I called him from the house. He sounded good. I'm still not sure how I let you talk me into this, I would give it all up just to get home safely now," Laura said with a little thank-you-for-asking smile back at Cal.

"But I have to say, this is going to make for some interesting reading if I can figure out how to incorporate any of this into my feature article, not to mention discussions around the family dinner table. No one in my family will be able to top this one."

With that, Laura closed her eyes, laid her head back and let the breeze from the half-open window and the warmth of the sun, which was only just now beginning to even start thinking of setting, and the steady hum of Cal's smooth driving carry her off to another place. With her left hand lying open-palmed on Cal's right thigh, just above where the wound was. Cal placed his hand gently on her left leg, just above the knee. With no shifting required for the long open road ahead, the old brown Ford F150 was quietly blending into a beautiful Mexican evening.

CHAPTER THIRTY-THREE

Neither Cal nor Laura had thought there was anything suspicious about the man who left the bank at the same time as Laura but then disappeared in the other direction.

But only two blocks away, the man opened the back door to a pristine white limo and slid inside where Carlos was waiting with another pistolaro.

"Well, what happened in there? Did the lady get anything?" Carlos asked the hired gunman impatiently.

"I couldn't tell what she did in there. She went back to a private room, but when she left the bag she had was definitely much fuller than when she came in with it."

"This is working out much better than I had hoped," said Carlos. "This way I get to keep all the money and no one will be the wiser. So don't fuck this up like those other two idiots and you'll be well taken care of. And remember, I know exactly how much money they should have on them, so if there is even one dollar missing it's coming out of your ass, is that clear?" Carlos waved his hand, dismissing the two thugs to get out of his ride and on with their jobs.

The two men, dripping with gold jewelry, scurried out of the limo and into their somewhat-less-than-mint-condition, older-model Cadillac. After a few minutes of double-checking their arsenal, they let the Caddy reach a very safe trailing distance behind the unsuspecting Cal and Laura.

A few hours later, Cal and Laura, hoping that their getaway had been as cleanly executed as it seemed to be, were hot and tired to the bone. They noticed a gas station up ahead—maybe a safe place to fill up and take a short break. Cal figured with all the old cars scattered about willy-nilly basking in the sun waiting for parts or to be worked on there was likely a good chance that a decent cup of coffee could be had there as well.

"Do you think it's safe to stop yet?" Laura asked, hoping Cal would say yes. Her frequent over-the-shoulder checks, she told Cal, assured her that they had not been followed.

"I was just thinking the same thing. It has been a few hours but bladder-wise I am pretty much at capacity anyway. So hopefully some decent coffee, gas and a pit stop coming up."

Laura took another long look in the mirror and over her shoulder; Cal also took a look around but saw nothing. Laura, who had taken the latest shift at driving, wheeled the pickup truck in by the pumps and shut the engine off.

The two experienced hit men had stayed well out of sight but not so far behind their marks that they would have lost them. There were not a lot of choices for changing direction out here, and they had been waiting for the perfect opportunity to strike where their prey would have less chance of getting away. This stop was exactly what they had been hoping for. At this point Carlos was just interested in retrieving the list and the money, so his instruction to the pistolaros was to obtain them as quietly as possible. He reminded them not to attract any attention whatsoever—which meant, in particular, no shootout.

The gunmen were hoping that offering not to shoot the fugitives in exchange for turning over the goods would be a sufficiently appealing deal for the fugitives to cooperate quietly.

✳ ✳ ✳

Cal wasted no time in hopping out of the truck.

"Remember, make sure the pump jockey clears the pump to zero before he starts filling us up. Arguing with him later will only prove futile," Cal reminded Laura. "I'll see what I can rustle us up for drinks when I'm done. Damn! Why could he have not hit the leg I already limped on? This looks ridiculous," Cal complained to Laura as he hobbled over to the door marked Amigos at the side of the building.

The late-model Caddy pulled up directly behind Laura just moments later, but she did not notice as she was concentrating on what Cal had said as well as paying close attention to the attendant's actions.

One of the pistolaros jumped out of the Caddy and went directly to the washroom behind Cal, while the other one got out and picked up the free nozzle. Laura glanced in the mirror and noticed the other person was starting to pump his own gas. She figured them to be locals and did not give them a second thought. Cal was just finishing his business when the other hit man came in and joined him at the urinals.

"If only I could piss cocaine, I would be a rich man," he said, showing off his two gold teeth with a broad smile, and grinning at his own joke. Cal figured he had uttered the same joke to strangers at urinals a thousand times before, and gave him a quick polite grin so as not to be rude or appear to be a snobbish tourist, but he was in no mood to start a conversation with anyone. Let alone this scruffy guy.

"You look like you've done all right for yourself," Cal answered, studying the man with a bit of trepidation. He had been in Mexico enough times to know that there were plenty of interesting and somewhat unscrupulous-looking people circulating around this beautiful country that you didn't have to become a complete paranoid every time one of them stood next to you at a urinal. It was nothing to see tough-looking people who were as gentle as pussycats down here. The tough-guy look was as much a fashion statement in Baja as it was an attitude, but still Cal felt uneasy and a little shiver went up his spine. This guy had confidence and an air of badness about him. He could see tattoos that looked like they ran all the way up his arm, and probably half his body, Cal guessed, but he had beautifully polished boots, gold teeth and he was loaded down with jewelry. Cal could tell something was not right. He did his zipper up as quickly as he could while keeping the corner of his eye on the stranger. Cal wanted to say *adios* and get out as quick as he could without appearing to be suspicious.

"Yes, I've done okay, and speaking of all right, I guess you thought you'd done all right for yourself as well," the pistolaro said aggressively, looking directly at Cal. "In fact, my boss thinks you've done too well and would like you to give it all back quickly and quietly and preferably while you are still alive. My partner and I would love to just transfer the money and the list to that lovely old Caddy parked behind you out there and head on home without any trouble, nobody gets hurt, no fuss no muss. You get your asses safely back to the US and forget this whole thing ever happened and we never see your gringo faces down here again."

Cal, still trying to comprehend what was going down here and who this man standing beside him was, calmly turned and smiled at him, then made a dash for the door. Unfortunately, with two bum legs he was awfully slow and with lightning speed the pistolaro was at the door pulling it shut again. The pistolaro's other hand brandished a knife just inches from Cal's face. Cal deflected the hand holding the knife with a quick move and lunged at the man. Cal's momentum forced them both against the wall and they began to wrestle.

✹ ✹ ✹

At the pumps, Laura paid for the gas and got back in the truck. She looked in the side-view mirror hoping to see Cal and wondering what was taking him so long. Then instead of seeing Cal strolling back, she noticed the second pistolaro crab walking along the side of the truck slowly towards her. Then she noticed the butt-end of a pistol he was concealing down by his side. Laura reacted in a flash, pushing the gas pedal to the floor and steering the truck towards the washroom door, knocking the pistolaro off balance and into the gas pumps.

In the washroom, the first pistolaro managed to free himself from Cal and stepped back, drawing his gun. Cal moved surprisingly quickly though and, grabbing an overhead pipe, swung his legs at his attacker with all the force he could muster, knocking the pistolaro through the cheap wooden door and sending him careening off the side of the speeding pickup as it sped by. Laura hammered on the brakes when she saw Cal as he rushed out, he yelled at her to keep driving. "Don't stop!" he hollered as he jumped on the sideboard. Laura pulled away with tires smoking and screeching.

"I'm sure glad this truck belonged to a motor head, it may look old but man it has gumption!" Laura shouted out the window to Cal.

"Tell me about it," Cal yelled back, hanging on to the side for dear life.

The second pistolaro came running around the corner of the building with his gun at the ready and managed to get off a few shots before Laura pulled out of range. He helped his partner up and they both ran back to their car and screeched away in a cloud of tire smoke. The young attendant left standing in disbelief at what had just happened—and screaming at the thugs to come back and pay. The mechanic and cashier came running out to see what the hullabaloo was all about, but the two vehicles were already disappearing down the highway, as gunshots were fired from the Caddy.

✳ ✳ ✳

"Why is it that with you around people seem to love shooting at us?" Laura said to Cal as he finally climbed into the cab through the open window and fell head-first into his seat. Laura realized that this was no time to joke when she noticed Cal clutching his leg and wincing with pain.

"Are you all right?" Laura asked. "Who were those men? They were definitely not the Feds this time?"

"I thought we were finished with all this shooting crap," Cal managed to say through clenched teeth.

Laura looked in the side-view mirror to see if the men had followed and soon got her answer when a round of bullets whizzed by the truck.

"How did they catch on to us so quickly, I wonder," Cal asked Laura, not expecting an answer.

"Why don't you just throw out the money? That'll at least get them off our backs and we'll maybe get home alive. I'm sure the money's all they want at this point."

"Wait a minute here. Have you been in the sun too long?" Cal replied. "We've still got the lead, and two damn good drivers now. That's not when a racer throws in the towel."

"All I want, all I wish for at this point, is to get back home and be with M. J. I don't care about the money," Laura said, fighting tears of frustration as another shot cracked the back window and lodged itself in the dashboard, inches away from Cal. "And I may not be a mechanic or know a hell of a lot about cars, but I can tell you that, as nice as this funky, supped-up old Chevy is, I'll bet it isn't any match for that big honkin' black Cadillac back there, no matter who's driving."

"That's 'souped-up,' and I believe it's a Ford F-150, but Andreas has this thing dressed pretty sweet. I hear what you're saying about M. J., though. I understand. I thought we were done with all of this as well, but I guess not. You are right—maybe if we toss them the money with the list they'll let us go. At least they'll be busy picking up the bags which should give us a damn good jump, but I do think they'll just head back." Cal reached down between the seats to pull out the bags of money. "At least half. We'll see if that stops them," Cal said quietly almost to himself trying to slip it past Laura as she was focused on driving as fast as she could.

"The whole amount, I don't want to take any chances at this point, I just want to get home alive and we are so close to the border now."

"Okay," Cal said, realizing she'd heard him. He was ready to concede on this one and do as Laura thought best when his fingers suddenly touched on something smooth, long and hard. His hand closed in tight around it and he hauled out a riffle from underneath the seat.

"Hmm, a Winchester model 70, beautiful. Too bad it's not a vintage Purdy, 28 gauge, but it'll do. Andreas knows his guns. If we're lucky it will be loaded, and should have about five rounds."

Cal checked and only found two bullets inside. He searched for more bullets, fingers grappling around below, but none were to be found. And there were none in the glovebox. "What kind of guy keeps a gun with only two shells?" Cal asked himself out loud, feeling rather perplexed.

"What the hell are you doing?" Laura asked as Cal straightened up in his seat.

"I was looking for more shells but it seems like we're limited to two shots," Cal said as he reloaded the Winchester, admiring its carved wooden stock and the Redfield accu-range scope that was attached. "We have two shots at freedom. Do I take them or do I just throw out the money?" Cal asked Laura, while he was holding the rifle in one hand and one of the bags of money in the other.

Laura sang a few lines from The Band's song "The Weight."

"My point being, these guys are obviously not Feds or we wouldn't have made it out of town; these two are playing for keeps and even if we give them back the list and the money, I suspect they are not going to just let us drive away now. They will still want revenge and to teach us a lesson for not just giving in back at the gas station." Cal sat still, looking intently at Laura. She did not respond she was focused on driving. She was not putting any distance between them and the pursuers but she was not losing any ground either.

"I could take just one shot with both barrels, or fire one barrel at a time," Cal suggested, hoping that Laura had already picked plan A of the first question and was ready to move on to part two.

"That's just great, put all the pressure on me," Laura replied, now weaving the truck back and forth so that the pistolaros' bullets might not hit the truck so often.

"I'm asking, do you want to try and get out of here with enough money to live out the rest of your life in comfort, able to send M. J. to the best schools in town, or do we throw it away and hope to God it's really all they want and leave us alone. I am prepared to live with ether decision. No regrets, where do you stand on this?"

"Even if we make it back home with the money, do you think they would just leave us alone?"

"I do, I think if we get back over the border with the money and the list I think they will weigh their options and figure they have bigger fish to fry, and it would be too risky for them to come after us. The list is a great security blanket and I think they will assume we don't want any trouble, and we don't, so they'll just leave us alone."

"What's your plan with the rifle?"

"I don't really have a plan, per se but I thought I could climb through the back window here to the back of the truck and take two shots, at best I can take out their tires, maybe scare them enough to fall back, or quit all together, but I don't think that will happen?"

"What happens if you get killed out there?" Laura asked her eyes watery, swelling with tears and fear.

"If I get killed out there?" Cal repeated as he finished pushing open the rear window and climbed out of the cab. "Throw the damn money out the window with the bags open so the money flies all over and they have to stop to gather it up. That should buy you more than enough time to get to the border at Laredo. Listen carefully, I will tell you right now, do not stop! Go through at night. Get as close as you can with your lights out, then barrel through and don't stop until you hit the US customs on the other side. I do not mean hit them literally. I'm sure with your American citizenship and a dead guy in the back of your pickup they'll want to detain you for questioning." Cal looked back at Laura with a crazy grin.

"What about you?" Laura asked, looking scared.

"Just leave me in the back and keep on driving as fast as you can. If you even think of stopping to help me, I will come back and haunt you," Cal said with his ass half out the back window. "Every time you even try to make love to a man, I will show up and make scary noises and rattle my chains until he high tails it out of there."

"You are definitely a certified nut-case, Mr. Redman."

"Besides, would you even miss me?" Cal's voice was barely audible as he finished.

"I just got over losing Mick. I don't want to lose you too."

Cal could not hear Laura with the rush of wind in his ears. He could not even hear how close the bullets were coming to hitting him. Cal stuck his head back in through the window, and leaned towards Laura, giving her a quick kiss on the back of her neck. Laura didn't dare turn her attention off the road.

"No amount of money is worth losing the best thing that's ever happened to me, so don't worry, I'll be fine," Cal said as he stuck his head back in the window."

Laura turned her head as close to sideways to the back window as she could. "Take your two best shots and if that doesn't stop them then I'll pass you out the bags, and we'll try plan B." Laura turned quickly and kissed Cal on the lips before pushing his head back out the window. "Now let me get back to driving this thing and you start shooting before one of us gets killed."

Laura concentrated hard on keeping the truck steady now as Cal prepared to take his first shot.

Cal crawled on all fours to the back of the truck with bullets whizzing all around him. As he stuck his head over the tailgate and readied to fire, a bullet struck and shattered the driver's-side mirror. It startled Laura, causing her to momentarily lose control of the truck and Cal's first shot missed the Caddy by a mile.

Cal readied himself for his last shot, crouched down behind the bullet-riddled tailgate. A million thoughts were racing through his mind. The first of which was that he only had one shot left and if he missed, the money would have to go. Mostly, he was marveling at the thought of how he was crazy about Laura and he gave a quick prayer that she at least would make it out alive.

Cal thought of Bob too, and hoped he was still alive—Cal was thinking a million mixed thoughts at lightning speed, but the steady plinking of bullets whizzing by and ricocheting off the truck brought him back to the realization that he had one last shot and he had better not miss. He steadied himself, took a deep breath and let it out slowly as he had learned, reached up and aimed directly at the windshield. He remembered not to pull the trigger back hard but to squeeze it slowly as he let his breath out.

As he steadied his arms and squeezed slowly on the trigger, the truck turned sharply, sending Cal tumbling on his back, and all he could see was blue sky and a puff of smoke coming from the end of the rifle barrel.

"Fuck!" Cal shouted.

"Sorry!" Laura hollered back. "It was a sharper curve than I thought." Laura did not dare look back. It seemed that plan A had not gone so well.

When Cal managed to get back up he watched in disbelief as the tail end of the Caddy disappeared off the road, skidding down a steep embankment in a cloud of dust and gravel.

What Cal hadn't seen was that after he fell back and accidentally pulled the trigger, the bullet he'd shot had not flown off into the sky, wasted, but in fact had ricocheted nicely off a sign that said Sharp Curve, taking out the driver's-side front tire of the Caddy and sending it sliding helplessly sideways off the road.

"Yahoo! Yes!" Laura heard from the back of the truck, then again almost right in her ear as Cal made his way into the cab. Maybe plan A hadn't gone so badly after all.

"Well done, lady, well done. That was some great driving you were doing there."

Laura smiled out of the corner of her mouth, but stayed focused on driving fast. "I can't see anything out of my mirror but I take it plan A worked?" Laura asked hopefully.

"I can't say for how long, or what happened, but the Caddy disappeared off the road."

Nobody said a word for the next few minutes. They both kept checking all the mirrors and Cal was constantly looking out his window. When Cal finally caught his breath he put his hand on Laura's leg and repeated his compliment. "Well done!"

"Me? You did all the shooting; I just kept the rubber on the tarmac."

"I'm not sure how steep that cliff was back there . . ."

"Pretty darn steep," Laura replied in relief. "I was praying the whole time that we ourselves wouldn't go over it."

"So I would think we've bought ourselves at least a few hours' leeway by the time they get back on the road. So if you want to pull over, I'll drive for a bit. I'm sure you could use a break?"

Laura looked over at Cal and smiled.

"Boy, you sure know how to court a gal. This has been one hell of a first date," Laura said with a smile as she pulled the truck over.

CHAPTER THIRTY-FOUR

It had been dark for quite some time and Laura was now sound asleep. Cal wasn't sure how long he had been driving but he was sure he had memorized just about every top 40 Mexican song on the charts. His neck was sore from turning to look behind him every chance he had. He noticed the glow of lights in the distance and surmised they had finally reached Algodones. Even though they were tired and anxious to get over the border they had decided to bypass the crossing at Mexicali because it was too big and Cal assumed officials would likely be expecting them there.

Unaware, of course, of what had transpired with Alessandra and Ramiros and the money, Cal was still expecting to maybe run into trouble at the border so his thinking was they would have a better chance of just making a break for it at the smaller crossing of Algodones. He had only been into Algodones once but remembered it as small and very busy with tourists who came in for the day or weekend. The border control checkpoint was a tiny outpost in the north end of town, with two officers running a declare or non-declare post. Depending on how well you knew them or how generous you were. Sometimes the wait could be an hour or more, but at this time of night he figured it would be a pretty short line and they would look like any other tourists. If they sensed any trouble there at all they could easily just barge on through to the US side and get pulled over by US Border Control. If all went well they would soon be on Interstate 8, heading into Yuma.

Cal turned the pickup down a secluded side street and pulled up near some bushes and trees. Algodones was quiet even for a weeknight; November wasn't its busy time of year. He shut the engine off and stepped out of the truck for a stretch, then walked around to the passenger side of the truck. He carefully opened the door and put his arm around Laura so that she leaned into him as the door opened.

"Okay, sleeping beauty, time to wake up. This is it." Cal gave Laura a little shake.

Laura's head drooped over onto Cal's chest and she put her arms around him and gave him a big hug.

"Are we home yet?" She sighed.

"No, sorry, you're not back in Kansas yet, Dorothy, but if you need any dental implant work done, fillings or whitening, you've come to the right place." Cal smiled.

"What are you talking about?" Laura asked, still groggy and rubbing her eyes.

"We are in the heart of Algodones, the oral Disneyland of the world if you live in the southwestern US and are looking for cheap, quality dental work."

"Really? I never knew that. People actually come all the way down here to get dental work done?"

"By the thousands, but—"

"There's always a but!" Laura interjected.

"No, this is all good. Because Algodones is also home to the buck-a-taco, the street-meat version or you can upgrade to a sit-down dinner in a cheap cantina for about six bucks, including beer or wine. And I think my haircut set me back a Lincoln."

"Gee, do you think we should hang out here for a while?"

"I'd love to and maybe we can come back one day when we need dentures, but we have one more hurdle to clear and then we will be home free this time—I promise." Cal helped Laura out of the truck and held her up while she steadied herself. He put both his arms around her, pulled her in tight and gave her a long, gentle, slow kiss.

"Hm! Death by suffocation or in a Mexican prison, are those my two choices?" Laura coughed out as she pulled back just a few inches.

"Sorry, I didn't mean to squish you so hard."

"I loved it, I just couldn't breathe." Laura smiled as she stretched up and returned the kiss.

"I guess that's going to have to last you for a while."

Cal got right back to business. "Okay, so the Algodones border is just a few blocks up the road. I'll pretend to be asleep this time and with a woman driving I think their guard might be down a little. The traffic should be just busy enough they may hurry us through." Remember."

"Do they inspect everyone's teeth as they leave?" Laura asked playfully.

"Remember," Cal said a little more sternly to Laura now that she was awake enough to remember what he was about to tell her, "you just say that we were down here for the race and we're coming back this way so we can visit your brother in Yuma."

"What if that doesn't work and they want to wake you up, or they tell me to pull over?" Laura asked nervously.

"Cry, and tell them I get really grumpy when woken up and that I said not to wake me until we reach your brother's. If that still doesn't work, just floor it and don't stop until we're safely on the US side.

Cal gave Laura one more quick kiss, and then hopped into the passenger seat.

"But don't run anyone over," Cal added with a smile. "We want them to like us regardless, just in case we get caught."

"Like I'd really hit anyone," Laura said seriously, settling in behind the wheel. "Now pretend you're asleep before I hit you." Laura put the truck in gear and pulled away. She had only rolled partway up the street when she suddenly hit the brakes and pulled over, shut off the engine and killed the lights.

"What's wrong?"

"Just nerves," Laura replied, taking a few deep breaths. "I'm okay now," she said, restarting the engine.

As Laura started to pull away, Cal abruptly leaned over and turned the ignition off.

"What is it? Is something wrong?" Laura asked; worry once again creeping into her voice.

"Well, I know you, it's not just nerves, and maybe you're thinking what I'm thinking, and in a way there is something wrong," Cal answered.

"What do you mean, thinking what you're thinking, in a way?"

"I mean, are you in a hurry to get home?"

"As in where the *H* on the tap really does mean hot water and I get to hold M.J. in my arms again and we don't have to worry about spending the rest of our lives in jail? Then yes, are you nuts? Of course I'm in a hurry to get home," Laura said, staring blankly at Cal.

"Now don't get upset, but I've been thinking this thing through," Cal said, turning to face Laura as he took her hands in his. "Ever since we left Tijuana I can't help feeling guilty about having this money."

"Well, we're sure as hell not going to give it back to those cops, who obviously obtained it illegally in the first place," Laura said, looking confused.

"No, I'm not talking about giving it back to the cops." Cal paused and looked at Laura a little puppy-eyed for a few seconds.

"Then what are you thinking we should do with it?" There was a minute's silence. Cal wanted to see if he and Laura were kindred spirits, and he watched carefully as Laura peered deep into his eyes.

"Momma's orphanage?" Laura said, a little unsure.

"Precisely!" Cal almost yelled with excitement. "I'd like to give it to Momma for her orphanage. I feel that is where this money belongs. I know it sounds like a very strange and whimsical thing to do, but my heart tells me after all we have been through there must be a bigger reason, a grander cause, a greater force than just you and me living like kings off of the blood of other people. That is where this money belongs. Maybe this was meant to be, why we had to go through this."

Laura took a deep breath and let out a heavy sigh. "God, will you ever stop surprising me. Where the hell did this come from all of a sudden?" Cal shrugged his shoulders and the two of them stared at each other for a few seconds. "You are one in a million, Cal Redman," Laura said, leaning over as best she could with the big stick shift in the way, giving Cal a tender hug and a kiss on the lips. "But can we do that thing that you do where we keep some for ourselves? I was just getting used to the idea of sending M.J. to a private school and not having to go back to work for a while."

"It's scary, you know me too well already—I did have that in mind but I wasn't going to tell you right away. There is this beautiful bungalow for sale only miles from the ocean in San Luis Obispo."

They both smiled.

"Really? Slowville?"

"I know, but Bob and I always have so much fun there, it seems like a great place to start over. I have a bit of money tucked away as well. I'm sure we'd do all right. But this much money would change the lives of those kids forever. Momma could run the orphanage for the next twenty years, maybe forever."

"We'll also have to at least buy Andreas a new truck. And we must owe Bob something."

"Yes, true. But now we better get a move on. You need to turn us around to head back to Momma's," Cal said as Laura started the engine and pulled away yet again.

"What? We are going to Momma's now. That's impossible!"

"You have to do a U-ey before we get too close."

"Why don't we just take care of Momma after we make it home?" Laura asked. "You know, deposit the money and send her a big check."

"We can't take that chance, you know it's a big gamble, we may not make it across cleanly, and if we don't, I doubt very much we'll get to keep the money. If either side gets hold of this money, we will never see it again, and neither will the orphanage. Unfortunately, this is something we have to do before we cross. At least we'll know for sure the money is being put to good use."

"You're right, I never thought of that. Five minutes from freedom and we are turning the truck around. God, I can't believe I'm doing this."

Cal squeezed Laura's hand.

"I was actually hoping you'd find a way to talk me out of that crazy idea. I didn't realize you would be such a pushover," Cal said, tilting his head back and closing his eyes, listening to Laura's soft laugh as it filled the cab and his heart.

"But can we can find some of those one-dollar tacos before we leave?"

"I think we can afford to upgrade to the sit-down dinner with a cold beer," Cal said, smiling as he sat up straight again.

"As long as it's on a patio." Laura laughed. "I am not letting this truck out of my sight for a second."

"Sure, but no dental work," Cal said, laughing. "If we hurry, we could make it back down to Momma's by late tomorrow."

CHAPTER THIRTY-FIVE

The pair watched silently from the shadows of the museum just up the road as the children were unloaded off a flatbed truck with rotted-out wooden side panels and in desperate need of a paint job. It was a very hot day, so they brought the children in from the fields early. Some of the kids would wash up for dinner right away, others would play a little soccer or baseball before they ate. The children were treated as kindly and lovingly as possible but all the older ones had to work in the fields to help pay for their time at the orphanage. Not an ideal life but still better than the alternative that many children there were faced with. Now back from a hard day's work, with little more than water, salad and corn bread to help get them through the day, they still seemed cheerful, knowing that a big dinner and a good night's sleep lay ahead.

The children started work in the fields at sunup. Chili peppers were a good source of income for the orphanage and the work gave the children a beginning understanding of taking pride in hard work, and kept them busy. All of the older children staying at Momma's worked at something. Some toiled in the fields while others who had gained Momma's trust helped in the restaurant, the museum, or around the house or the gas bar and some even found employment in nearby towns. Over the years, some of the children had moved on to community colleges, become farmers, owned restaurants, or other businesses.

"Reminds me of my days as a teen, picking grapes in the valley," Cal said with a lump in his throat.

"Yeah, but you got paid for it, and had a mother and father to go home to who would tuck you into bed at night," Laura said sweetly to Cal, reminding him of why they had risked their own freedom to come back here.

"I don't know," said Cal, changing the subject and getting back to the task at hand. "Something just doesn't feel right. I know we took out the pistolaros, but I'm sure someone would have been lookin' for us at the border knowing we were heading that way and now that we haven't been seen there they could be out looking for us. There are way too many players in this thing for it to just go away."

"We don't know what happened back in Tijuana, but I'm sure no one would think in a million years that we would come all the way back down here, even to Momma's. They probably think we're hiding out in some end-of-the-world town in the desert," Laura added not very convincingly.

"Well, they know we have enough money to hide out for as long as we need to down here as long as we don't get caught. I'm just very curious as to what happened up north and to the pistolaros and whoever stuck them on us. But we can't bicker about this all day," Cal said, feeling a little apprehensive as he lurched the truck forward over to the barn and out of sight. He was puzzled by the fact that they had not seen a single police officer on the way down.

With a gentle tap on the door, Cal pondered why Momma had not come out to meet them. But there she was at the door and, looking somewhat puzzled, invited them in. Cal and Laura entered carrying the money with them.

"So you did come back," Momma said.

"How did you know we would?" Cal asked, surprised.

"She didn't but we did," Ramiros said as he exited from behind one of the closed bedroom doors. "It was a long shot, but we figured you wouldn't try to cross the border with a huge sum of money—once we found out how much it could be—and take the chance of losing the whole thing, or worse, spending life in jail down here. We weren't sure what you would do but we sent some guys to stake out Mike's."

"Again," Ramon added as he came out of the room.

"And we came here, hoping you would too," Ramiros finished.

"So where does that leave us?" Cal asked.

"The way I see it"—Ramiros shrugged—"you have two choices. You can hand over the money and leave quietly of your own accord and at leisure. We understand what happened now and you are free to go. Or you can try to keep the money."

"Well, we were actually going to give it to Momma anyway," Laura said, smiling at Momma.

"Or you can make Ramon and I use our weapons and we will take great pleasure in shooting you anyway," Ramiros said with a smile.

"Two very distinct and different endings. Hmmm . . . let me think about this!"

"Cal!" Laura said as she moved forward very slowly and passed two of the duffle bags to Ramon, who nodded with a polite smile. Cal gave his to Ramiros. Then suddenly Ramiros caught Cal with a surprise left hook and sending him to the ground. Ramon pulled his pistol out as Cal staggered up slowly.

"What the hell was that for?" Cal asked, rubbing his chin, as Laura helped to steady him, both looking totally surprised.

"That was for back at the jailhouse. My head still hurts." Then Tony reached into the bag and counted out one hundred thousand dollars and handed it to Laura.

"This is for everything we have put you two through. I apologize on behalf of all the good hard-working officers that got dragged into this mess, but also thanks to you, we are unwinding a pretty thick, knotted ball of corruption to which there seems to be no end. But getting this money back and the list will surely help."

"I'm sorry, Momma, but we need to take all this back in for evidence." Tony and Ramon headed for the door.

"We should be on our way now. We have a lot of work to do. I wish you all the best, and a safe journey home this time," said Ramiros as they both tipped a nod to Cal and Laura and headed out the door.

Just as the two men reached the door and opened it, gunshots from a few different directions came screaming in at them, and bullets ricocheted off the walls as everyone ran for cover.

The two officers pulled out their guns and divided up the front windows.

"Can you see anything, Tony?" asked Ramon. Then they heard a voice coming over a bullhorn.

"Throw out your weapons and come out with your hands up! You are surrounded. There is no hope of getting out of there alive unless you surrender," the voice ordered.

"Who are you and what do you want? Ramon hollered back through the window, making sure to keep his head low.

"I am Governor Gonzales. And I want the money and the list." If you surrender, we will make sure no one is harmed. If not, you will leave me no other choice but to use all the force I have at my disposal and it is more than enough to make sure no one walks out of there."

"I don't trust him, Tony," Ramon said. "I knew something was fishy with him. This thing goes even higher than we have found out already."

"Well, we can't just let him kill everyone here."

"You have one minute to make up your mind, and then we are coming in. Please, I just want the money and the list. Do not make us come in there." Then there was silence.

Everyone in the room crouched down behind something.

"Do you have a gun?" Cal asked Momma.

"Yes, I have a rifle and a box or two of shells. I can get them for you."

"That's very noble, guys, but if I know the governor he has his whole goon squad with him. The rest of our gear is safely stowed away in the trunk of the Jeep, which is hidden up the road, so I'd say we're going to have to take him at his word, but I don't like that option either. I'm sure he won't hurt you guys as you pose no threat to his career. Ramon and I, that's another story." The two officers looked at each other.

"Well, you and I could do the Butch Cassidy and the Sundance Kid thing and hopefully they would let everyone else go when they get what they came for," Ramon said with a bit of humour.

"Not sure I find that ending all that appealing either," Tony said.

"Ten seconds, what's it going to be?" Gonzales shouted.

"What are our choices again, Governor?" Tony hollered back sarcastically.

"It's nice to see you keeping a good sense of humour in times of trouble, Sergeant. You are a good officer. I will make sure no harm comes to you and your partner. But you have to throw out your weapons and the bags of money and the list and come out with your hands in the air or we are coming in. On the count of three."

A flurry of shots began coming from various directions riddling the house. Some found their way in through the windows. Luckily, the walls were made of very thick brick, adobe timbers in the old traditional style, but the onslaught of bullets was taking its toll on the outside walls. Momma ran to her bedroom and retrieved the rifle and shells for Cal, and then crouched down behind the big sofa again. Cal and Laura were under a love seat they had turned upside down and Ramiros and Ramon were still each in position under a window.

By now the girls in the restaurant had had heard the gunfire, and came running out but had to retreat into the restaurant for fear of being shot. Miguel, who had stopped in after his shift kept moving forward, sneaking around behind to where the gunfire was coming from.

After another minute or two, which seemed like an eternity to the captives, the firing suddenly came to an abrupt halt.

After a few seconds of no sound at all the hostages inside the house could hear the governor instructing his men to stop the shelling and put their weapons down. To the surprise of all inside the house they stood up and listened carefully for any sound outside.

Then they could hear Miguel calling out: "Hello in there, I could use a hand out here, please come out slowly whoever you are?"

The big brown wooden doors to Momma's house creaked open slowly as the two police officers stepped out first as if being pulled forward by the guns that were clutched in their hands. Then Cal came out sporting Momma's rifle.

"Aw, it's you again," Miguel squeaked out. His hands trembled. He was holding a gun point-blank to Gonzalez's head.

The other few men in the goon squad had put their guns down and were standing still with their hands in the air.

"Okay, what the hell is going on here now?" asked Miguel, slowly starting to put his arms down, thinking he had done the wrong thing.

Together Ramiros and Ramon hollered at him: "No! Keep your gun on him."

One of the goons thought he had caught a break and bent down for his gun, but Cal let go a shot from the rifle that threw a spattering of dirt up into his face, and he quickly resumed his position as a non-hostile captive.

"Okay, I'm asking again. Someone explain to me what the hell is going on here," Miguel said with his gun barrel now back resting on the governor's skull.

The governor and Tony both started yelling at him at the same time, when Momma appeared from the house.

"Miguel!" she snapped. "Keep your gun on the governor and listen to the sergeant here. Do not take your eyes off him for a second. He is a snake."

"Okay Momma," Miguel said a little hesitantly, but when it came to Momma he knew he had better follow orders.

After a brief explanation from the sergeant the three officers and Cal put the goon squad and the governor into separate squad cars and Ramon phoned in for a Special Forces unit to come and help out.

✳ ✳ ✳

By the time the Special Forces unit left with their charges, and Tony had explained to everyone what had transpired in Tijuana the sun was just a sliver in the amber sky and beautiful lines of golden sun lit up everyone's faces as they said their goodbyes in the yard.

"I hope you are happy with the amount we have chosen to give Señor Redman, and that this may be the last we see of you for a good long while. Although I must say we could use some good drivers down here like you two to help capture some of these drug runners."

"You never know what can happen, as the events of the past week prove, but hopefully Laura and I can find something a bit safer to do for a living," Cal said, smiling at Laura as she took his hand.

"So no legal action against the force then?" Ramiros asked shyly.

"Nah, I figure we are all even. Happy to be getting out of here up a few grand, and a lot wiser."

And they both knew instinctively not to mention the hundred thousand they had already taken out. They weren't about to look a gift horse in the mouth.

Cal counted out half from the bundle of cash Ramiros had given them and handed it to Momma.

"I hope you don't mind," Cal said, looking at Laura.

Laura gave Cal the biggest smile he had ever seen and then Cal and Laura gave Momma the biggest hug she had ever received. They both swore that once they got back home and settled in they would do whatever they could to help, and come and see her again as soon as they found the time. Momma whispered to Laura to focus on getting M. J. back and not to worry about her and gave her an extra-hard squeeze and wished her luck with Cal.

"You have your hands full, but he will be worth it in the long run," Momma added, giving Laura a knowing smile.

"Well, seeing that we are no longer in a hurry to get back home, I suggest we partake in some fine Mexican dining over at Momma's before we head out, I myself am going for the Redman Ranchero Deluxe, and an ice-cold beer. Then we're going to find us the nearest hotel with a pool and an air-conditioned room with a king bed, and get some much-needed rest," Cal said as he put his arm around Laura.

"That sounds great, let's call over to Emilio's and see if they can join us for dinner?" Laura offered.

Cal looked at Laura with a broad smile, and then kissed her.

"Excellent suggestion, I think I have me a keeper, Momma."

They all laughed and you could see the tears welling up in Momma's eyes as she watched the love birds head off to the restaurant.

Tony tapped Ramon on the shoulder; Ramon had made himself busy talking to Momma's daughter Maria while everyone was saying his or her goodbyes.

"So you think next Saturday would be okay?" Ramon asked Maria quietly, hoping no one else heard the question as the yard went suddenly quiet with the departure of Cal and Laura.

"Let's get going," Ramiros said. "We have a long drive ahead of us and a lot of complicated investigating to do, along with all the damn paperwork to fill out when we get back to the station."

As Anthony turned to walk away, he caught a glimpse of the sadness in Momma's eyes, which he correctly attributed to the fact that she had only moments earlier serendipitously come across enough money to run the orphanage for at least her lifetime, and then lost it all in the same moment.

"I'm sorry, Momma, but I'd be no better than the men who acquired this money in the first place if I didn't hand it back in. I could possibly lose my job, or worse the men behind it, illegally making all this money, might get off, but now I have very good evidence to get them behind bars. I might even get a promotion and be in a better position to help you out down here. But worst of all, if the owners of this money ever caught wind that it was given to you, you would never have a day's peace until they had wrestled it back from you. There may be safer and better ways we can help in the future," Ramiros imparted sadly.

"I am more than grateful for the money that I have received, Sergeant. One cannot dwell for long on what may have been. It serves no good purpose," Momma replied.

✳ ✳ ✳

Ramon and Tony headed for their car, both men knowing in their hearts that there was no better or more deserving place on earth for the money to go than to this orphanage.

"I wonder how high up this conspiracy really goes," Ramon said. "I wonder how much of this money will just disappear, and I wonder if the colonel or the captain will ever be brought to trial?" The two men walked towards their Jeep, dust swirling around them with each step. Yet in the middle of the dust they could see Momma's rose gardens and the beauty she had created within this dust pit, with the kids playing soccer in an open field behind the barn. The youths were laughing, screaming and sweating after a hard day of picking peppers as if nothing had just happened, as if they had not a care in the world.

After a few more steps, Ramiros stopped and looked at Ramon with a grin, the likes of which Ramon had never seen on his friend before, or anyone else. The grin created wrinkles all the way along both sides of his face up to the corners of his eyes. "You know, Ramon, you just might be right," Ramiros said.

"What do you mean?" Ramon asked.

"I wonder how high up this ugly mess goes and if we can even make a dent in it at all?" Tony replied as he turned around. "I wonder what would really happen to all this money if we just handed it over to Momma."

Ramon watched as his best friend and moral compass walked back to Momma's, laughing, as he placed one of the bags beside the orphanage's donation box, then he banged hard on Momma's door to make sure she would come right away.

"May God have mercy on our souls if any of this ever gets found out, my new friend," Ramiros hollered in at Momma through the screen door. He hoped Momma heard him.

As Tony returned to Ramon he draped his free arm around his shoulders and they walked back to the Jeep with a newfound confidence that they had chosen the right career and that they would be able to make a difference as police officers in a tough and sometimes unforgiving environment.

Neither man ever spoke another word to the other about what had transpired there that day. But they would always remember Momma's squeals of joy as they ducked into their Jeep feeling comfortable that they had made the right decision.

They weren't sure what web of lies they would have to spin, or if the real amounts of money and names would ever be known, but as the two best friends drove off in silence under the great wide Mexican sky, they both knew life was never going to be the same.

AUTHOR'S NOTE

Someone asked me about the title *Tijuana Crossing* and intimated that I may be using the name to misrepresent the book and take advantage of the current political climate between the US and Mexico.

So I would just like to take a moment and set the record straight.

After spending time working in the Baja on various film projects (mainly the Baja 1000 off-road race) in the early 1990s, I started making lots of notes and doing interviews for what I hoped would be a future project but with no concrete idea at the time. The situation even then in Mexico was not much different from today, and my working title for these notes was *Tijuana Crossing*.

Life gets busy; my work, kids, and family took me in other directions and subsequently I did not do much work on this book again until an unfortunate accident happened during a routine operation in 2012 which after several corrective operations left me mostly blind in the left eye. Knowing that I would eventually need the same operation in my right eye I decided to focus on completing this book as soon as I could (and also started work on others).

That brings us to this day in June 2019 and the first edition of the novel *Tijuana Crossing* is being sent out into the world. To change the title at this point would be like changing the name of one of my children.

Simply would not feel right.

ACKNOWLEDGEMENTS

Firstly, in order to stay happily married and possibly even alive I would like to very much thank my loving and understanding wife, Keltie, who, with amusement, puts up with all my creative undertakings, and also had to read a few very early drafts of *Tijuana Crossing*. Love you!

Thanks to my long-time friend, an intellectual debater of all things that are, ever have been, or will be; are mechanically powered, physically played, or simply enjoyed. He too read and conjectured on a few early drafts: Pat Gidlow.

Another very long-time friend who suffered through an early edit for me to make *Tijuana Crossing* initially readable: Jane McIver.

Brother in-law Scott Duncan also contributed to an early edit.

Other readers include: Nancy Abba, Steve Abba, Greg Brown, Mark Cantania, Harry Strothard, Muriel Truter, Michelle Walker, Adam Weitner.

If I have omitted anyone, it's only because it took so damn long to finish this book and I have completely forgotten: my apologies.

I cannot thank you all enough for your time and input.

Marijke Friesen: for your outstanding work creating a wonderful look and feel to this book.

Editor (task master) Chandra Wohleber. Honestly cannot thank you enough for all the hours you spent working on and discussing this book with me. You make me want to be a better writer. And God knows you are trying.

BRADLEY H. LUFT is an award-winning screenwriter, director, and producer who worked in the film and television industry for over thirty-five years. Although he has had articles and poetry published, *Tijuana Crossing* is his first novel. He lives with his wife in Toronto, Canada. Brad enjoys road trips, writing and reading, and playing the guitar. He enjoys spending time with his children, friends, and family, and preparing large meals at home or at their cottage in Northern Ontario.